Forget Me Knot

Forget Me Knot

THE LOVE GAME: BOOK NINE

ELIZABETH HAYLEY

WATERHOUSE PRESS

This book is an original publication of Waterhouse Press.

Cover Design by Waterhouse Press
Cover Images: Shutterstock

ISBN: 978-1-64263-358-0

To new adventures . . .

Chapter One

OWEN

"I don't think it's gonna fit."

"If you'd both just relax, I'm sure it'd slide right in," Inez barked at Roddie, her voice exasperated.

"It's too tight," I said. "And it's starting to hurt."

"You guys are such babies," Vee countered. "Inez and I have handled way bigger things without any complaints."

I scoffed. "I've seen what you've handled today. Bigger is a gross overstatement."

"Maybe not at one time," Vee said, "but in terms of total volume, we definitely have you beat."

"Let me try giving you one more shove from behind and see if it goes in." Inez positioned herself behind me. "Don't be so tense."

My arms started to shake. "That's easy for you to say."

"Hey, guys?" Natalia's voice yelled from the top of the stairs. "I couldn't help overhearing you down there . . ."

"Because you were eavesdropping so you wouldn't come down too early and have to help?" Vee interrupted, accusation clear in her tone.

Silence fell for a moment before Natalia recovered, completely ignoring Vee's question. "And it sounds like... Well... Are you guys pegging Owen? Because as his ex-wife, I feel like I have a right to be part of that experience."

"What? No!" Vee yelled, looking flustered. "Why would we be doing that?"

I could almost hear Natalia's shrug. "I don't know what you guys are into. Owen's pretty open-minded."

"And you thought *I'd* want to watch?" Inez asked as Natalia appeared in the doorway to the basement apartment I used to live in when Minnie was still alive.

"Voyeurism is a pretty popular kink. And I don't know you that well, so..."

"What's pegging?" Roddie asked.

"That's it," I said as I lowered Inez's bed frame to the floor. "I cannot have this conversation while holding a bed."

"So you can talk about it now that you're *not* holding the bed?" Natalia looked at me like a Labradoodle puppy being taunted with a stuffed toy. "Because I gotta say, I'm insanely curious what your stance is."

Instead of replying, I looked over at Vee. "Can you please deal with your cousin?"

"Honestly, at this point, I feel like we just gotta chalk her up as a loss," Vee replied.

"Hey!"

I watched as the cousins began to squabble, oddly happy to see them joking around with each other, even though their topic of choice left a lot to be desired. I wasn't sure their relationship would survive my ill-conceived marriage to Natalia, but the annulment their uncle Ricky had procured for us had allowed the last of the hostility to fade away.

And with that behind us, we were all ready to move forward. Which included allowing Inez to move into my old basement apartment so we could have extra income to help us pay utilities and for renovations on the house Minnie had left me.

Since Natalia had already been living with us rent-free for a few months, it felt weird to suddenly make her start paying. But she and Vee had a discussion, and Natalia was going to take over some of the utility bills to help out. Inez's rent payment would help Vee and me cover the rest of the expenses.

Things were finally on track. We could continue working on the house while keeping the lights on, Inez no longer had stress about an unreliable landlord, and I got to live with the love of my life. The only thing that could make it more perfect was if we could be done moving Inez's stuff into the apartment.

As I focused back on the conversation happening around me, I heard Natalia say, "I bet if you used water-based lube, it would be fine."

"Whoa, whoa, whoa, what are we talking about here?" I asked, alarmed.

Vee looked exasperated, but also fond. "Natalia was explaining what pegging was to Roddie, who seems... interested."

"From a purely academic perspective," Roddie quickly tacked on.

Inez's brow furrowed. "What's academic about being penetrated by a dildo?"

Roddie shrugged. "I like to learn new things."

"Okay, well, I hate to interrupt this fun tutoring session Natalia's running, but can we get back to the task at hand?"

I said. "I don't think the frame is going to fit in this corner." Which was weird because it was where I'd put my bed when I'd lived down here.

Maybe it was because I'd left the box spring on the floor. Inez was clearly at a different point in her life than I'd been in when I'd lived down here.

Inez looked around with her arms akimbo. "I'm not sure where else to put it. Anywhere else and it'll jut out into the middle of the room."

We all looked around as if we'd somehow see the same space differently. The apartment was a studio with a little alcove nestled behind a storage unit Minnie had installed some time ago to make up for the lack of a true closet. It was the most logical place to put the bed because the unit gave the illusion of a semiprivate bedroom.

"Does the storage thing move?" Roddie asked.

I shook my head. "It's screwed into the drywall." Looking at Inez, I asked, "Do you need the frame?"

Inez looked at me as if I'd suggested using our blood to draw a pentagram on the floor. "What would I sleep on?"

"The box spring and mattress," I answered carefully, a little afraid of the intense way she carried herself.

Inez was effortlessly cool in a way most people couldn't pull off. The few times we'd hung out, she'd struck me as someone who didn't put much stock into physical appearance. But if that was really the case, genetics had been kind to her. Her light-brown skin was flawless, and her brown hair had beautiful honey-colored highlights. The result was an afro that looked like a glinting crown in the right light.

She seemed to ponder my suggestion for a moment before replying. "Do you have somewhere I can store the frame?"

"Sure. We can keep it in the unfinished section of the basement."

The basement apartment Minnie had built took up the majority of the space below the house, but she'd left a portion unfinished that was accessible from the main floor via a second set of stairs. Inez had a door that gave her entry to this space, as well as a second door that led to the outside.

She thought for a second longer before smiling. "Then I guess that's what we'll have to do. I'm sorry you guys have to take the frame apart after just putting it together. I should've measured."

I shrugged. "It's no big deal." And it wasn't.

Inez could give a moving company a run for their money. She'd had everything that could be disassembled apart when we arrived, everything that could fit in a box was packed away and labeled, and she'd even organized it in her apartment in the order she thought it would best fit in my truck.

Putting the frame back together had taken minutes because she'd put the screws into a bag and taped them to the metal. I was just sorry she wouldn't be able to use it.

Roddie scratched the back of his neck. "Maybe we can find a slimmer frame?"

Inez shrugged. "It's not a priority right now. I'll be fine." She rubbed his back as she passed him, missing the way his cheeks flushed.

I eyed Roddie, wondering how deep his crush on Inez ran and if she noticed it. But I forced my curiosity down. Looking over at Vee, I couldn't help my smile. The universe had a way of making things work out how they were meant to. Whatever would be between them would be.

VERONICA

"I'm sore in places I didn't know could be sore," I groaned after face-planting on Owen's bed.

He chuckled. "Like where?"

"My hair," I muttered.

He climbed in beside me, and I opened my eyes to see his dazzling smile directed down at me.

"Your hair?"

"I pulled my hair back too tight. And now, it's not only my scalp that hurts, but like the individual strands. I didn't know that was possible."

"I'm not sure it is," he said, clearly amused. "Maybe you have magic hair."

I reached out and flailed a hand in his direction, lightly hitting his chest. "Don't pick on me." I didn't withdraw my hand, instead letting it linger on his chest for a minute before it began its own journey along the planes of his body.

He shifted closer, letting his body align with mine so he could trace my spine with his fingers.

I pushed my face into his neck, suddenly wanting to crawl inside him. I pecked light kisses along the column of his throat as my hands wandered lower, caressing him lightly through his jeans.

"I thought you were sore," he whispered, sounding breathless.

"Aren't you supposed to work out sore muscles? Keep them… limber?" I squealed as I was suddenly rolled onto my back, Owen hovering over me, his lips a hair's width away. "Owen," I breathed, my voice plaintive as he stared as if trying to memorize me.

My voice seemed to break through the haze, as his lips descended on mine in an erotic kiss that made my head spin and my body react. Only Owen had ever had this effect on me. He was probably the only one who ever would.

Our bodies came together as explosively as they always did. Since he and Nattie had finally gotten the annulment finalized, things between us had been even better than they had before. It was like almost losing each other made our bodies ravenous, desperate.

And as we sank into the afterglow some time later, I hoped we always remembered not to take our time together for granted. I wanted him desperate and ravenous for me... always.

Chapter Two

VERONICA

Owen sighed beside me for the millionth time as he continued to scroll through his phone. We were sitting in the two-seater swing chair he'd come home with after his boss at the hardware store had gotten a couple in. Owen said he'd immediately pictured us swinging in it. So he used his employee discount and brought one home. And here we were, swinging in it just as he'd imagined.

It was actually really relaxing when it wasn't being shared by someone who appeared to be on the verge of a meltdown. When he sighed again, I dropped the textbook I'd been perusing in an attempt to get a head start on the upcoming semester and stared at him.

It took him a few seconds to get the feeling he was being watched. "What?" he asked when he finally looked over at me.

"Don't what *me*. What *you*?"

His face scrunched up. "Are you sure you got into law school?"

I stuck my tongue out at him, and he laughed. But he

sobered quickly, looking down at the phone in his hands.

"I'm graduating this year," he finally said.

"Yeah," I said, dragging the word out in my confusion at where he was going with the conversation.

He sighed again—*I am gonna kill him*—before looking back at me. He seemed almost sheepish, which worried me. Owen hadn't been uncertain around me in a while.

"I can't picture myself in an office," he said.

I snorted. "I can't see it either."

"But I'm an accounting major. That's pretty much the definition of an office job."

I thought for a moment before asking, "Does it have to be?"

He stood abruptly, sending the swing careening back. I put my feet down to keep from smacking into him as it swung forward.

He paced in front of me, his hands pushing through his hair. "I chose accounting because my advisor said I had to pick *something*, and I'm pretty good at math. Accounting seemed . . . stable. And like a mature choice. Something a responsible person would pick. But it just seems so . . ."

"Boring?" I supplied when he didn't continue.

He huffed out a breath. "Yes. Which makes me feel shitty because I'm sure that's not the truth. There are probably people out there who *love* accounting and are great at it and—"

"Owen, you don't have to defend all the accountants in the world to me. You feel how you feel."

It was such an Owen thing to attempt to not offend anyone, even if no one was around to be offended. He had such an empathetic spirit, and I loved him for it. But I also hurt for him because of it too. He spent so much time focused on the feelings of others, he didn't think about himself nearly enough.

"What is it you really want to do?" I asked him. "What makes you the happiest?"

He leered at me, making a laugh burst out of me. "As much as I wish being with me could be your full-time job, I think you may need a break from time to time."

He sat beside me again and nuzzled into my neck. "I'd like the chance to prove you wrong."

I giggled and pulled back, pressing a quick kiss to his lips. "Focus."

"Oh, I'm definitely focused."

I kissed him again, because how could I not? I let my forehead rest against his. "What do you *want*, Owen? Without the expectations of anyone else weighing on you, what do you want?"

He pulled back just enough so he could look behind him, at Minnie's house. After a long moment, he turned back to me.

"I want to restore houses."

I smiled. "Really?"

He nodded. "At first, fixing up Minnie's house was daunting. But once I got started, I... enjoyed it. I enjoyed making it mine. Ours. And I want to do that for other people."

"So do it," I urged.

He sat back and rubbed his hands over his face. "So... what? I just quit school with a semester left and learn construction? I put so much time into school. To not finish or use my degree feels—"

"I'm not telling you not to finish."

"Then what are you telling me?" He looked so lost, my heart ached.

"Get your accounting degree. It'll probably be really

helpful if you start your own business."

His eyes widened as he looked at me like I was crazy. "I can't start my own business. Half the stuff I'm doing in there, I'm learning from YouTube."

"I didn't say you had to start a business *today.* But someday, it would probably be helpful."

"I don't know. It feels like I'd be starting all over. And I don't even know what I'd need to do to get started in a career like that."

"Hmm." I tapped a finger to my chin. "If only you knew someone whose entire family was in construction."

He gave me a dry look. "Being a smartass doesn't suit you."

I laughed, earning a small smile in return.

"I'm not sure your dad and brothers will be too excited to help me out after everything that happened."

He was right. They probably wouldn't be thrilled. While my dad and brothers let me live my own life and make my own choices, they were also fiercely protective. And they'd been really caught off guard by Owen marrying Nattie. They'd never thought he'd do something like that to me, and it made them hesitant to even contemplate trusting him again.

But at their core, they wanted what was best for me. And that was Owen. I had to have hope that they'd see that eventually.

"Maybe not," I replied. "But they'll help anyway."

He gave me a small smile and gripped my hand as he gently rocked us.

Everything would be okay. I'd make sure of it.

OWEN

"Are you sure they don't mind?" I asked for what was probably the three hundredth time since Vee had told me her brothers agreed to call and talk me through becoming a contractor.

Vee gave me a pissy look. "How many times are you going to ask me that?"

"I didn't have a set number in mind, but—" My smartass reply was cut off by my phone ringing. It startled me so badly, I dropped it. Thankfully, the carpeted floor of the living room cushioned its fall.

When I picked it up and looked at the display, I turned what I was sure were wild eyes on Vee. "Oh my God, they're calling."

She looked at me as if I'd gone insane. "How shocking," she replied dryly. "Are you going to answer it?" she asked when I continued to look down at my phone.

"I'm not sure."

"Jesus Christ," she muttered as she reached over and took the phone from me. "Hey," she greeted her brothers when she connected the FaceTime call.

"Hey. Where's Owen?" one of them asked.

"Standing next to me freaking out like Taylor Swift is calling instead of you two losers."

"We weren't losers when you asked us to do you a favor and talk to your boyfriend."

"Yes, you were."

"I guess we'll just hang up, then. Maybe he can find some non-loser guys to help him."

I used my eyes to plead with Vee to not piss off her brothers before I had to talk to them.

"So sensitive." Vee *tsk*ed.

"Is Owen there? Because I can think of a lotta things I'd rather be doing than talking to you."

"I told you he was right here," she replied, flashing the screen in my direction.

I waved like a simpleton. "Hey, guys," I added.

"So Vee said you wanted to get into renovating houses?" Manny asked, skipping the pleasantries.

"Uh, yeah, yes. I think that would be... good. That I'd enjoy. And be good at. Hopefully." I couldn't have sounded any dumber if I'd tried. "I've done a lot to Minnie's house, even since the time you guys were here. I hung new drywall, put up crown molding, repaired some wiring, swapped out a few pipes—"

"We don't need your résumé," Franco cut in. "Just listen, and we'll tell you what things you need to do to get started."

So I shut up and listened as they explained diploma programs, getting certifications from technical programs, and who I'd need to file paperwork with to be legit. There were a few options, especially since my state didn't have an actual licensing procedure. The trick would be getting the experience I needed so customers knew they could trust me to do a good job.

And I wasn't sure how to go about getting that while going to school full time. Would someone let me work weekends? Even if they did, what would happen to my job at the hardware store? I didn't want to leave Mark in the lurch.

"Owen? Owen! Are you even listening?" Manny's voice broke me out of my panicked spiral.

"Yeah, yeah, I'm listening. Sorry, it's just . . . a little overwhelming. Figuring out how I'm going to make it all work."

He sighed. "You want my advice?"

"Absolutely." The emphatic way I responded seemed to relax him. His jaw lost some of its rigidity, and his eyes softened slightly. It was still obvious he was less than thrilled to be speaking to me—which I couldn't blame him for—but maybe it was possible for me to worm my way back into their good graces. If Vee could forgive me, maybe her dad and brothers would too.

"Stop being such a fucking wimp and figure your shit out."

Or maybe forgiveness was not in the cards.

"You've identified the end goal, so that's a step," he continued. "Now you gotta figure out what you need to put in place to accomplish the goal. To me, your first step is to finish school. Having any kind of business degree is gonna help you out. Whether it gives you another marketable skill to bring to an interview or whether you need to keep yourself organized in a solo venture, your accounting degree is gonna come in handy."

While Manny had gotten off to a rough start with the whole wimp thing, he'd really turned this pep talk around. There was a lot of good insight in what he was saying. It was basically what Vee had already said—which I'd agreed with—but it felt good to have it confirmed.

"Yeah, and that hardware store probably brings in all kinds of vocational workers. So network there, get to know people," Franco added. "Meanwhile, keep working there and fixing up your house. That way you'll have funds coming in and projects to build a portfolio with."

"That's all...great advice," I breathed, appreciation overflowing that they'd made it sound so manageable.

What they were saying was ultimately good old-fashioned common sense. But I'd been so focused on needing to get the wheels on my future moving, I hadn't stopped to think that I'd already been on the path I wanted. I'd gone from feeling I was in the absolutely wrong place in my professional life to understanding I was exactly where I needed to be.

Franco scoffed. "Of course it's great advice. Did you ask us to call you thinking you'd be getting shit suggestions?"

"No! No way. I knew you'd be able to help. I just... didn't realize how much you guys would be able to calm me down while *also* giving great advice."

Manny smirked. "He was just giving you shit. But glad we could help."

"Is that all you needed?" Franco asked. "I have a date later, so I gotta go get waxed."

"Ew," Vee said. I'd almost forgotten she was next to me, she'd been so quiet while her brothers and I spoke.

"What?" Franco asked. "Gotta look good for the ladies." He pulled the phone back a little so we could see him run a hand down his chest as he spoke.

"You probably look like one of those hairless cats," Vee replied. "All wrinkly and alien-like."

Franco shrugged with a smile. "Never had any complaints."

"Other than the ones filed with the police," Vee retorted.

Franco pointed a finger at the phone. "That's not funny. I've never been inappropriate with any girl I've taken out." He smirked again. "Unless they've asked me to."

Vee groaned as she turned to me. "Is brain bleach a thing? Because I need some."

"You're just jealous because your little surfer boy over there has no game."

"Hey," I said, affronted. I had game. Didn't I?

Vee squawked in outrage on my behalf. "Owen has tons of game. I'll have you know, just last night, he—"

"No. Nope. Nuh-uh," Manny interrupted, holding a hand out as if he could physically keep her from saying anything else. "I am not listening to my little sister talk about her sex life." He smacked Franco on the back of the head. "That's for making me say the words *sex* and *my little sister* in the same sentence."

Vee smiled as if having them turn on each other had been her plan all along. She scared me sometimes. "Okay, well, I guess we'll leave you two to . . . whatever it is you two do. And hey."

They both settled down and gave the phone their attention.

"Thanks," she said, her words dripping with sincerity.

"Anytime," Manny replied before ending the call.

Vee put the phone down on the coffee table and relaxed back into the couch. "That went well, right?"

I settled in beside her. "Definitely. It feels good to have some info and a plan."

"Good," she said, smiling at me before leaning over and giving me a soft kiss.

I returned it, taking it from something soft and light to something deeper and more meaningful—the perfect metaphor for my feelings for her.

Chapter Three

VERONICA

Even though Inez was a tenant, she was also a friend. And so it seemed only fitting to have our other friends over to meet her. Granted, most of them had met her at least in passing because she worked with Ransom and Taylor, but we wanted something more… formal.

Sure, she was paying us for her room, but we also wanted her to feel like part of our endearing yet dysfunctional found family.

Since we were nearing the end of summer and some of us would be returning to school or were getting ready to start new ventures, it was also a fun way to close out the season together. Two birds, one cookout.

As Owen did… whatever he was doing outside on the grill, Nattie and I prepped things in the kitchen. She looked out the window where she could see the large *Welcome* sign I'd hung as well as the balloons I'd tied to every object I could find.

"Don't you think this is a little… much?" she asked.

I shrugged. "It's fun."

"You didn't have this much fun when I moved in," she muttered.

"Maybe that's because you moved in as my boyfriend's wife."

She rolled her eyes. "You just can't let that go, can you?"

The truth was, I *had* pretty much let it go. The fact I was able to casually throw it into conversation instead of hurling it like a grenade was proof of that. But I enjoyed holding it over her because I was maybe a teensy bit sadistic when it came to torturing my cousin.

"Hey," Inez said as she came into the kitchen from the hallway.

"What can I do to help?" she added.

"You can't help with your own party," I scolded.

She narrowed her eyes. "You said this was a party *with* me, not *for* me."

"The over-the-top decorating would imply otherwise," Nattie muttered.

"Decorating? Wha—" Inez looked out the window before giving me an unimpressed look. "Seriously?"

"We want you to feel at home here," I defended.

"I don't think making a spectacle of me is going to achieve that."

"It's not a spectacle. It's a casual party with friends."

"Your friends or mine?" she asked.

I opened my mouth to reply, but no words formed. How had we not thought to invite any of her friends? We were the absolute worst.

"Exactly," she said. "You're having a party so your friends can meet *me*. Therefore, a spectacle."

I squinted as if contemplating her words. "I still think *spectacle* is an exaggeration. Especially since everyone has already met you."

She rolled her eyes. "Semantics." Looking around, she asked, "What still needs to be done?"

She seemed content to let the subject drop, so I refocused on the various snacks spread out on the counter.

"Wanna put the salad together?"

"Sure." Inez set to work, as did I.

When Owen reappeared sometime later, he asked, "How's everything going in here?"

I scanned the countertops. "I think we may have gone overboard."

Inez snorted as Owen came over and dropped a kiss on my cheek. "With this crowd? No such thing."

Which was true. There was genuinely no overfeeding a group that included Brody. The guy was a bottomless pit.

We bustled around, cleaning up and setting food out on the table so people could grab it at their leisure. Then there was nothing left to do but wait.

It didn't take long for us to hear the front door thrown open and the booming voice of Carter say, "Everybody decent?"

Gimli began to bark in excitement, and I heard Carter coo at him as we walked to meet them in the foyer.

"Who's a good boy?" Carter asked as he rolled around on the ground and let Gimli lick and jump all over him.

My eyes caught Toby's, who shrugged in a *What can ya do?* gesture.

Carter eventually stood, bro-hugged with Owen, and then leaned in to give me a kiss on the cheek.

I stopped him with an outstretched hand. "No way."

He clutched his chest. "You don't want a kiss from me?"

"Not after you just made out with our dog."

"*Our* dog, huh? How domestic." Carter waggled his eyes as he stepped up to Toby and pressed a chaste kiss to his lips. "At least my boyfriend will let me kiss him."

"Against the advice of everyone," I mumbled.

Carter ignored me as he quickly hugged Nattie and then moved to Inez. "Nice to see you again," he said. It was so cute when he used his manners.

"Thanks." She smiled.

"Drinks are out back," Owen said. "Food's in the kitchen."

We all turned to head toward the back of the house when the door flew open again, almost hitting Nattie.

"Doesn't anybody knock anymore?" she grumbled.

"Sorry," Brody said with a smirk as he let himself in. Behind him trailed Aamee, Sophia, and Drew.

Despite Sophia always arguing with her brother, they seemed to spend a lot of time together. Maybe because Brody and Drew were working on opening a bar together it put them in a kind of forced proximity.

Once greetings were over, Brody looked at Owen with a wicked smile on his face. "Quite the harem you got going here, O-Man."

Aamee smacked him as soon as the words were fully out of his mouth, and Owen gave him a reproachful look.

"Not cool, man."

"What?" Brody asked, hands and eyes spread wide. "It was a joke."

"Jokes should be funny," Sophia said seriously, as if truly reminding him of this fact.

"Everyone is so sensitive," he muttered.

Ignoring him, we made our way out back. It was warm, but the trees provided enough shade to make it bearable. I loved the space out here. A lot of houses built nowadays didn't have the land Owen's did. His backyard was substantial, probably over an acre, though I'd never thought to ask the exact size.

But other than mowing it, the back half of the yard was untouched. Maybe we should think about putting something out there. A garden or volleyball pit or something.

I tuned back into the conversation around me as our friends teased each other. Taylor and Ransom arrived, followed closely by Xander and then Cody. Roddie was the final person to turn up, and I felt a small sense of victory shoot through me that we had invited one of Inez's friends after all.

These were my people, my surrogate family while I was away from New York. I'd met them under the strangest of circumstances, but somehow, I couldn't imagine it happening any other way. We were bound by the bizarre—and those bonds were unbreakable.

OWEN

Nothing beat hanging out with friends on a summer night, casually drinking and eating. Everyone had made an attempt to get to know Inez better and welcome her into the fold.

"Why would you move *here* from California?" Well, everyone had made an attempt except Natalia. Her question would've been harmless if not for the derision in her tone.

Every comment she made to Inez seemed to carry a sharpness to it, and I didn't understand why. They'd been living together for over a week and hadn't seemed to have any problems. But today, Natalia seemed to have an issue.

Inez shrugged, seemingly unbothered by Natalia's tone. "Here's as good a place as any."

Natalia gave her a dubious look but took a sip of her drink rather than reply.

"You moved here from New York," Vee pointed out. "People could ask the same question of you."

"I came here because I got married, which you know."

"You're not married anymore," Aamee pointed out.

Natalia sniffed. "No, but I have a job here now."

"Doesn't she work at a mechanic's shop?" Brody whispered loudly enough for us all to hear.

"Yeah," Carter replied, also whispering loudly. "They must not have any of those in New York."

Natalia shot them a dry look, and the rest of us fought smiles.

We bullshitted for a bit longer, catching up on what everyone's next steps were. I was the only one who didn't have much to contribute. Even though I was close to the same age as everyone else here, Xander was the only one who was still completing undergrad, even though someone had said he already had multiple degrees. He and I had never been super close, and I wasn't fully sure what his deal was.

Cody was younger than I was, but he'd always said school wasn't for him. He worked a few jobs to make ends meet and always had crazy stories about things that happened to him. Despite not having a firm career path, he seemed content with where his life was as well as where it was heading. So even he was in a better place than me.

Granted, talking to Vee's brothers had given me a better

grasp on what I wanted next, but there were still a ton of doubts swirling in my head. I didn't know what was best in the long run, and I hated that. Considering I used to mostly exist by letting life come to me, it felt odd to suddenly feel so adrift at not having it all figured out. Home ownership, a failed marriage, and a serious relationship made a guy grow up, it seemed.

As I looked around at my friends, I saw people who knew what was next for them. Vee was off to law school, as was Taylor. Ransom was working as an athletic trainer at a local university. Drew and Brody were almost set to begin renovations on a building they purchased for their new bar. Sophia had gotten hired at a marketing firm in town, and Aamee . . . did whatever Aamee did. Something in public relations, I thought. She kind of scared me a little, so I tried not to ask her too many questions.

Inez didn't seem to have it all figured out, but she also seemed to almost intentionally structure her life that way. Kind of like Cody. And Natalia was . . . Natalia.

Then there was me. The guy who'd graduate in less than a year with an accounting degree even though he wanted to renovate houses. And I knew, logically, that those things weren't mutually exclusive. But I still felt like I was biding my time until I could put my real plans into action—and hope those plans actually worked out to my benefit.

Someone nudged my arm, and I looked over to see Vee looking at me, concern evident in the furrow of her brow.

You okay? she mouthed.

I reached over and took her hand, giving it a squeeze. "I'm fine," I answered, hoping it was true.

Chapter Four

OWEN

I pulled onto campus and drove through the parking lots, hoping I'd get lucky and find someone leaving. Parking on campus was always a hassle, but it seemed especially bad the first couple of weeks.

Miraculously, a student arrived at their small red Honda just as I rolled past. She vacated the spot quickly, and I pulled in. Despite enjoying the stroke of luck at easily finding parking, I wasn't in a great frame of mind to start classes. Slinking back in my seat, I closed my eyes and tried to do a quick meditation to find a better head space.

Vee had been almost giddy to begin school. She had a few days of orientation before classes began, and she was excited to get started. I, on the other hand, had practically had to drag myself out of bed.

When I couldn't put it off any longer, I grabbed my book bag and clambered out of my truck. My trek to my first accounting class could only be classified as a trudge, and I wasn't sure what the hell my problem was. I'd always enjoyed school before. But I already felt over it.

The class passed quickly, the professor reviewing the syllabus and then sending us on our way to prepare for the next session. I had an hour before my music class, so I headed toward the quad and found a bench, cracked open the accounting book I'd purchased the week before, and began the first assignment.

As I covered the material, I felt myself slipping back into the old Owen. The guy who enjoyed learning. Maybe with all the drama of the summer, I'd simply forgotten how fun school could be—even accounting.

When it was time to head to the Fine Arts building, I was feeling better. I arrived at the classroom surprised but thankful to see a familiar face.

"Yo, man. What's up?" I asked as I lowered into the open seat next to Xander.

He looked over at me, startled for a second before his features relaxed. "Hey, how's it going?"

We did a bro-shake and settled back in our seats.

"Have you heard anything about this professor?" I asked.

"Nah, I think he's new."

"At least he didn't require us to buy a book."

Professors typically knew these classes were only being taken as general requirements by people who didn't have more than a passing interest in the subject, and they typically acted accordingly, which I appreciated. Having to pay a million dollars for a book for a class I was only taking because the university told me I had to wasn't ideal.

"Definitely off to a good start," Xander agreed.

"So, you picking up a minor in music or just fulfilling a requirement?" I asked.

Xander shrugged. "Neither, really. I was just trying to fill out a schedule with something in a department I hadn't taken before."

I nodded like that made sense even though it didn't. Was he just taking random classes for fun? To be well-rounded? To find his calling? I tried to think of how to tactfully ask but was interrupted by the professor coming in.

At least, I assumed with the way he strode to the lectern that he was the professor. Nothing else about him would have implied that, though. He was dressed in jeans with holes at the knees, flip-flops, a threadbare T-shirt that said *Dream Waves* on it, and his blond hair was pulled back at the nape. He had a five-o'clock shadow at eleven a.m. and carried a small bongo drum.

"This is either going to be really good or really bad," Xander whispered.

Within ten minutes, we learned it was the latter. The guy rapped on the drum after nearly every statement, as if punctuating a joke with a cymbal. Except nothing the guy—Ted, as he instructed us to call him—said was remotely funny.

"For fuck's sake," Xander muttered as he banged the bongo for at least the tenth time.

"So, yeah, I couldn't find a book that had all the things I want to share with you guys. And gals," he quickly added with a finger point in the direction of a girl in the front row. "Don't wanna be accused of sexism on the first day." He said that with a wink and a bang of the drum. "So I put my own book together. The university said I could." He smiled as if this was insider information only he had instead of common knowledge.

I'd had to get secondary materials from the University Press for multiple classes over the years. But I had a feeling

Ted's materials would be unlike any others.

"We also have a Myspace page you'll need to join. I have a lot of music uploaded there that you'll need. A lot of it from my own band." He pointed at his shirt. "Dream Waves."

"Myspace?" I muttered to Xander.

"Yeah, clearly Ted's living in the wrong decade. I think it became really popular with musicians, but I don't know if anyone still uses it."

"I know you all wanna know what inspired the name of my band," Ted continued. "People always ask about it because it's so unique. It combines my two favorite things: following dreams and chasing waves."

And that was when it became abundantly clear that I was going to have to drop this class.

VERONICA

As I pulled into the driveway, I still felt a frisson of excitement across my skin that had been there all day. I was doing it. I was officially a law school student. I'd already been invited to join a study group, I'd done all the reading I needed to complete before classes started, and I'd made friends with the woman who ran the law library. Things were amazing.

Owen's truck was also in the driveway, which excited me even more. Nothing could make a good day even better than celebrating with my boyfriend.

I let myself into the house and yelled for Owen.

"In here," he replied, the sound coming from the kitchen.

I walked in and found him sitting at the table, hunkered over a laptop. I walked up behind him and slid my arms around him, pressing a kiss to his cheek. Then I settled my chin on his shoulder and looked at his laptop.

"Is that Myspace?"

He sighed. "Yeah. My professor, *Ted*, told us we had to follow his band Dream Waves."

"Like, as an assignment or a recommendation? And Dream Waves? Really?"

"A requirement. And yeah, really. The guy's a total lunatic. He has all these insane things on the syllabus. Like going to one of his shows in addition to a variety of other ones that will 'enhance our music education and simultaneously change our lives.'"

Owen's use of finger quotes dislodged my chin a bit, but I stayed put, gripping him a little tighter. He seemed like he needed it.

"We also need to form a band with our classmates and create an original song that we'll perform on the quad at the end of the semester."

"What? Can he do that?" The class wasn't performance based. No one would've taken it with the understanding they'd have to learn an instrument and play for a crowd. The idea was ridiculous.

Owen shrugged. "He said he can when someone asked. Said he already got the approval of the dean."

I gave him another kiss. "Sounds like a class you need to drop."

He sighed. "I thought that, but I already joined a band. I don't want to leave anyone hanging."

I had to hold back a laugh because only Owen would let his loyalty to a bunch of strangers override his best interests.

"I'm sure they'd get over it."

"Xander probably wouldn't."

"Xander's in the class? And *staying* in it?"

"He said the professor's bound to do something outrageous that gets him fired, and Xander wants a front-row seat for when it happens."

"Sounds fatalistic. Classic Xander. But still, I'm sure he wouldn't hold it against you if you dropped the class."

"Oh, I think he would."

"Really? Why?"

"Because he said he'd never forgive me if I dropped the class. Ted recommended we group up in fours, and he doesn't want to get stuck with the other two alone."

"Maybe they'll drop it too."

He shook his head. "Not a chance. One is actually a fan of Ted's music, and the other was in high school marching band. They were actually good drafts by me, since Xander tasked me with finding our bandmates, but they're also both *super* into the assignment. Like they actually think we're going to be a real band. Xander said if I abandoned him with those two, he'd make my life miserable. It seemed like a credible threat."

I kissed him again. "Sounds like you've had a rough day."

He groaned. "It hasn't been one of my best."

"Maybe I can improve it a bit." I trailed my lips down his neck and lowered my hands so I could run them over his chest.

"Hmm. How would you do that?" He tilted his head to give me better access.

"I have lots of . . . ideas."

"I would love to hear about some of these ideas."

I smiled against his skin. "Maybe instead of telling you about it, we could go upstairs, and I could show you."

"I do learn best that way," he murmured.

I gave him one last kiss before pulling back so I could

stand up straight. "Then let's go upstairs so I can teach you a few things."

He slammed his laptop lid closed as he stood, whirling around and grabbing me in a hug and lifting me off my feet. "You're moving too slow."

I giggled as he did his best to run for the stairs while holding on to me. Thankfully, he set me down before we started up the stairs. He gripped my hand as he led me up to his bed, and I knew in that moment, despite all the great things happening in my life, being with him was still the best.

Chapter Five

VERONICA

Later that night, Owen and I sat cuddled on the couch. I was reading some course material, and he was researching instruments that wouldn't be difficult to learn to play.

"What do you think about the kazoo?" he asked.

"I . . . don't?"

"I feel like that or a tambourine might be my best options."

"I wonder if you guys could just pretend to play instruments. You could tell Professor Ted that it's an avant-garde approach to music. The audience gets to imagine whatever music they want to hear while you all stand onstage with instruments made of cardboard."

Owen slowly turned his head in my direction. "Do you really think that could work?"

I shrugged but was cut off from replying by the front door swinging open and Nattie's voice yelling, "Anyone home?"

"Yeah, in the living room," Owen called back.

A moment later, Nattie appeared in the room with a girl shadowing her. "Hey. This is Wynter."

"With a *y*. It's Wynter with a *y*," the girl, *Wynter with a y*, said vehemently.

Gimli, who'd been snoozing at our feet, got up to sniff the new arrival. But he stopped abruptly about three feet from her, leaned forward as if to sniff more closely, and then tucked tail and booked from the room. Which was . . . concerning.

Though I was too busy trying to figure out why the spelling of her name was something I needed to know to analyze his reaction further.

Then Nattie continued. "She's our newest roommate."

Owen and I both sat forward quickly, as if we'd both barely restrained ourselves from leaping off the couch.

"I'm sorry . . . what now?" Owen asked.

"Wynter needs a place to live, and I figured since you were renting out rooms now, I may as well offer one."

Owen looked gobsmacked for a moment before he recovered. "I'm sorry, uh, Wynter with a *y*, but I think taking on another roommate is something we all need to discuss first."

Nattie, with her arms akimbo, snidely replied, "You didn't discuss Inez moving in with me. Why do I need to discuss Wynter moving in with you?"

"Because it's not your house, you psycho," I shouted at her. Seriously, what the hell was she thinking?

"It's not *your* house either," she argued back.

"Right. Which is why I'm not inviting strangers to live here. No offense, Wynter."

"But Inez was *your* friend. She only lives here because you talked Owen into it."

"No, I suggested to Owen that it might be a sound financial decision to rent out the basement to someone I knew had a steady income."

Nattie looked at me smugly. "Wynter has a steady income. She agreed to pay first and last month's rent up front if she could move in immediately. Right, Wynter?"

Wynter didn't answer right away. She'd moved farther into the room, allowing me to see her more clearly. She was tall and thin, almost gaunt, with a pale complexion that was made all the more pasty by her long dark hair that fell down her back in dreadlocks.

As we stared at her, awaiting her reply, she looked around the room, mostly at the ceiling, her head whipping from side to side.

I had the sudden urge to follow Gimli's quick exit.

"Wynter," Nattie practically snarled.

Wynter jerked back to herself and said, "Sorry. Did an old man live here recently?"

Owen and I looked at each other before Owen replied with a cautious, "No."

"Hmm. A woman who looked like a man?"

"No," Owen repeated, more firmly this time.

"A younger person who just looked old?"

"Jesus Christ," I couldn't help but mutter.

"No, it's not Him," she replied.

I shot Nattie a wide-eyed look that I hoped screamed *What the fuck!* "Where did you two meet?"

Even Nattie had begun eyeing Wynter curiously. "Uh, downtown. They closed one of the streets for a kind of block party thing. There were vendors there selling stuff, and Wynter was one of them. We got to talking, and she mentioned needing a place to live, so I figured"—she shrugged—"why not?"

"So you've known her approximately, what, two hours?" I asked.

"Give or take." Nattie's reply was said with the ease of someone who probably shouldn't have made it this far in life without being abducted by a stranger with candy.

"Uh, hey, Wyn-Wynter?" Owen said, trying to get the girl's attention from the corner she'd begun staring at.

Wynter looked over at him. "I think I figured out what's going on with the old guy. He didn't live here. He just likes the house."

"That's . . . great for him," Owen replied. "But, uh, I hope you understand, we weren't planning on taking in any more tenants. The only thing we have is one spare bedroom. They're not full apartments or anything."

Wynter, her attention back on the walls, put her hand inside the leather satchel she had hanging from her shoulder and withdrew a wad of cash. She then finally turned to completely face us and held out the money.

"I have fifteen hundred dollars to put down. I don't need much space, so just a bedroom is fine as long as I'm free to burn sage and other incense in there. I may also need to put some warding marks around the room, but I'll be sure to use chalk so it wipes off easily."

Owen stared at the cash in her hand for a moment, seemingly trying to wrap his brain around being handed a stack of bills by someone discussing warding marks.

I tried my best to smile genuinely. "Could we, maybe, have a minute? To discuss . . . everything."

Wynter offered a half smile that was really more of a twitch than anything. "Sure. Could Natalia maybe show me the room while you . . . discuss?"

"Uh, yeah, that sounds like a good idea," Owen said.

Nattie pouted. "Don't I get to be part of the discussion?"

Owen opened his mouth to reply, but I beat him to it with a firm, "No."

Nattie huffed but motioned for Wynter to follow her and then led her from the room.

"Okay, seriously, what the hell was Nattie thinking?" I whisper-shouted when they'd left the room. "That girl is... out there."

Owen's lips twisted. "Yeah, but she also has fifteen hundred dollars ready to hand over. That could go a long way to helping me make more repairs."

"You can't be serious. You're not actually considering letting a total stranger who stares at walls while claiming to see invisible old men move *in*. Are you?"

"We can offer her a short-term lease. Then if it's not working out, we can just not renew it."

"Do you even have a lease lying around? And are we not going to discuss the seeing-ghosts thing?"

"Yeah, I printed off a few when Inez was going to move in. I can just amend one to reflect the different time frame. And you know about the poltergeist from my old room, so I don't find it impossible to believe she really did see an old man."

I sighed. "This has disaster written all over it."

Owen put an arm around me. "Yeah, but since when has that ever stopped us?"

The man made a fair point.

"Should we go up and see how she likes the room?" Owen asked.

"I guess," I said, sounding as unenthused as possible.

He pressed a kiss to my hair before taking my hand and leading me out of the room and up the stairs.

"I'm sure everything will be fine," he said as we

approached the room. “How bad could she be?”

When we reached the room, Wynter was sitting on the floor, eyes closed, palms facing up on her knees, as her lips moved in a silent chant.

Even Nattie had started to look as if she’d miscalculated.

“You were saying?” I snarked at Owen.

Owen stared at the scene before him as if he were willing it to make sense.

He cleared his throat. “Wynter?”

Her lips stopped moving, and she sighed heavily before opening her eyes. “I was communing with my spirit guides. I sense a . . . presence in this room.”

“A presence?” Nattie asked, sounding terrified. Served her right.

“Yes. But I can’t tell if it means me harm or not yet.”

If said presence had ever met her, I was pretty sure I knew what its intentions would be.

Wynter got up off the floor. “I’m confident I can handle it, whatever it is. Do we have a deal?”

Owen cast a worried look around the room before fixing his gaze back on her.

“Yeah. Yeah, we have a deal.”

OWEN

Wynter was happy to sign a short-term lease because, as she said, who knew where the wind would take her.

She moved in that night, which worried me a bit. Where had she been and why had she needed to leave so quickly? These were questions I probably should’ve asked, but I felt too far in by the time I thought about it.

Wynter returned to the house in an old blue Honda and pulled two trash bags out of the back seat. I offered to help, but she said she didn't want me to get my aura all over her things.

Okay, then.

Joke was on her, because I'd had my aura read a couple years ago, and the woman had said it was beautiful.

We barely saw her in the days that followed. She was either out or in her room. She didn't keep food in the kitchen, and she never watched TV or anything in the living room, even though we'd made sure she knew those were communal areas we were willing to share with her.

I'd begun to think that maybe *she* was the ghost.

But then she appeared in the kitchen looking decidedly . . . haggard.

Vee and I were cooking dinner, and I caught sight of her first, her long dreadlocks piled atop her head in a messy bun and wearing a baggy T-shirt that said *The Doors* and a pair of green cargo shorts. Her eyes looked a little wild.

"Hey, Wynter with a *y*," I said, hoping a joke would lighten the ominous mood that seemed to emanate from her.

Vee's head jerked up at my words, first looking at me and then turning in the direction I was looking. After catching sight of Wynter, Vee looked back at me in what could only be classified as alarm.

"Do you have any issues with me running salt along the boundary of my room?" Wynter asked.

"Uh . . . salt?" I asked.

"For the spirit."

"Oh, um, no? I guess not. Still not friendly I take it?"

Honestly, I truly didn't think there was a spirit up there.

Since dealing with my own poltergeist for years, I considered myself fairly sensitive to those beyond the veil, so to speak, and I'd never picked up on anything in the house. And while I'd never slept in that room, I'd gone in and out of there frequently enough to feel confident nothing dwelled in there.

Wynter shook her head. "The only way forward is through."

I shared a look with Vee before saying, "I'm not sure what that means."

"Trying to ignore the presence isn't working. So I'll have to deal with it directly. If I can't keep it out of my room, I may have to banish it more permanently."

"Like an exorcism?" Vee asked.

"Yes. I have some acquaintances who may be able to help. But don't worry. I'll consult you before I move forward with anything like that."

That was good because there was no way I was letting Wynter plan an exorcism in my house. Before I could come up with a tactful way of telling her that, she backed out of the room and disappeared.

"I truly don't mean to judge," Vee started, "but that girl is weird as hell."

"Yeah, she's . . . something."

We went back to fixing dinner when Natalia came in. "Hey, so the crazy chick you let move in here is dumping salt all over the place."

"The crazy . . .? Are you serious right now?" Vee asked, her voice accusing. "You're the one who invited her to move in."

Natalia clearly had balls of steel, because she rolled her eyes. "You know I'm a horrible judge of character. You should've never said yes."

"Your ability to blame everyone else for your mistakes is truly incredible."

Natalia smiled. "Thanks."

"It wasn't a compliment," Vee grumbled.

"Everything's a compliment if you choose to take it that way," Natalia chimed. "What's for dinner? I hope it's nothing you need salt for, 'cause—" She gestured upstairs rather than finish her sentence.

Vee looked seconds from committing murder, so I quickly cut in. "We're having baked chicken and salad."

"That's so boring and healthy," Natalia whined.

"It's a good thing we didn't invite you to eat any of it, then," Vee replied.

"But you guys are like my parents now. You're supposed to feed me."

"There's a box of Kraft Macaroni & Cheese in the cabinet if you want to make that," I offered.

Vee sneered. "You could get less sodium from licking Wynter's floor."

"I could also probably get high as a kite. She's been burning all kinds of shit in there." Natalia retrieved the box from the cabinet and set about making it. "Do you really think there's a ghost in there?"

"No," Vee answered before I could.

"I was asking Owen."

"Why aren't you asking me?"

"Because you're too . . . logical," Natalia explained.

"I'm going to try not to be offended by that," I said. "But I also say no. I think Wynter is . . . projecting."

"Projecting what?" Natalia asked.

"Her untreated mental illness," Vee sniped, and I shot

her a withering look, to which she mouthed *Sorry.*

"It's not okay to joke about someone's mental health," I chided.

"I know, I know. I said I was sorry."

Natalia looked pensive for a second before saying, "I don't mean to sound offensive . . ."

Which pretty much guaranteed she was going to.

"But that girl is definitely a few fries short of a Happy Meal, so is it really *joking* to talk about it?"

I opened my mouth to reprimand Natalia for her insensitivity when a loud bang came from upstairs. We all shared a look and then bolted for the stairs. When we reached Wynter's room, we stopped and looked at each other again before I reached out and knocked.

"Wynter?"

"One second," she yelled from inside.

We heard scrambling around before the door opened and revealed an out-of-breath Wynter.

"Everything okay?" I asked.

"We heard a bang," Vee added.

"Yeah, sorry, that was just me."

We stood there waiting for more information, but none seemed to be forthcoming.

"Were you jumping or something?" I said.

"No, I fell off the dresser."

"Oh, jeez, are you okay?" I asked at the same time Natalia said, "What the hell were you doing on the dresser?" And if I was being honest, I hoped Wynter answered her question in lieu of mine.

"I'm okay. It's just hard to get the salt to stay on the ceiling. I lost my balance."

"Salt on the... ceiling?" I shifted a bit so I could look around her, and that was when I saw a bunch of little baggies—nickel bags I was pretty sure—taped to the ceiling.

"Salt on the floor isn't keeping him out. He can still appear through the ceiling. But don't worry. I'm using that sticky stuff that doesn't ruin paint."

"I, um, thanks... for that. That's considerate. Do you want, like, a ladder or anything?"

Vee looked at me as if *I'd* lost my mind, and truthfully, I was beginning to feel like I had.

"No, I'm just about done. Thanks, though." And with that, she closed and locked the door, leaving us staring agape on the other side.

"So have we decided where we stand on discussing her mental health?" Natalia asked.

I shot her a glare before heading for the stairs so I could eat my boring, healthy, salt-free dinner.

And if I looked into how to commit someone while I was eating it, well, that was my own business.

Chapter Six

OWEN

It was only nine in the morning when I heard my doorbell ring for the third time in two minutes. At least it had *seemed* that long from my spot under the covers.

"Who *is* that?" I heard Vee groan beside me.

"I don't know, and I don't wanna find out." I flipped over and pulled her closer to me.

"We need to get one of those doorbells with the cameras like everyone has."

"But then we'd feel obligated to answer if it were someone we cared about. This way I can pretend it's some Bible beater waiting to warn me about my ticket to hell or one of those guys passing out info about lawn care."

"Our lawn *does* look like shit lately," Vee joked, though the comment wasn't incorrect and we both knew it.

"It's the end of summer, and it hasn't rained in like three weeks. Totally expected. I'll fertilize in the fall, and it'll be all good. No way I'm paying someone to do that shit."

She laughed a little before she turned over and kissed me.

"What was that for?" I asked.

"Nothing really. Just turns me on when you talk about doing things yourself. You're so manly." She kissed me again, this time long enough to make me fully hard.

"I'm also so poor," I said when our lips parted. That made Vee laugh again. "You think whoever it was is gone?" I asked, already rolling her over so I could position myself on top of her. But thoughts of pulling off Vee's white tank top were interrupted by a male voice yelling up the stairs.

"Yo, Owen, you here?"

"Is that Xander?" Vee looked completely confused. I was too, though not quite as much since I knew he was supposed to come over around ten thirty.

"Unfortunately." Reluctantly, I got out of bed and walked toward the door. "He and the other band members are supposed to come over later to get started on this project."

It had only been a few days since Professor Ted had assigned it, but when we'd returned to the second class yesterday, Xander and I had been surprised to learn that almost all the other groups had gotten a jump on things.

It was probably more due to them being completely delusional and seeing this as an opportunity to play out some musical fantasy they'd had since childhood than the fact that they cared about their grades, but who was I to make assumptions?

"On a Saturday morning?" Vee's confusion seemed to be mounting. "Everyone was available and willing to work on that thing today?"

"Yeah, I guess. I mean, Xander wasn't thrilled about having to get up early, which makes me wonder even more why he's here right now. And Brae and Jagger seem to go along with whatever. Something tells me their social calendars don't fill up too quickly."

"I can hear you up there," Xander called. "Come down."

Opening the bedroom door, I said, "I'm not trying to hide from you. I was in bed . . . you know, because it's nine on a weekend. And you're not supposed to be here until ten thirty."

I made my way downstairs and was surprised to see Xander standing alone. He was holding a box of coffee, which made his presence here so early a little more tolerable.

"Where are Natalia and Inez?"

Xander shrugged the shoulder of the arm that was holding a paper bag I figured was filled with creamers and sugar.

"Who let you in?"

"I let me in." He pointed at the front door. "I know this house is old and things not working is part of its charm and everything, but that lock doesn't even work. I turned the knob and gave it a hard push, and it opened pretty easily."

"Perfect. Something else I gotta fix. Also, you realize you're like an hour and a half early, right?"

"Of course. I learned to read an analog clock when I was nineteen months old."

I didn't think that was true, but I knew with Xander it might be, so I didn't question it aloud.

"Thanks for the coffee. I figured I could set up in the kitchen when the other members of our *band*," I said with an eye roll, "get here."

"That's actually why I came early," Xander said. "I was up most of the night learning to play the piano, and I didn't go to sleep, so I figured I'd just head over."

"You learned how to play the piano in one night?" I knew the dude liked to be prepared, but that seemed ambitious—and pretty much impossible—even for Xander.

"Well, I did have a bit of a background in it because my dad made me take lessons as a kid, but I haven't played since I was about eight, and even then I wasn't any good. But I guess you could say I wasn't starting from scratch."

"Do you even have a piano?"

"No. I bought one of those little keyboards toddlers play with. Same notes. It'll be fine."

I doubted that.

"So what are you gonna play?" He poured himself a cup of coffee.

"Dead," I said. "I'm hoping I can just play dead."

VERONICA

Once Owen had taken a shower and gotten dressed, he and Xander spent the next hour or so in the kitchen talking about possible band names. And once Nattie and Inez had joined the conversation, the guys had quite a list going.

They claimed they were going to narrow it down before Brae and Jagger got there in the hopes that leaving them with just a few choices would make picking a name easier, but so far the list had only grown. If they couldn't even pick a *name* for a band that didn't technically exist, I had no idea how they were going to *function* as one.

Inez and Nattie had tossed out a few suggestions too, ranging from the mundane The Classmates all the way to the absurd Four Bamboos, which Nattie had just suggested moments ago.

"What does that even mean?" I asked.

"Band names don't need to mean anything," Owen said.

"Especially when it isn't a real band."

He had a point there.

But Nattie then explained, "Giving someone three stalks of bamboo is lucky. Four means you hate them and want to curse them."

"I'm definitely giving Professor Ted four bamboo stalks at the end of the semester," Owen said.

The doorbell rang a few seconds later, and Owen went to get it. He returned with a man who had to be almost seven feet tall with pink hair that was shaved on one side and down to his shoulder on the other. He also seemed to be wearing some sort of contacts that made his eyes look like a wild animal's and was holding a guitar without a case.

He introduced himself as Brae.

We then all introduced ourselves to him as well as the petite woman who followed him into the kitchen. She looked to be about five feet tall and wore a yellow sleeveless dress with flowers. It reminded me of something my grandmother would've put me in for church when I was a little girl.

I assumed that was Jagger, though she spoke so softly, I couldn't hear her for sure. Her straight black hair framed her face, and her bangs practically covered her eyes completely. Jagger took a seat at the kitchen table and pulled her computer out of the backpack she'd been wearing, which was when I noticed it had cartoon kittens all over it.

I didn't even know why one would need a computer for this kind of project, but I also didn't want to find out, so I decided I'd finish doing the dishes that were in the sink and then excuse myself to go do . . . well, anything that didn't involve being in a room with these two.

Brae plucked at his guitar, which I was thankful was

electric because it was quiet since he hadn't brought an amplifier.

"Oh, I almost forgot. You had a bunch of mail in your mailbox, so I brought it in for you." He removed a bunch of white envelopes from inside his raincoat. The raincoat he'd worn on a sunny ninety-degree day.

"It's illegal to go through someone else's mail," Xander muttered to no one in particular, though it had obviously been in reference to Brae. "Felony actually."

Brae glared at him but didn't bother replying.

Since most of my bills were electronic, I'd only gotten a few things in the mail here since I'd moved in a few months back. I wasn't in the habit of checking the mail frequently, and it appeared neither was Owen. Or maybe it was because we now had four adults living here.

"Anything for me?" I asked.

"Nah, I don't think so." Owen flipped through the stack of envelopes Brae had handed him. "Damn, we need to get Inez her own box with the rate she's getting mail here. There were like seven things for her the other day, and they all looked interesting."

"What do you mean 'looked interesting'?"

He shrugged. "One was in a purple envelope, so it was probably a card or something. And I think she got like three wedding invitations."

"Wedding invites are as bad as bills," Brae said.

Jagger nodded, and I saw her lips move but still couldn't make out what she'd said.

Brae's mouth fell open as he stared at her for a moment before looking around at all of us. "Can anyone hear what the fuck she's saying?"

Jagger flipped him off and then typed something into her phone.

Then came the robot voice from the cell phone that said, "My cousin's wedding is how I got laryngitis."

Brae laughed in a way that I would've found insulting if it had been toward me. "What's that got to do with bills?" He seemed genuinely confused, but Jagger didn't bother typing a reply into her phone.

Owen made three stacks of mail on the counter. "Even Minnie still gets things sent to her sometimes." He pointed at one of the piles. "She's more popular than I am."

"What are they?" I asked.

"No clue. They're not addressed to me, so I don't open them."

I thought back to Xander's felony comment. "So what do you do with them?"

"Sometimes I write *Deceased, return to sender* and put it back in the mail. Other times I just toss it in recycling if it looks like junk." He held up an envelope with a clear window and Minnie's name and address typed out. "Boring equals recycling. If it's something that looks like it came from a person, I send it back so people know she's no longer living."

I wanted to point out that if it was anyone who mattered to Minnie, they'd probably already know she was dead, so those were probably the ones that mattered least.

"You mind if I take a look?"

"Go for it. We should probably get started on this project anyway," Owen said, taking a seat at the table.

As the group discussed band names and previous musical experience, I flipped through Minnie's mail. Owen was right that most of what was there was junk: magazines asking her to resubscribe, landscaping companies offering end of the summer deals on fall seeding. Most of it wouldn't have been anything Minnie was interested in, and I knew Owen wouldn't be.

But one piece of mail caught my eye because not only was it from the county, but Minnie and Owen had both received one. They looked nearly identical and also official enough that I was surprised Owen hadn't opened it.

"You should probably take a look at this one," I told him.

"You can open it if you want. Just let me know if it's important."

I had a feeling it would be since it had the words *Final Notice* stamped across both envelopes. Starting with the one addressed to Owen, I opened it and found a letter inside, followed by some sort of invoice behind it.

It wasn't in my nature to read things, especially time-sensitive things, word for word from the beginning to end. My brain didn't work that way. Instead, my mind processed most of the information simultaneously as my eyes scanned the page for important words. And the words that jumped out at me weren't ones Owen would want to hear.

So before I filled him in on exactly what was going on, I made sure to fully understand what was happening so I could give him a thorough rundown of the situation and his options—which it turned out weren't many.

"What's wrong?" I heard Owen ask, and it occurred to me that my expression must've revealed at least the connotation of what had been in the letter.

"You wanna talk in private?" I motioned to him to follow me out of the kitchen, and once we were there, I handed him the letter.

He looked at it for a second or two before saying, "What is

this? Why would I owe this?" His eyes must've gone straight to the number at the bottom of the page, which read $22,658.35. "I don't get it. Why would I owe over twenty-two thousand dollars?"

"It's the property taxes that haven't been paid."

"I see that, but this is the first time I've seen anything about this. And Jesus Christ! Twenty-two thousand dollars! For property taxes? This isn't the OC."

I could see the fear on Owen's face, the uncertainty of what would happen to him—to the house.

"It looks like Minnie hadn't paid them in a while, so it says they put her on some kind of payment plan, but she defaulted on that too."

"Okay, so that's probably just a misunderstanding. When I took ownership of the house, I should've taken over the payment plan too, but I didn't know about it. I'll just call the county Monday and explain what happened, and I'm sure they'll let me pick up where Minnie left off."

"Unfortunately, I don't think it'll be that simple."

The relief that had been on Owen's face when he'd decided to call the county vanished as quickly as it had appeared.

"They already put a tax lien on the house."

"I don't speak lawyer, so can you dumb all this down for me?"

"Basically, the crux of it is that Minnie's been behind on her taxes for a while, and the county wants their money."

"It was probably an honest mistake because she didn't have a mortgage, so the taxes weren't included in there. I bet it just slipped her mind to pay them."

"This is years' worth of taxes," I told him.

I didn't know how something like that could slip

someone's mind, especially with bills as reminders and then a payment plan. But I also knew Minnie didn't have much money, so I guessed it could've been a combination of the two: she didn't have the money when the bills came, and then as time passed without paying, she forgot about them entirely.

"It looks like they gave her adequate time to pay them, and she didn't. The county's tired of waiting for its money, so they're doing away with the payment plan."

"What does that mean exactly?" Owen said with a gulp, probably already knowing the answer.

I sighed heavily. "It means you either pay the debt in full or they're selling your house in sixty days."

Chapter Seven

OWEN

The news Vee had shared with me felt almost crippling. My entire body seemed completely immobilized, and even as Brae and Jagger performed a duet using only a toy whistle and a fork, I couldn't make the muscles in my mouth move enough to smile, let alone laugh.

I'd never been good under pressure, preferring to take my time and do things the right way if possible. But with this, it seemed there was no right way. That ship had sailed when Minnie had forgotten—or *decided* not to pay taxes and then done the same with the payment plan.

But when I thought back to when the title to the house had been transferred to my name, I realized I wasn't much better. I'd signed some paperwork, and there were invoices for the sewer as well as some tax forms, but I hadn't bothered to look closely at anything beyond putting my signature down. I figured that when the bills came, I'd pay them. And I would've if the first one I'd received hadn't been twenty-two fucking grand.

I tried to contribute to the group when they argued over what instrument I should play or what genre we should even focus on. But ultimately, our first meeting as a band probably foreshadowed our future as one: a complete clusterfuck.

By the time Brae and Jagger left, we'd come up with a name and a logo. I tried to act like I cared enough about what they were, but being a member of a group called Kenso Gummers that apparently played a cross between alternative rock and EDM was now on the back burner of the stove that held all my problems.

"Making our music more EDM was a good idea," I heard Brae say to Xander as they headed out. "Hopefully the tech'll hide the fact that none of you can play anything."

"I can sing," I heard Jagger's phone say.

Brae turned back to stare at her blankly for a moment before he said, "You can't even talk."

Somehow Jagger was able to grunt out some sort of noise I recognized as pure frustration as she stormed past Xander and Brae.

"I'll see ya in class Monday?" Xander asked because apparently he wasn't sure.

"Unfortunately," said Brae.

Brae and Xander thanked me for offering my house up as a place to meet.

"Yeah, anytime." But as soon as the words left my lips, I realized they'd been a lie. *Anytime within the next sixty days* is what I should've said.

Brae pulled me into an awkward-as-fuck bro-hug that resulted in my face leaning against his bony chest.

Xander could barely contain his laughter.

That made one of us.

VERONICA

As much as I wanted to bombard Owen the second Xander and their classmates had left, I could tell Owen wasn't in the mood to talk, so I let him keep to himself for the remainder of the day. He wasn't being rude or distant necessarily. Just… pensive in a way I'd rarely seen him. I wondered if this was how he handled any type of major stress.

The only other problem I'd seen him face was his marriage to Nattie, and I couldn't exactly use that as a gauge for his future behavior since most of his emotions and reactions had been rooted in our interactions with each other more than the marriage itself. But this felt different. This was a problem we should be able to solve *together,* and I hoped he would let me be a part of that when he was ready.

Inez and Natalia had left, and I hadn't seen Wynter with a *y* since last night when she'd come downstairs to grab some sage and oregano out of the spice cabinet.

She'd mumbled something about needing white vinegar too as she opened and closed cabinets abruptly in no particular order. Then she'd disappeared into her room immediately after and hadn't been seen or heard from since.

I wasn't complaining, necessarily, because Wynter with a *y* wasn't the most pleasant to be around, and I hadn't really gotten a good grasp on her schedule yet—if she even, in fact, had one.

The last thing Owen needed right now while he was contemplating how to come up with more than twenty grand was for our new roommate to come down complaining about spirits and demons or whatever the fuck she claimed lived with her.

He'd been on his computer for the last two hours or so,

and every time I'd looked into the dining room, he was staring at it with the intensity better suited for a doctor performing neurosurgery than an in-debt college kid.

Around three in the afternoon, I approached him holding a beer and a sandwich. "I come bearing gifts," I said with a cautious smile because I was pretty sure he wasn't in the mood to return it.

"Thanks," he said. He took the plate from me, and I set the beer down next to his computer. "You even put both types of mustard on it."

"Of course I did."

He took a big bite, chewing slowly and still staring at the screen in front of him. "This is so fucked up."

"It is that," I agreed.

"I filled out some stuff online to see if I can get a loan, but I doubt I'll be able to. They all ask what the loan is being used for. I thought that was weird because, like, what's it to them what I use the money for, ya know? But when I Googled it, it made sense. If I were buying a car or something, they could have that as collateral or whatever if I don't pay, but I doubt any kind of financial institution is rushing to approve a twenty-three-year-old college senior for a loan to pay off back taxes. If I owe the township money, why would a bank think I'd pay back a loan to *them*?"

He put his sandwich down on the plate and dropped his head into his hands. He looked like he'd given up, and it had only been a couple of hours.

"What about an advance on your credit card or something like that?" I didn't know anyone who'd ever done that, and the idea didn't sound like the wisest financial decision, but at least it would give us all more time to come up with the money.

Owen shook his head. "Already tried that. They won't do it. I haven't had the card open long enough."

Sighing, I looked over at him, but he didn't return the gesture. "We'll figure something out," I told him. "We always do. Look, I have a little money saved of my own that I'm happy to contribute. And I'm sure if I ask my dad and unc—"

He jolted up. "No. Absolutely not. I'm not taking your money, and I'm definitely not taking your family's."

"It's not a handout, Owen. You can pay it back. They trust you. *I* trust you."

Shutting his computer with a loud smack, he looked at me. His eyes softened, revealing the boyish charm I loved so much.

"I know all of you would be happy to help," he said softly. "And I'm grateful. I didn't mean to sound so abrupt."

"I get it."

"I just . . . I already feel so indebted to Ricky for the whole annulment thing, and your dad and brothers have helped with the house a few times. I can't ask them for anything, and I won't take it." He took my hand in his and squeezed it gently. "This is my mess. I have to clean it up myself."

We held each other's gazes for a long moment before a tiny smile creeped over one side of his mouth. I was sure it was forced, but I wasn't sure if it was for my sake or his. Maybe both.

But the moment was interrupted by the sound of Wynter with a *y* stomping down the wooden steps and dragging the trash bags she'd brought her belongings in behind her. It looked like she was headed toward the front door, but she stopped short when she saw us.

"You got a real fucking problem up there, and it's just

gonna get worse if you don't do something about it."

I looked to Owen, who raised an eyebrow in confusion at the dark-haired, pale-faced woman who was obviously crazy. I also thought she had a few more dreadlocks than she'd had the night before. I wondered if she'd been creating them by tying her hair in knots rather than letting them develop naturally.

Wynter with a *y* let out a frustrated huff. "I'm done with this. I don't need this kind of negativity in my life. It's not good for my aura." And with that, she headed out the front door, still dragging the partially ripped Hefty bags behind her.

We were both quiet for a moment before Owen said, "Could've done without *that* today."

Chapter Eight

OWEN

Xander had sent out a cryptic group text asking the entire Scooby Gang if they'd be available to help him with something the following weekend, and if so, which day worked best. Since Xander never asked anything of anyone, we all complied, but inquiries about what exactly he needed our help *with* went ignored, which didn't do much for my already stressed-out mental state.

Though hopefully a night out with friends would get my mind off the loan for a while.

Unlikely.

Everyone was available Saturday night, or at least had plans they could cancel. Once that was decided, we all received an invitation—a formal one we had to click a link to RSVP. It invited us to a celebration at a ritzy bar downtown called Ambrosia, where we'd all have access to an open bar and appetizers.

He didn't clarify what we were celebrating, despite

multiple people calling him for answers. He ignored their calls and replied with a simple text.

You'll find out Saturday.

Vee and I had been tossing out possibilities all week. With Xander, it could be anything from brainstorming some new app he wanted to build to asking for our help disposing of a body.

"Just so you both know," Natalia said from the back seat as we drove to Ambrosia, "I'm not doing anything that will make me sweaty, dirty, or an accessory. And I'm not playing any games or trivia or anything nerdy like that."

"I expected nothing less. Or more, in your case," Vee said sardonically.

"I probably shouldn't have come," Natalia added. "Your friends are nice and all, but you guys get up to some strange shit. I'm actually surprised I was even invited."

Honestly, I was surprised too. Xander had barely ever even spoken to Natalia. But for better or worse, she'd married into the group, so to speak, and was therefore invited to most things. If she hadn't been invited, I was sure she would've been bitching about that even more than she was complaining about *being* invited.

Dealing with her was a no-win situation sometimes.

We had to circle the block a few times before finding a parking spot, and then we trooped toward Ambrosia. Drew and Sophia were walking up to the door at the same time.

"Did you ever get anything out of him?" I asked Drew. He was closest to Xander and therefore had the best shot of pulling info out of him.

"Not a word."

"This is a really nice place," Sophia said.

It was decorated in varying shades of brown. The walls were made with furnished wood that gleamed under the white light fixtures that adorned them. The tables matched the wood on the walls, but the chairs were lighter, almost beige. Paintings depicting gods and goddesses hung around the large, open room. And at the far end sat a long bar with wooden, high-backed stools. The liquor behind the bar was backlit, and a gold chandelier lit up the rest of the room from above.

"I feel like we can't afford to be here," Vee whispered in response.

Drew stepped up to the hostess and gave Xander's name.

She smiled and said, "Right this way."

She led us to the left of the hostess stand, down a small alcove I hadn't seen initially. It opened to a decent-sized room, decorated in a way that made it look how I imagined an old-fashioned study would. There were large leather armchairs gathered around tables that were low to the ground like coffee tables. There were books lining shelves built into the wall. A smaller bar filled a corner, and a bartender stood behind it mixing a drink while a server walked around offering appetizers.

I felt like I'd stumbled onto the set of a *Clue* remake.

"Hey, guys," Xander said as he approached. He hugged everyone and then gestured behind him. "Brody and Aamee have already found the bar. Help yourselves."

"You ready to tell us what's going on?" Drew asked.

Xander smirked. "I'll wait for everyone to get here."

We fell into easy conversation from there, getting drinks

and helping ourselves to food. Ransom and Taylor came in shortly after, followed by Carter and Toby.

Cody was the last to arrive, immediately announcing, "This place is awesome," and heading for the bar.

We mingled for a bit longer before Xander asked for our attention.

"I bet you're all wondering why the hell I brought you here," he said with a smile. At our nods, he continued, "This is my graduation party." He raised his glass. "Thanks for celebrating with me." He swigged back a large pull of his drink, but the rest of us didn't move, too shocked to do anything other than stare.

Toby was the first to collect himself. "What do you mean? The semester just started."

"Not for me," Xander replied with a grin.

"But... I don't understand." Poor Toby looked genuinely confused.

The rest of us probably wore similar expressions.

"Can you explain from the beginning?" Drew asked.

"There's not much to it. I originally planned to stay in school for a couple more years, but I changed my mind. I'm ready to join the working world."

"Don't you want to finish your degree?" Aamee asked, looking genuinely concerned. I'd never seen that expression on her face before, and it was a little unnerving.

Xander shrugged. "I finished my business degree last winter."

"You did? Why didn't you tell us?" Drew asked.

"It was just another piece of paper. It didn't feel like anything worth mentioning."

"Is this about your dad?" Drew asked.

Xander was contemplative for a second before saying, "Yes and no."

"I feel like there's a backstory here that I'm missing," Vee said to me.

"You guys are really bringing down my vibe," Xander said, but his tone was still light. "My dad agreed to pay for me to go to school until I was twenty-five. So I've just been kind of hanging around, wasting his money. But it all got kind of… boring. I was at the campus bookstore, buying my books for the semester, and I just didn't want to do it anymore. He'd transferred money for tuition into my account because he couldn't even be bothered to write a check to the school or sign up for an account and pay online. So," he said, "I decided to use it to throw myself a kick-ass graduation party instead."

"Isn't he going to be mad?" Carter asked. "When he realizes you didn't use the money for school?"

Xander let out a short, humorless laugh. "He doesn't care enough to find out what I spent it on. As long as he doesn't have to actually see or talk to me, he's happy."

"So you're not even going to tell him?" Taylor asked.

Xander looked at her intently before looking around at all of us. "I know this is really difficult for a lot of you to understand because you have good parents. Well, most of you," he said with a meaningful look at Aamee.

She raised her glass in salute.

"But trust me when I say," Xander continued, "my dad couldn't care less about what I do or what happens to me. I've only seen the guy a handful of times since high school."

"I'm… I'm really sorry to hear that, Xander," I said. I couldn't imagine having a parent like that. As much as my family drove me crazy sometimes, their annoying actions came from a surplus of love, not a lack of it.

"I'm not," Xander replied, but the waver in his voice told us that wasn't strictly true. "Staying in school is only prolonging the misery for both of us. It's better to just be done and cut ties completely. I don't need him. It's time to start acting like it."

"What are you going to do?" Toby asked, his voice quiet.

"I got a job with a cybersecurity firm. A rival of my dad. I couldn't resist the opportunity to be petty," he said with a smirk, though it was obvious in the shine of his eyes that the conversation was weighing on him. "And now we can both just be done with each other. Neither of us has anything to offer the other."

"It's his loss," a voice said from behind us. We all whirled around to see Aniyah standing in the doorway.

"Niy," Xander whispered.

"You and I are gonna have some words," she said to Xander. "How are you going to have a graduation party and not invite me?"

Xander didn't reply. Instead, he pushed through us to get to Aniyah, enveloping her in a giant hug when he reached her.

We couldn't hear what they said, but it was clear they were murmuring something as they embraced. It almost felt too intimate to observe. I'd always assumed something was going on between them, but by the time I'd firmly joined the friend group, Aniyah had moved over an hour away for work.

After a few more moments, they pulled away from each other, both dabbing their eyes.

Then Aniyah reached out and smacked Xander. "And don't think you're off the hook. Why did I hear about this party from Toby? Why didn't you tell me?"

"I know how busy you are with work, and I didn't want

to add something else to your plate. Besides, it's not that big a deal."

She looked around. "Seriously? You couldn't have found a more pretentious place to have this. No offense," she said to the server who chose that moment to come into the room. "It's obviously a big deal."

He shrugged. "I just wanted to blow my dad's money on the most expensive place I could find."

"Well, I, for one, am thankful for that," Brody said as he raised the cocktails he held, one in each hand.

"Hear! Hear!" Carter yelled.

Drew went over and slung an arm around Xander. "Don't worry, buddy. Your chosen family is more than happy to help you spend Daddy's money." The words were said with a teasing lilt to his voice, but there was a sincerity to his eyes that revealed the heartfelt truth in his words.

The people gathered in this room *were* a family. A great one. Many times better than the ones some of them had been born into. And watching everyone rally around Xander let me know that, when the time came, I could lean on them with my problems too.

And it was that sense of goodwill that kept me from punching Xander square in the face for telling me not to drop Professor Ted's class, even though he went and dropped the whole college. Sometimes the best revenge required exceptional timing.

VERONICA

Everyone, excluding Owen, was drunk. He'd had a couple of

beers, but he hadn't done much drinking since his accidental marriage to Nattie. She hadn't learned the same lesson. I watched as she and Cody laughed hysterically at something on his phone.

The rest of us had pulled all the chairs to make a large circle around one of the tables.

"I'm so sorry I forgot to put you in my wedding," Aamee said as she practically fell into Aniyah's lap.

"You actually forgot to tell me you were having a wedding at all," Aniyah replied, humor evident in her voice.

"I know! You moved away, and I forgot all about you. So crazy."

"Crazy's one word for it."

"But it's in the Masons' backyard. Like Vee and Brody's."

"Wait... what?" Nattie's head popped up like a Labrador retriever at Aamee's words.

"What *what*?" Aamee asked.

"Did you say your wedding is going to be like Vee and Brody's?" Nattie asked.

"Uh, yeah," Aamee said, clearly implying the *duh*.

Nattie's gaze narrowed, but it seemed to take a lot of effort. My girl was hammered. "Do you mean to tell me that you were married? After all the shit you gave me for marrying Owen? You... you... you... What's the word I'm looking for?"

"Hypocrite," Cody supplied.

"Yeah, hypo... That word he just said."

I rolled my eyes. I'd never told my family this story because there was really no need. I also didn't want them to get a bad impression of the people I'd met down here.

"We weren't really married. It was all pretend to piss off Brody's parents."

"Well, Owen and I only got real married to piss off you. So it's basically the same," Natalia argued.

"It's not even remotely the same," I replied.

"Eh," I heard from beside me.

I turned an accusatory glare on Owen.

"It's got some similarities," he defended.

"Oh, really? Did I abscond to Connecticut, drag an officiant out of bed, and then have to become a drug mule for someone while I tried to procure an annulment?"

"Drug mule?" Carter asked.

Owen shook his head. "I wasn't a drug mule."

"Not technically, but you thought you were," I supplied. "He almost killed a man in prison."

Owen shot to his feet. "I did not! I gave him aspirin. And I knocked it out of his hand before he could take it anyway."

"Your life sounds even wilder than mine," Ransom said. "Who'd've thought."

"Can we come back to this story another time?" Sophia asked. "Because it sounds amazing, but I'm too drunk to remember it."

"I'm a little hurt we don't already know it," Taylor said.

"It's embarrassing," Owen explained. "But if you can remember to ask another time, I'll tell you all about it."

This seemed to appease everyone, and I expected the conversation to move on, but Nattie wasn't done.

"I want to hear more about this backyard wedding."

"It's going to be beautiful," Aamee responded. "Kate planted her back garden with these absolutely gorgeous—"

Nattie waved a hand at her. "Not *your* wedding. Her wedding." She pointed at me. Well, she pointed in my general direction at least.

"I didn't have a wedding."

"I'm going to have to disagree," Taylor said. "I was there. And I believe that was you up front standing in front of, like, fifty members of Brody's family in a wedding gown saying vows."

"You had a wedding dress?" Nattie screeched.

"I really don't want to talk about the dress. I still feel bad that Mrs. Mason paid for that."

"Oh my God, your mother-in-law bought your wedding gown?"

"Are you just going to repeat everything everyone else says?" I snapped.

"It was a really pretty dress," Sophia commented.

"It was okay," Aamee added.

"Oh my God, were you there?" Nattie asked Aamee. "Were you and Brody together then?"

Aamee opened her mouth to answer, but I cut her off. "Isn't tonight supposed to be about Xander? Doesn't anyone have embarrassing stories about him?"

Many of them shared a look as slow smiles spread over their faces.

"The library!" they all said in unison. What followed was a detailed story about a library fire Xander had accidentally set. From there, they talked about Xander creating an app for a delivery business Brody, Drew, and Sophia used to run, followed by how he'd helped Taylor and Ransom when her ex had tried to blackmail them, and on to what an amazing bartender he was.

Xander seemed embarrassed by the attention, but he also seemed to bask in it. I realized that Xander truly hadn't understood how integral he was to this group until they all sat around bragging about him.

He'd come into tonight thinking he was saying goodbye to something, but as we all sat around, it was clear he'd found something instead. Or maybe he'd finally just accepted it.

This group of people would never abandon him. He wasn't a burden or someone they felt obligated to hang out with.

Everyone here loved him without conditions or expectations. I'd grown up with a family like that. Xander had needed to go to college to find it. But now that he had, I was confident he'd have it forever.

Chapter Nine

OWEN

I wanted to tell the gang about the tax issue ever since I found out about it. But I also wanted—almost as badly—to find a way out of this mess on my own for once. Plus, I didn't want to ruin Xander's party with my problems or make a night that was about him about me instead.

So I waited until Tuesday, and it nearly killed me. I Googled ways to get money quickly—a search I regretted immediately once I hit Enter.

Suggestions ranged from selling electronics and other expensive items, which I didn't have, to taking a loan from a retirement account, which I also didn't have. Another option was taking loans from credit cards, which I'd already looked into.

And then there was amateur porn.

The only options that seemed like viable ones were to take some online surveys and ask for an advance in my pay at the hardware store. The surveys took hours—I knew because I'd taken a few—and left my computer so riddled with so many viruses that I wasn't sure I'd be able to use it again.

And while I did plan to ask Mark if I could have some type of advance, I didn't work a ton of hours to begin with, and it was a small business. He'd have to pay me for the next ten years for it to make a significant impact on my debt. I knew every little bit helped, but I couldn't come up with enough *little bits* to make a dent in twenty-two grand.

By the time Tuesday rolled around, I knew it was time to bring in the big guns.

And by big guns, I meant the group of people whose first suggestion to earn some extra money was to take part in a human experiment.

"I'm not looking to die," I said.

"You won't die," Carter said before looking to Xander. "Will he?"

Xander shrugged and hopped down off the small stone wall that ran the perimeter of my backyard patio. "Probably not."

"See," Carter said. "Totally safe."

Vee looked concerned. "He never said it was safe, just that Owen probably wouldn't die."

"Students do them all the time."

Cody snapped his fingers at me. "What about selling your sperm?" He looked around to the group. "Or we could all sell our sperm! Think about it. There'd be a bunch of Cody Juniors running around out there somewhere. I'm not sure I ever want kids, so this'll be the next best thing." He paused like he was imagining a world filled with miniature versions of himself—a fantasy that apparently brought a satisfied smile to his face. "My DNA will live on for eternity," he said, lifting his beer bottle in the air like he was giving some sort of toast.

"Isn't that a reason *not* to do it?" Drew asked, never missing an opportunity to tease his little brother.

"Oh, like people are begging for *your* sperm."

"I beg for it," Sophia said with a shrug.

That made Cody snort, but Brody didn't look so amused.

He visibly gagged. "Too bad you can't sell vomit, because I can feel a bunch coming up."

"It says you can make some pretty decent money," Toby said, looking up from his phone, where he'd obviously already googled sperm donation. "Seventy bucks when the deposit is made." He laughed after that. "And thirty when your sample is released."

Carter raised his eyebrows, looking suddenly interested. "What does that mean? Like *as* you're coming, they give you thirty bucks?"

Too wrapped up in whatever he was reading, Toby didn't even seem to have noticed Carter's comment. "According to this article, sperm banks are pretty particular with their requirements, but overall, they look for educated, good-looking men who are at least five feet eight and have no history of mental illness. And get this," Toby said, sounding increasingly excited. "It says you can make upwards of a thousand bucks a month."

"I'm so in!" Cody said.

"It also says," Toby continued, "that you have to refrain from any type of ejaculation for several days leading up to each deposit."

Cody's smile faded quickly. "I'm out. Sorry, Owen."

"It's fine," I said. "Maybe we can table the sperm donation idea for a bit until we discuss some other options that have fewer moral, ethical, and personal implications." I didn't really know what any of those would be, but I felt it was best to move on as a group.

"Ooh," Taylor piped up. "What about selling *plasma*? There's no moral reason not to."

"Ew, needles are cringe," Aamee said with a shiver. "I think I'd die."

"You wouldn't die," Taylor said with an eye roll. "And you'd actually be helping other people so they *don't* die."

Aamee was about to reply, but I beat her to it. "Does anyone have any ideas that don't involve bodily fluids?"

The way everyone exchanged glances told me no one did.

"First of all," Xander said. "How much money can each of us comfortably afford to give?" He looked around at the group and then over at me. "I wish you would've told me about this before I threw myself an extravagant and unneeded party. I could've chipped in another fifteen hundred or something."

"Another?"

"Yeah, I just Venmoed you twenty-five hundred. I wish I could have given you more, but I need to keep some until my job starts."

"Xander, I can't take that from you. I can't take money from any of you."

Brody and Aamee were saving for their wedding now that Aamee's parents were no longer helping. And Brody and Drew were in the process of purchasing a bar together. Everyone else was still in school, so even if they had the money to give—which I knew they didn't—they had to worry about paying their own bills, not mine.

"I appreciate the offer," I said, "but we'll come up with something."

But it seemed no one was listening to me. The couples

were conferring and chatting in hushed tones.

Vee and I just looked at each other.

"We're not robbing a bank or something," I said. "My life is crazy enough right now without worrying about getting arrested." My recent visit to the prison had been more than enough for me to know a life of crime wasn't for me. "Hello?" I said when still no one was paying attention to me.

"I think they're coming up with a plan," Vee whispered. "I'm scared."

"I'm scared too," I whispered back.

"Done?" Drew asked Cody.

He nodded back. "We just sent you a little over four grand."

If my eyes were able to open any wider, they would've dropped out of their sockets and rolled across the floor.

"Four grand! I just told you not to send me anything. I can't… How did you even…? I have to send it back."

Ransom crossed his arms over his large chest and smiled. "That's why it came from Cody. We all sent the money to him so you wouldn't know how much each of us gave you. If you wanna risk our four thousand dollars being blown on pizza and horse races, then return it to Cody immediately."

"Listen," Cody said with a finger extended at Ransom. "How was I supposed to know that horse was gonna break his leg? I could've been twelve hundred bucks richer."

Ransom raised his eyebrows like Cody's comment helped to prove his point.

"The money's yours now, O," Carter told me. "Now we just have to figure out how to get the rest of it."

VERONICA

Once we accounted for Wynter's first and last month's rent and deposit—which she'd told Owen to keep since the room was cursed and she believed taking it back would transfer the curse to her—we calculated that we needed about ten thousand more. That included Inez's rent for next month as well as what she'd already paid.

Between Inez's and Wynter's rent and what his friends had given him, he'd amassed over six thousand dollars. Though I knew Owen didn't want to take money from our friends, we also both knew he had to. There was no way he could come up with that much in a matter of weeks.

I'd watched as he said teary-eyed *thank yous* to the group, and I hoped their efforts hadn't been for nothing. Of course, they knew how much each of them contributed, and if we couldn't raise the rest of the money, Owen promised that he'd be returning every dime to them.

But we all hoped it didn't come to that.

"Oh my God," Roddie said, looking up from his phone. "How did we not think to start a GoFundMe?" He smacked himself in the head. "Duh, crowdsourcing is literally the staple of raising money for stuff like this."

Roddie was still rubbing the spot on his head where he'd hit himself when Inez spoke up. "There probably aren't a lot of people lining up to donate to a college kid who can't pay his bills."

We all knew there was more to Owen's situation than that, but Inez's summary was probably what most people would see when they encountered the page. GoFundMes were for paying medical bills for dying children or covering funeral costs for families who'd died in fires. They weren't for . . . this.

Roddie looked around to the group, probably hoping his idea would have more legs than it did, but several of our friends muttered their agreement with Inez even though it seemed like they didn't want to.

"It's fine," Owen said. "I'd rather earn the rest anyway instead of accepting donations. I was thinking with Halloween coming up, we could throw a banger with a cover charge. We talked about a party anyway, but we could charge enough to make a profit. Sophia's great at marketing, so maybe she can hype the thing up. Who doesn't want to go to a Halloween party in an old house like this?"

"It *is* pretty creepy on its own," Drew said.

"I saw a bunch of cobwebs on the front porch. You wouldn't even have to decorate," Brody added.

"Yeah, and most of the floors creak," Aamee said. "I certainly wouldn't wanna live in this place, but I agree it'd be great for a party."

Owen's face scrunched up at Aamee's comment before it seemed like he'd decided it wasn't worth responding to.

"That settles it, then. Halloween party's a go." He wrote it down in the notebook I brought him from the kitchen.

"Okay, thinking along those same lines," Taylor said. "What about a fair type of thing? Like over a weekend or even just one Saturday. Maybe you can borrow some farm animals and do like a petting zoo or pony rides or something."

"Borrow some farm animals?" Ransom asked. "Where can you borrow farm animals?"

Taylor glanced around the room at the rest of us, seemingly looking for the answer to Ransom's question, but when no one provided one, she said, "I haven't figured that out yet."

Owen wrote it down anyway. "I think it's still a solid idea. Maybe we could use it to promote local restaurants and businesses. People could set up stands with food or little things to give away. It'll be a win-win. Businesses'll get exposure, and people'll get free shit."

"It's a decent idea," Xander agreed. "You can do a lot with that."

"Thanks," Owen replied, looking slightly surprised at the compliment. "Let's just start planning these for now since they're both pretty involved, and then we can see if any other ideas pop up as we go."

"I got a million of them," Cody said. "An ultimate frisbee tournament, pie-eating contest, cook-off, lemonade stand—"

"I don't think a lemonade stand is gonna bring in the money we need," Owen told him. "But some of the others aren't too bad. Maybe we can include them as part of the fair."

"Also," I added, "I feel like we're over the age limit where setting up a lemonade stand is socially acceptable."

"I'm surprised it's ever been socially acceptable, to be honest," Xander said. "Parents teach their kids not to talk to strangers or take anything from them, but it's okay for kids to set up lemonade stands in front of their houses and sell drinks to strangers? Feels a little hypocritical if you ask me."

"Good thing no one asked you," Cody said, though it was clear there was no malice behind it. "You know what *is* really fuckin' weird, though?"

"Your desire to populate the world with your offspring but not raise any of them?" Xander replied with his usual dry wit.

"No," Cody said, not further entertaining Xander's comment. "Those events where you eat candy from strangers' cars in parking lots. That shit has Pedophile Party written all over it."

We all exchanged confused glances, but no one questioned him.

"What the fuck are you talking about?" Well, no one but Roddie questioned him.

Drew let out a long sigh like he'd been having to explain Codyisms for way too long. "He's talking about Trunk-or-Treats," he said with a shake of his head. "He's mentioned them before."

"That's because it's insane to me that there's any event that *encourages* kids taking candy from strangers."

"You do realize that Halloween on its own is exactly that, right?" Brody pointed out, surprisingly the voice of reason for once.

Cody thought for a moment and then shrugged. "It's just creepier when cars are involved, I guess. I can't explain it."

"That's good," Drew said, "because none of us want to hear your explanation." Then he grabbed two beers from the cooler and sat back down next to Sophia.

Listening to them bicker reminded me of Franco and Manny. Or maybe it reminded me of *me* and Manny and Franco. And as they continued, more of our friends joined in—arguing over this or teasing someone about that.

Everyone was so...good together despite driving each other crazy at the same time. It was a paradox only a family could pull off. And I was thankful these people were mine.

Chapter Ten

OWEN

I was stumped. The Scooby Gang had given me a ton of ideas, but very few of them were *good* ideas. I was still tossing around the suggestion of hosting events for local college kids, but it made me hesitant. Anything could happen when a bunch of co-eds got together, and I didn't want anything to happen to my house or the people who lived in it. Saving my house wasn't worth people getting hurt.

I was sitting around looking through my laptop for inspiration when Inez opened the basement door, followed by Roddie.

"Hey, Owen. You got a second?" Inez asked.

I moved my computer from my lap to the coffee table and gave them my full attention. "Sure. What's up?"

Gimli went over to say hi to our guests, and Roddie bent down to pet him. After a few moments of neither of them speaking, Inez bumped Roddie with her leg.

"Ask him."

Roddie looked hesitant as he stood upright.

Inez rolled her eyes. "Dude, he's not going to care. Ask him."

I smiled at Roddie to try to make him feel more at ease. He didn't strike me as the shy type, which made me wonder what he could possibly want to ask.

He looked between Inez and me for a second before blurting, "I need friends." His eyes widened as if surprised by what had just come out of his mouth. "Shit, I didn't mean that. I mean, I *did*, but I didn't mean to say it like that."

I looked to Inez for help because Roddie seemed to be having some kind of mental breakdown I was ill-equipped to deal with. I was busy with my own, thank you very much.

"What he means," Inez began, "is that he needs to convince his parents he's mature enough to live on his own."

"I'm not sure that's a better way to phrase it," Roddie muttered.

"And I can help with that how?" I asked.

Roddie sighed. "Okay, so listen, the truth of it is, I was a major screw-up in high school. Barely graduated and it took me a while to get my shit together. But since starting at Safe Haven, I've been doing well. But my parents, they... aren't really impressed. I want to move out, but they worry I'll fall right back into old habits. So I thought since Inez said that Wynter chick moved out, that maybe I could move in here to show them that I can handle it."

I narrowed my eyes in confusion. "I don't understand. If they don't want you to move out, why would they let you live here?"

Roddie scratched the back of his head. "Well, that's the thing. I'd need all of you to meet my parents and help me convince them."

He must've seen the doubt in my face because he rushed to continue. "It wouldn't be that hard. Vee's a lawyer, you own your own house, and it's a residential area away from bars and frat parties and all that stuff. I really think they might go for it."

"Vee's *studying* to be a lawyer and I'm about to *lose* this house unless a miracle happens. I'm not sure how convincing that would be. Not to mention we might all have to be out of here in less than sixty days."

"They don't need to know any of that. And I just need to convince them that I can handle it. Sixty days is plenty of time to show them that, and then I can move somewhere else on my own."

I thought it over. While I could definitely use the money, this seemed like a lot of hassle for very little profit.

"I don't know, Roddie. This is just really bad timing."

"But you need the money, right?" he asked.

"Well, yeah, of course. But two months of rent isn't going to be enough to—"

"Tell him the other thing," Inez interrupted.

I stared at Roddie expectantly.

"The reason I want to move out is because I want to start my own business."

"A business?"

He nodded. "A hotel for dogs."

"Hotel for dogs? Like the movie?"

"Yeah. Kind of. Eventually. See, in addition to Safe Haven, I work as a dog walker. My ultimate plan is to get my own place and turn it into a doggie day care and boarding facility. A plan that my parents think will leave me eternally broke. But I can make it work. I know I can."

"I'm sure you can, Roddie." It always helped to support people's dreams. "But what does that have to do with me?"

"While I'm here, I can use your backyard as a trial day care. You won't have to do anything. I swear, I'll take full responsibility for the dogs. And in turn, I'll pay you rent for a room *plus* rent for use of your property."

Inez smiled at me, looking hopeful. But I couldn't say yes. Could I?

No, there'd be dogs everywhere, using my lawn as a bathroom and barking, and no, there was no way I could even consider it.

"How much were you thinking of paying?" I heard myself ask. *No! Bad Owen.*

"What were you charging Wynter for the room?"

"She paid fifteen hundred for two months."

"Okay, then I'll double it. So that would be fifteen hundred for the room and another fifteen hundred for the backyard. I can pay it all up front." He smiled. "One positive to living at home. I saved a lot of money. But you'd also need to meet my family. It all hinges on them giving the go-ahead."

"Why?" I asked. "You're not a child. They can't legally keep you home if you don't want to be there," I said.

Roddie bit his lip. "Legally, no, but my family is . . . difficult to explain. And they mean well. I'd rather have their support than start throwing ultimatums at them."

I knew there was more of a story there, but Roddie didn't seem willing to tell it, and it didn't feel right to pry. I already knew Roddie was crazy.

"I need to run it by Vee and Natalia first."

Roddie bounced on his toes. "Yes, great, I totally understand."

I looked at my watch. "Vee has a study group and Natalia's at work, but I should be able to let you know later tonight. Is that okay?"

"Absolutely. Oh, and Gimli can of course come to day care for free." His smile was wide and happy, and I suddenly desperately wanted to give Roddie this chance. It was like giving a kid the *one* gift they'd asked Santa for.

I smiled. "I'm sure he'd love that."

Inez and Roddie excused themselves after that, and I looked down at Gimli. "You wanna let some friends come over and play in the backyard?"

Gimli's tongue lolled out of his mouth as his tail wagged.

"Guess that's a yes. We just have to hope our other roommates are as excited about it as you are."

VERONICA

I was *not* excited about this. When Owen had presented the idea of letting Roddie run a doggie day care out of our backyard, he'd been animated. Not that I could blame him. Someone offering three grand when he desperately needed money probably seemed too good to be true.

Which it probably was.

Though it didn't sound all that good to me to begin with. Having a yard full of dogs running around, whether I had to interact with them or not, was not ideal to me. What if one of them ran away? What if they somehow bit a neighbor? Or another dog? Or me? There were a lot of unknowns, and we weren't prepared for any of them.

"What happens if it rains?" I asked Owen as we set the

table for dinner. I'd been randomly throwing questions at him as they occurred to me, and he hadn't had an answer for a damn one of them.

"I dunno. I'll add it to the list."

He'd begun writing down our questions on his phone so we could remember them all when we finally talked to Roddie, which we'd be doing tonight. But I wasn't sure how much information we'd get because we weren't only meeting with Roddie but also his parents, who we had to somehow convince we were well-rounded, responsible adults rather than a couple of kids who hadn't been smart enough to remember that paying taxes were a thing.

Not that I blamed Owen for the oversight, but it still didn't make us feel like the dependable roommates we were pretending to be.

All that considered, it had been impossible to tell Owen no. I'd never stand in the way of Owen doing what he needed to save the house. And if I secretly hoped no dogs showed up for Roddie's day care, well, that was something I'd keep to myself.

I expected Nattie to be a more vocal opponent of the whole idea, but she simply shrugged. Maybe after the whole Wynter debacle, she realized she didn't have a right to be negative.

"How long do you think this is going to take? Because I'm missing my spa night for this." Nattie stood at the entrance to the dining room with her arms crossed, watching us finish up with the table.

So much for not being negative.

"It's just a dinner. Can't be more than a couple of hours," Owen replied.

"A couple of *hours*. Why so long?"

Owen opened his mouth, but I put a hand on his arm to stop him. "Don't even answer her. She thrives on being dramatic."

We went back into the kitchen where Inez was taking out the lasagna she'd made. Roddie had told her his mom favored Italian food, and Inez's grandmother evidently had an incredible lasagna recipe, so we'd left her to it.

"They should be here any minute," Owen said, looking at his phone.

"Let's put the salad and bread on the table so we can start eating right away," I suggested. "The quicker we get started, the quicker it'll be over."

As we carried things out, the doorbell chimed.

"I'll get it," Nattie called as I caught the back of her as she moved toward the door.

"Shit," Inez whispered. "No offense, but your cousin is not the first impression we wanna make."

"None taken."

We all basically dropped the food on the table and hurried down the hall to the foyer.

"Oh my God, is that blouse from the Eva Halloran boutique downtown?" Nattie asked Roddie's mother, who smiled and affirmed that it was. "I love it there."

She was a tall woman with blond hair swept into a French twist. Her features were thin and symmetrical, and her makeup was impeccable. In short, she was not at all how I pictured Roddie's mother.

Slightly behind her stood an even taller man who looked . . . stylish. His hair was graying at the temples, but he still looked fit and strong, with his wide chest and defined biceps that peeked out beneath the sleeves of his polo shirt.

And beside them was Roddie, wearing a vintage Rolling Stones T-shirt and jeans. Roddie was cute in a messy, haphazard way. His look and personality were endearing in their unpredictability.

But his parents looked like they had every moment of their lives scheduled, had color-coordinated their closets, and had routine beauty treatments.

It took me a second to realize everyone except Nattie was staring at them, and the air around us was awkward.

"I'm sorry, how rude of us," I rushed to say. "Please come in."

Their smiles seemed reserved as they joined us inside.

"Mom, Dad, this is Owen, Vee, Natalia, and Inez. These are my parents, Eva and Jack."

"Oh, wow," Nattie said. "You shop at Eva's and your name is Eva. How cute."

Roddie's mom cleared her throat and seemed to be attempting to suppress a smile.

"She *is* Eva Halloran," Roddie informed us. "That's her shop."

Nattie's mouth opened so wide, I thought the lower half of her face might actually come unhinged.

Nattie began to gush as the rest of us greeted our guests.

"Dinner's ready if you're hungry," Inez said as we led Roddie's parents into the house.

"I can always eat," Jack said with a laugh and a pat to his flat stomach.

As we entered the dining room and chose seats, it occurred to me that it was probably weird to eat as soon as guests arrived. Should we have made appetizers? Maybe offered cocktails in the living room first?

But Roddie had said to skip the alcohol so his parents wouldn't think we were boozers, so I guessed it was good we'd forgone that. Though this was definitely the kind of gathering that called for drinks. Lots of 'em.

"This looks lovely," Eva said.

"Inez made it," Owen said. "It's her grandmother's recipe."

"And you live here too?" Eva asked Inez.

And that was how the inquisition began. Over the next forty-five minutes, Eva had asked enough questions to write a full biography on each of us. The single-minded focus she rained on us was intimidating in its directness. It was how I imagined being questioned by the CIA would go.

Once we'd cleared dinner and dished out dessert—a cheesecake Roddie had ordered from his mom's favorite bakery downtown—Eva seemed ready to pronounce her sentence.

"How much has Roddie told you about himself?"

Roddie groaned. "Mom, they know me."

"Do they?" Her question was pointed but not unkind. Even though Eva had asked most of the questions that evening, I had learned one thing I didn't doubt in the slightest: she loved her son.

I also got the sense that there was a reason for her overprotectiveness beyond what Roddie had told Owen about his troubled high school years.

Roddie looked at his mom for a moment and sighed. "I have ADHD."

All of us looked at each other because he said it with a gravity that I would've found more fitting for a revelation concerning a terminal illness.

"Okay," Owen said, uncertainty bleeding into his voice.

"It's pretty severe," Roddie continued. "But I'm good about taking my meds."

"Now," his dad said.

Roddie took a deep breath. "Yeah. I'm good about taking them *now*. A few years ago, not so much. And I made some mistakes when I wasn't taking them how I should have been. But I haven't had any problems in almost a year. At least none that I couldn't handle."

Eva seemed to be debating something with herself before she pushed her plate back a bit and rested her arms on the table. "I want to be frank with you. You all seem like very nice people. But you're perhaps a little . . . young to fully understand what living with someone like Roddie entails."

"Mom, I'm not a child."

"I know. I know, and I'm sorry I'm treating you like one. I just . . ." She shrugged. "I love you. And whether it makes you hate me or not, I have to make sure you're safe."

"You're going to have to trust me at some point."

Eva looked at her son, and her chin wobbled.

Her husband put a hand on her back and rubbed soothing circles on it.

"You'll have to excuse us," he said. "We almost lost Roddie a couple years ago. We're a little overprotective of him now."

Eva dashed at her eyes, and said, "Have you told them?"

I assumed her question was to her son, who stared down at his lap.

When Roddie raised his head, his jaw was set. "During my senior year of high school, I forgot I was making a pizza and went upstairs to play video games. I ended up falling asleep. When I woke up, I was in the hospital."

"You nearly died," Eva said, her voice catching on the final word. "And you burned almost our entire house down. What if something like that happens here? It isn't just you we have to think about, Roddie. What about your roommates' safety?"

He looked at us with pleading eyes. "That had never happened before, and it's never happened since. And I'm much better on my meds. Not perfect . . . I still struggle sometimes, but my therapist has taught me strategies to help. I've put in the work. I just need a chance. Please."

Owen and I shared a look. He looked as torn as I felt.

I couldn't blame Eva for feeling as she did. It was hard to even imagine how terrified she must've been when she'd seen her son in the hospital. But I could also relate to Roddie, who just wanted a chance to grow up.

I tried to convey to Owen that this was his decision, and I'd support him in whatever he decided.

After a few seconds, he straightened his spine and faced Roddie's parents. "I know a little about what it's like to be a son parents have to worry about. I won't pretend to have faced anything like what Roddie described, but I do know that my parents spent more time worrying about what would become of me than they should've needed to."

He looked at me, then Nattie, and then Inez, before continuing. "Yes, we're all young. But we're also all trying. To be good people. To figure out what we want to do with our lives. To become functioning adults. If Roddie was ever going to have the space to learn those things, it's going to be here. I can't make you any promises about how it's going to go. We're all going to have to take a leap of faith."

Eva released a shaky sigh. "That's . . . not as reassuring as I'd hoped it would be."

Owen smiled. “I’ll work on my inspirational speeches for next time.”

She returned his smile, and though it was small, I was hopeful it was a good sign. Turning to Roddie, she said, “Okay. We can give it a try. But you need to be prepared for me to be overbearing. I’ll try to work on it. Maybe. A little.”

Roddie beamed. “I can handle that.”

I hoped that would be true for the rest of us.

Chapter Eleven

OWEN

Roddie moved in the next day, thankfully with actual boxes instead of trash bags, and settled into Vee's old room.

After some discussion, we decided she'd move in with me so Roddie could have her room. She spent every night with me anyway, and this way we didn't have to worry about Roddie being tainted by whatever had gone on with Wynter. The room seemed somehow cursed after she'd been in there, and we wanted to give Roddie the best shot he could at making things work.

He also wasted no time getting his doggie day care set up. Thankfully, he started with only three dogs, not including Gimli, so it was manageable for all of us.

After he moved in, we sat down and ran through our questions with him, and we were pleased to hear he already had answers for all of them. It went a long way to making us feel better about his plans that he was well organized.

Since the backyard was already fenced, half the battle was already won. He brought over some tents to provide shade and hoped that those would suffice if it rained.

He did sheepishly ask if it was okay to bring the dogs inside if there was a thunderstorm or dangerously high heat, and I said it was fine as long as he had some way of keeping them contained. He went out and bought baby gates later that day.

The next day, I got ready for school and noticed Roddie's car was already gone. He'd told us he was picking up two of the dogs because their owners left early for work. Another would be dropped off later.

As I rinsed my cereal bowl, the doorbell chimed. Maybe Roddie had forgotten his key? While things had been pretty smooth over the couple of days he'd been living with us, I did notice that Roddie put forth a lot of effort to keep himself organized and on top of things. It wouldn't surprise me if he'd rushed around that morning and forgotten it.

I answered the door, clad only in my boxers and white undershirt, and found a middle-aged woman holding the leash of a Great Dane. Her eyes widened as she took me in, and I looked down at myself in embarrassment.

"Sorry. I was expecting Roddie," I rushed out.

She looked confused. "Doesn't he live here?"

"Yeah, I just thought maybe he forgot his key." God, I sounded stupid. I pointed at the dog. "I guess he's here for Roddie's day care."

The woman eyed me warily and seemed to clutch her dog's leash a little tighter. "Yes. Is Roddie here?"

"He went to pick up some other dogs. I'm sure he'll be back any minute."

She looked down at her watch and shifted her weight.

"Do you want me to take him?" I offered.

She looked at me like I'd just invited her into my basement with promises of ice cream.

But at that moment, Gimli stuck his head out of the door between my legs, and her entire demeanor relaxed.

"Who's this?" she said sweetly as she bent down to give Gimli some head scratches, which was slightly awkward because it put her hand precariously close to my boxer-clad dick.

"This is Gimli. I rescued him from a truck stop last year."

She went from looking at me like I was Hannibal Lecter to the second coming of Christ. "Aw, how sweet." She handed me her dog's leash. "This is Apollo. He's very friendly, and he loves other dogs, so I'm sure he and Gimli will get along well."

Apollo moved into the house quickly, lured by the scent of Gimli.

"We'll take good care of him," I said, instantly wondering when Roddie's venture became a *we* thing.

She hurried off after that, and I closed the door behind her. When I spun around, I saw Natalia standing on the stairs, looking at me disapprovingly.

"What?" I asked.

She waved her hand at me and the dogs. "I knew you were gonna get all involved."

"I'm not involved. I'm just helping until Roddie gets home."

"Please. By the end of the week, you'll be picking up dog shit with one of those weird shovel things and carrying around a dog whistle."

I rolled my eyes as a reply as I led Apollo and Gimli to the backyard. Once there, I let Apollo off his leash and watched the two dogs get to know each other. After a few minutes, I figured they were getting along well enough for me to sneak upstairs and change for school.

I dashed upstairs and got ready for my day. When I was done and had returned downstairs, I saw Roddie out back playing with two other dogs. I went out to join him.

"Hey, how'd pickup go?"

He looked up from where he was playing tug-of-war with what appeared to be a pit bull.

"Good," he replied. "You can let Gimli come out if you want. These guys are all friendly."

I looked around quickly. "He's already . . . out here." My voice trailed off as I realized Apollo and Gimli were not, in fact, out there. "Wait. Where did they go?"

"They?" Roddie said, his voice concerned.

"Yeah. Apollo's owner dropped him off, and I left him and Gimli to play out here while I got dressed for school."

Roddie's face grew an alarming shade of white. "I opened the gate this morning before I left so I wouldn't have to bring the dogs through the house. Did you close it?"

"No, I didn't realize it was open." We kept a padlock on it to prevent anyone from being able to access the backyard. It made sense Roddie would've unlocked it, but it hadn't occurred to me he would.

"Oh my God," he muttered. He ran to the gate and undid the lock, me following close behind. He pushed it closed once we were out and ran down the street, scanning up and down it for the dogs.

He yelled for them, but there was no bark or appearance of either animal.

"Roddie, I'm so sorry."

He pushed his hands through his hair and pulled slightly.

"Shit. Shit! What am I going to do? I can't believe I screwed up on the very first day."

"You didn't screw up. I did."

"My mom was right. I'm clearly not ready for this."

I grabbed his shoulder tightly. "Stop. You didn't do anything wrong. I messed up, and I'm going to help fix it."

He shook his head. "You need to go to school."

"No, what I need to do is find some dogs. Gimli's missing too. I can't sit in class while he's out wandering around. But we're gonna need reinforcements." I pulled my phone out of my pocket and opened our text thread.

"Who are you texting?"

"Everyone."

VERONICA

Owen's text came through as I was sitting through my morning lecture. I was supposed to go to a study group session after that, but I begged off and hurried home.

When I pulled up, there were a ton of cars in front of our house, all of which I recognized. The cavalry had arrived.

I rushed inside and found it empty. Going out back, I saw Nattie and Inez sitting on the porch swing watching two dogs.

"You're here," Nattie said, sounding surprised.

"Of course I'm here. Where else would I be?"

"At law school." She enunciated the words as if *I* was the one missing something. "Learning to become a lawyer."

I stared at her as if doing so would make her make sense.

"She thinks being at school is more important than finding Gimli," Inez explained.

"Because it is."

"It is not," I said, offended. "Gimli's part of the family. If you were lost, wouldn't you want me to hurry home and look for you?"

"With all the times you threatened to hide my dead body, I think I'd actually rather you pass."

I ignored her in favor of talking to Inez. "Is everyone already out looking?"

"Yeah, and they split up. Ransom took playgrounds because he said he has some kind of experience with runaway dogs and sliding boards." Her tone conveyed how ridiculous she found that explanation. "Xander went with him. Brody and Drew headed toward Dayton Street, while Carter and Toby went the opposite direction. Owen and Roddie went toward the woods at the end of the street because Owen said Gimli likes it there. We were told to hang out here in case the dogs came back."

"I can't believe all those people came."

Not that I expected less of them necessarily, but they all had their own lives. That they'd drop them to help us look for a couple of dogs maybe shouldn't have surprised me, since that's who our friends have always shown themselves to be, but it did.

Nattie shrugged. "I can't believe *anyone* came. Don't get me wrong," she said, holding up a hand when she saw my mouth open, "I care about Gimli too. But don't any of your friends have lives?"

I couldn't even with her anymore, so I said, "I'm gonna walk the neighborhood just in case the dogs circled back."

As I walked, I shot off a text to Owen telling him I was home and looking. He sent back a thumbs-up and a heart emoji.

After thirty minutes of yelling for the dogs, and without word that anyone else had found them, I began to lose a little hope. What if we didn't find them? What if someone stole them? Or they got hit by a car? So many things could go wrong, and while I knew it didn't help to focus on them, I couldn't stop myself.

I circled back to the house so I could use the restroom and change into shoes better suited for all the walking I was doing. I climbed the stairs, seeing Gimli's toys littering the steps, and tears pricked at the back of my eyes.

As I went into the bedroom Owen and I now shared, I plopped down on the bed, and some of the tears fell down my cheeks. I took a minute to compose myself before retrieving my sneakers, used the restroom, and then headed back into the hall.

I headed toward the stairs when a noise behind me stopped me in my tracks.

Is that... nails?

I spun around and looked at the closed door to the room Wynter had stayed in. The one she'd said was haunted. The one I now heard a scratching sound coming from.

Oh my God, was she actually right?

I slowly backed away from the door, staring at it as if a demon was going to spring through it at any moment. I just made it to the stairs and began to turn when I heard another noise.

Whimpering.

"Oh my God!" I ran to the door and threw it open. As I did, two blurs of fur booked out of there like their asses were on fire.

I chased them down the stairs, calling for Gimli as I went.

Both dogs hid under the dining room table, the gigantic one jostling it as he climbed underneath. I dropped to my knees to try to get to them. Once I saw that they both seemed content to stay there, I pulled out my phone and called Owen.

"I found the dogs," I said by way of greeting.

"Thank God. Where?"

"In the spare bedroom."

There was a pause. "What? How'd they get in there?"

"I have no idea. The door was closed so they couldn't get out."

"The door was closed. They shouldn't have been able to get in there in the first place," Owen replied. "Did you go in there?" he asked someone who I assumed was Roddie.

"No way, man. After the story you told me about the salt girl, I don't want anything to do with that room."

"That's so weird," I said almost to myself.

"We're on our way back," Owen said. "I'll text everyone that you found them."

We hung up, and I did my best to coax the dogs out to no avail. Not even a treat moved them. It wasn't until Owen and Roddie came back that they left the table.

Gimli practically dived for Owen—which, okay, not gonna lie, that stung a bit—and the other one followed his lead, knocking over a chair in the process.

When everyone returned, I repeated the story about the room, which everyone listened to with rapt attention. Once I was done, everyone stood silently for a second before Brody spoke up.

"Dude, your house is haunted as fuck. That's so cool."

I wished I shared in his enthusiasm.

Roddie looked like he was going to be sick. "Please don't say that."

"No, no, this is a good thing," Brody said.

"In what way is a haunting a good thing?" Ransom asked. "Not that I'm saying I think your house is haunted. But after the past couple of years, nothing seems impossible anymore."

We all nodded because yeah, we'd all been through some weird-ass stuff together. And besides, this wasn't the first time someone had mentioned the house having a ghost. It was just the first time it seemed possible.

"Because Halloween is coming," Brody said, answering Ransom's question.

"So?" Owen asked. "I mean, don't get me wrong, I *love* Halloween. But you know, in the Druid tradition, it was actually—"

Brody put his hand over Owen's mouth. "Please nerd-out on your own time. For now, we have a haunting to publicize."

"What are you talking about?" I asked.

"I'm talking about how you're going to make enough money to save your house," he replied. When all of us stared at him blankly, he spread his arms wide. "It'll be more than just a Halloween party. We're going to turn this place into the haunted attraction of the year. People love scaring the crap out of themselves. It's perfect."

I opened my mouth to explain just how *not* perfect it was, but the words wouldn't come. Because maybe, just this once, Brody was actually on to something.

As we all looked at each other consideringly rather than shooting the idea down, he began to look smug.

"Yes, I know," he said patronizingly. "You can thank me later. For now, we have work to do."

Chapter Twelve

VERONICA

Owen and I headed outside after we had our morning coffee to play with Gimli for a bit. Roddie only had one other dog here—a bulldog named Paulie, who Gimli loved with such enthusiasm I started to think Owen had some competition.

The two animals jumped and rolled around in the one patch of the yard that didn't have grass. They kicked up clouds of dirt with every flop to the ground and then let it fall back onto their fur and collars. We'd definitely be giving Gimli a bath later. There was no way he was sleeping in our bed looking like a farmer during the Dust Bowl.

Eventually, the dogs settled down into some shade on the grass where they had extra cool water, and Owen and I began to assess the situation that was Owen's backyard. It definitely needed to be mowed again even though Owen had done it at the end of last week, and the garden desperately needed to be taken care of.

We'd grown some cherry tomatoes and peppers, which I considered a win since it was my first real try at gardening.

We'd never had enough room for a garden in our yard growing up, but my mom had grown a few vegetables in pots on our small patio out back. Ever since then, I'd always wanted to plant something in the ground and see if I could get it to grow. Turned out I could, and I planned to pick every last little tomato until there was nothing left on the plant.

I was pulling a few of the last red ones off and preparing to put one in my mouth when I heard a voice coming from behind me that I didn't recognize.

"Hi there." It sounded a little deeper than Owen's, and when I turned around, I saw a man standing on the other side of the gate with a hand in the air midwave. He lowered his hand and pointed at the gate. "You mind if I . . .?"

He didn't finish his question, and he also didn't wait for an answer.

Owen was already walking toward him from across the lawn. "Hey, man. Can I help you?"

I could tell by Owen's tone that he didn't know him, but maybe he was Paulie's owner. Neither of us had met either of his owners, but I didn't think he was supposed to be picked up until later in the day.

Heading over to also greet the guy, I noticed he had a clipboard in his hand. Probably someone asking if we wanted our windows replaced or maybe our lawn treated for insects or something.

Owen reached the gate before I did, but he didn't open it. The man was a little shorter than Owen, with a shiny bald head he probably shaved every day and a short graying beard. He looked like he was in decent shape with a physique that he probably obtained from years of physical labor rather than countless hours at the gym. He was dressed in a light-blue polo and dark chinos and was pointing around at various parts of Owen's property.

"Hi, I'm Veronica," I said, extending my hand over the gate when I reached it.

Owen didn't exactly *need* backup when salespeople came around, but he tended to be less . . . blunt than I was, probably because he had more of a heart than I did and cared about everyone's feelings.

I'd tried to explain that everyone in sales was used to rejection and couldn't possibly take it personally or they'd be perpetually depressed, but Owen's kindness always won out. And most salespeople knew a soft *no* really meant a hard *yes* if they pushed long enough.

I, on the other hand, was totally fine with being the bad guy.

"Rich Cappello. Nice to meet you."

There was no company name on his shirt, and I didn't see anything on the black truck he had parked in the driveway that indicated even his occupation.

"I'm building some homes down the street on that piece of property." He pointed to the woods a few houses down at the end of Owen's street that backed up to God knows where.

I'd never been in them, but I think some of our friends had when they went looking for the dogs when they'd slipped out.

"Oh, wow. That'll be nice to have some new neighbors," I said, thinking he was going to be handing out some sort of marketing materials to us any second to see if we were interested in moving or had anyone in mind who might like to live near us.

"Yeah, I've already had a lot of interest. You guys see the development over on New Street yet?" Rich pointed toward what I guessed was the direction of New Street, though I didn't actually know where or what he was referring to.

It occurred to me how little I actually knew about this neighborhood despite having lived here a few months. I tended to just travel the roads I needed to to get to work or school.

Owen nodded and said he knew which spot Rich was talking about.

I nodded too for no real reason. I didn't care what this guy thought about my knowledge of the community, but it just seemed easier to go along with it rather than ask questions.

"You familiar with the current market?"

"Not really," I said with a shrug.

Owen looked at me and then back to Rich, who'd already pulled out what I assumed was a business card. "Yeah, we aren't in a position to buy, so I haven't paid much attention to it, to be honest."

Rich let out a laugh through his nose, and I swear I saw a few nostril hairs move with it. "Wasn't talking about you buying. Was more thinking you might be interested in selling."

My attention immediately shifted to Owen, who looked like Rich had just suggested donating half of his brain to science.

"Nah, we're good here," was all he said.

Rich leaned in so his arms crossed over the fence, and he seemed to let some of his weight settle against it as he looked into our yard. "You sure?"

"I'm sorry?" Owen said, a little more defensive than I was used to seeing him.

"You said you're good. Just wondering if you're sure." He looked toward the direction of the sun and squinted before raising his arm to block it. With his other hand, he pointed at our neighbor's house. "Just gave her a good offer for her home, and I'd be happy to do the same for you."

My eyes narrowed at him, trying to gauge just what he was getting at exactly. "I thought you said you were building new. What would you want two old houses for?"

"My company's small and has been in my family for the last forty-eight years. It started out as my grandfather's construction business, actually." Finally, Rich handed over the card he'd been holding.

Cappello's Custom Homes

The name didn't do much to clarify.

"When he started out," Rich continued, "he mainly worked on already-existing homes that needed renovation, but once my dad got involved, it expanded pretty fast. The last couple of decades, we've been building from scratch, but there's nothing like bringing new life into a property that needs it, ya know?"

Owen nodded, but he looked hesitant about whether to reply otherwise.

"Yeah, we've actually been fixing up this place gradually too," I said. "My dad and brothers are all contractors, so they've been helping here and there, and Owen's naturally good at that stuff." I put my arm on his back and leaned in a little closer to him.

The word *naturally* might have been a stretch, but Rich didn't need to know that, and I figured a boost to Owen's ego couldn't hurt. He'd become quite good at home projects, but some hadn't been easy. Though I could see how, as time went on, he could become skilled at even the tasks that were tougher now.

Owen smiled back at me and, without looking back to

Rich, said, "Yeah, we're all set here. We'll let you know if we ever need anything, though. Thanks for stopping by." His last two sentences came out in a rush with barely any space between sounds.

But Rich didn't take the hint. Or at least he didn't want to. "So you got the money, then?" he asked, his lips twisting while he waited for one of us to reply.

We were both quiet for a moment before Owen said, "Sorry?"

"The tax money," he clarified, though both of us probably had a feeling that was what he'd been implying. "You have that ready to pay?"

"How do you know . . ."

"Public record," Rich said.

I hadn't even thought about how anyone could have access to that information, though I'd known they technically could look it up. And Owen probably had too. But neither of us had been prepared for someone to approach us about it.

"We're done here," Owen said. "Now if you can kindly remove yourself from my property, that'd be fantastic." His voice was even, intimidating in its calmness. It would've turned me on a little if I hadn't been so incredibly irritated.

"Sure," Rich replied. "But if you don't come up with the money soon, this property won't be yours for long." His tone was almost a direct mirror of Owen's—calculated, deliberate. "Just think about my offer," he said before smacking his hand on the fence and standing upright. "It would be financially advisable for you to get rid of the property before *it* gets rid of *you*."

"Get off my property," Owen said again, this time opening the gate so there was nothing between him and the asshole on the other side of it.

It seemed like Rich hadn't been expecting Owen to leave the yard. The two men stared at each other like dogs before a fight, waiting to see if the other would cower. But I knew Owen wouldn't fight him. Not unless the guy hit him first. Owen was smarter than that, and he wouldn't give Rich any reason to take legal action against him. It would only make the struggle to hang on to the house more difficult than it already was.

"We're not interested in any deal you have to offer," Owen told him, his face only inches away from the other man's. "And my financial status is none of your goddamn business, so it would be in your best interest to forget about me and my house entirely."

Rich smiled from one side of his mouth, like he couldn't allow his whole mouth to commit to the act without it looking genuine. "You know how to find me if you change your mind."

Then he walked over to his truck, leaving Owen to mutter, "We won't," in a voice so low I wasn't sure if he meant for me to hear it.

Chapter Thirteen

VERONICA

We were ruminating over the meeting with the land developer, wondering if we'd done the right thing. Not that I was in a position to *do* anything. It was Owen's house, and ultimately all the decisions concerning it were his to make. But I also knew that while his name was the one on the deed, he considered it *our* house.

And honestly, I considered it that as well.

Which was why I was going to do everything in my power to save it. Even if that meant turning it into a haunted house.

"Do you really think we can pull it off?" Owen asked as we leaned against the kitchen counters and picked at leftovers.

"I think we have to try."

"It'll require us putting money out, though. That seems silly to do with no guarantee of earning it back."

"If we go like we've been, you lose the house anyway. We're not even halfway to the goal at this point."

"I can sell my truck," he said.

"You can*not* sell your truck."

"You're right. I may have to live in it," he muttered.

I moved next to him and cuddled against him. "You need a car to get to and from work and school."

"Maybe I could get a refund on this semester like Xander did?"

"Didn't your parents pay for this semester?"

He nodded.

"So even if you could still get a partial refund, the money would need to go back to them. Do you think they'd front you some of next semester's payment for the taxes, and you could just work from now until then to make back what you used?"

He exhaled loudly and rubbed his hands down his face. "I know this isn't the mature thing to do, but I just . . . can't tell them. They were already disappointed in me with the whole marriage thing. If I tell them I've lost a house that was left to me free and clear, they'll never trust me with anything again."

"It *wasn't* free and clear, though. And you aren't to blame for not knowing that."

He looked down at me and pressed a kiss to my forehead. "It's understandable that I didn't know it, but I'm still to blame for it. I should've sought someone out to explain everything to me instead of just hoping it all worked out. Ignorance isn't really an excuse here."

I hugged him tighter. "I still think they'd help you."

"Oh, I know they'd help me. That's the kind of people they are. But how much money can I continue to take from people? My college fund is one thing. They've been saving that since I was born. But to borrow *more* from them, on top of what our friends have offered . . ." He shook his head. "Maybe selling the house is the way to go. I'm obviously not ready to be a homeowner."

"That's bullshit," I said, pulling away so I could glare up at him. "You're a great homeowner. You've fixed this place up on your own, made it yours, and you *love* it. You're happy here the way June intended Minnie to be happy here when she gave it to her. Like Minnie hoped you'd be when she gave it to you."

I took a minute to try to get my thoughts in order so I could convey to him what I was truly trying to say. "This house passes between people who love each other, Owen. And that's why you need to do everything you can to keep that seedy, soul-sucking developer the hell out of here."

He looked at me for a second before reaching out and cupping my chin, letting his thumb rub along my jaw. "That was quite an impassioned speech."

"Thanks. It felt pretty solid, but it's tough to tell sometimes."

We both laughed softly for a moment before falling silent.

"So you really think I can do this?" he asked.

"No."

His face dropped until I wound my arms around his waist.

"But I think *we* can. You, me, and the rest of the gang. I think we, against all odds and common sense, can accomplish anything when we work together."

He pressed his lips to mine, and we rested our foreheads against each other's.

"Then let's plan a haunted house."

OWEN

I had to give them credit. My friends got shit done.

A few of them asked their parents for old Halloween decorations we could use, Xander did some research on surrounding attractions and how much they charged so he could draft a business plan for us, Cody offered to take pictures to post on social media, and Roddie promised to keep the yard clean so we didn't have to worry about any doggie accidents.

But Brody and Drew came up truly clutch. They offered to come up with haunted mocktails and put up signs to promote the bar they were in the process of building. That way, they said they could record it as a business expense, and I could sell drinks for a profit.

Beyond the drinks, we'd decided against offering any other food. Drew said he could talk to Sean, Drew's former boss at Rafferty's, and Vee had suggested asking June if her family café wanted to donate anything, but none of it seemed worth the hassle. Besides, having to tell June I was turning her childhood home into a haunted house so I could save it from being seized didn't seem like a fun conversation.

All that was left to do was to come up with the actual plan to decorate it. Everyone had offered to come over the following weekend to brainstorm ideas and get started. Hopefully, we'd be able to open with still a few weekends left in September and capitalize on the season.

But until then, I had to try to focus on classes... and practice for Professor Ted's band assignment. I walked into the room where I had music class—the class Xander was supposed to be sitting in with me, but he betrayed me and left me to suffer through not only the class but the goddamn band as well.

Though the money he'd offered me had gone a long way to buying my forgiveness.

"Hey, Owen," Jagger said.

"Hey," I replied, planning on moving past them to the seat I'd chosen on the first day.

But Brae motioned to an empty seat I could only assume they saved for me, and I couldn't think of a tactful way to say no, so I sat.

"How's it going?"

"We were thinking," Brae began, and I instantly wanted to find a way onto the roof and hurl myself off. There was no way anything good was coming from those two thinking.

"Have you ever heard of bluegrass music?" Jagger finished.

"Yeah," I replied, drawing the word out with my hesitance.

Jagger and Brae looked exceedingly excited at my admission.

"We think that would really jibe with our vibe," Brae said.

"Our vibe?" I wasn't aware we had one.

"Yeah, relaxed and simple. Do you think you can learn to play a fiddle by any chance?" Jagger asked.

I wanted to ask what the hell was simple about playing a fiddle, but instead I pinched the bridge of my nose and counted to ten.

"No, I do not think I can learn to play a fiddle. Or any other instrument. I thought you guys were okay with me playing the triangle?"

They shared a look. "We were. Until Xander backed out. Now we need you to play something with a little more . . . pop."

"I thought you wanted to play bluegrass."

"We do," Jagger said, clearly confused even though she was the one who said *pop*.

Brae rubbed a hand through his pink hair. "What about

the washboard? I bet you could learn to play that."

"Where would I even find something like that?"

He waved me off. "I'm sure we can find one somewhere." He pulled out his phone and began clicking away.

"We also have to talk about where we're going to perform," Jagger said. "I know Ted said we could play in the quad, but he also said he'd give extra credit if we could book an actual venue. I think that'd be so cool."

Her excitement was palpable, and I almost wished I shared it. But not quite, because she had clearly lost her mind.

"We've barely even practiced. No one is going to give us a chance . . ." I trailed off because suddenly I had the best worst idea I'd ever come up with. Or maybe it was the worst best.

Leaning in, I asked, "How do you guys feel about haunted houses?"

Chapter Fourteen

OWEN

"Tell me you're kidding," Vee said.

"Nope."

"What would possess you to let your band play at our haunted house?"

I held my hands out in front of me like a zombie. "Maybe it was the evil spirit who chased away Wynter and kidnapped our dog."

"Is it called kidnapping when it's a dog?" she asked.

"Dognapping, then."

She sighed. "Well, one thing's for sure. It'll be interesting."

I walked closer and enveloped her in my arms. "Are you doubting my musical abilities?"

She hesitated. "Not to sound unsupportive, but yes."

I huffed out a laugh before drawing back just enough to kiss her. Things between us quickly escalated the way they almost always did when I was near Vee. I ran my hands under her shirt, smoothing along the silky skin of her lower back, and dipped my fingers below her waistband.

For her part, she slid her hands up my chest and rested them there.

"These are in my way," I said, tugging lightly on her shorts.

"Hmm, maybe you should move them, then."

"Uh, I'm sorry to interrupt."

Vee and I broke apart as if we'd been caught doing something wrong and turned wide-eyed to Roddie, who was standing in the doorway.

"There's some lady looking through her bushes at us. The dogs keep running over to where she is, and she keeps hissing at them to go away. I think she's trying to be stealthy, but she's doing a shit job of it."

I groaned. "I'll be right there."

"Sorry, man," Roddie said sheepishly before heading back outside.

"Hold this thought?" I asked her.

"Absolutely."

I pressed one more kiss to her lips before I headed for the front door.

Even though Roddie hadn't said, I figured the snooper was Mrs. Aberdeen. I didn't know her well. Minnie had despised her, and as a result, I'd always kept my distance. Other than a wave and a smile and a handful of casual conversations about missed trash pickups or a late mailman, we each kept to our own properties.

But I did know that she was a relentless gossip who wasn't particularly invested in the truth.

Her property wasn't fenced, so I was able to go out the front door and walk up her driveway, where I could easily see her huddled behind the shrubs she had planted along her property line, peeking through our chain link fence.

"Did you need something, Mrs. Aberdeen?" I asked, my voice sounding a tad more sarcastic than I'd intended.

She straightened so fast, I worried she'd pulled something. "Oh, uh, no, no, I just... heard barking and wanted to make sure your dog was okay."

I bet.

"Yeah, we're just dog sitting." That seemed a simple enough explanation without going into detail about what was really going on.

Her gaze turned shrewd. "Dog sitting? Every day? Because I see dogs get dropped off and then picked up. You running some kind of service over there?"

Christ.

I shrugged. "One of my friends really likes dogs." It was a dumb response, but I didn't want to tell her that we were running a business out of the house. I had no idea if there were certain rules we needed to follow to do so, and I was damn sure she'd look into it if she knew.

She was quiet for a moment, and the look on her face turned calculating. "I heard you've run into some trouble with Minnie's house," she finally said.

I shoved my hands into my pockets, hoping to seem nonchalant, but I was pretty sure she saw it for the defensive posture it was.

"Not sure where you heard that." I wondered if that Cappello guy had told her about it when he'd offered to purchase her house.

She smiled, but it was predatory. The old biddy smelled blood in the water, and she was circling.

"I have my sources." She sighed. "Such a shame. Minerva never was good with money. Surprised she was ever able to buy it in the first place, let alone hang on to it all those years. Though, of course, there's all sorts of rumors about that."

And I bet she'd started at least half of them.

"I wouldn't know," I lied.

She hummed as she assessed me. Seeming to come to some decision, she moved closer.

"If you want my advice—"

I barely restrained the urge to tell her I didn't.

"I recommend you get out from under that house before it drowns you. Smart thing to do. A young man like you isn't ready for all that responsibility. Think of what you could do with the money you'd make from the sale. The places you could go. The adventures you could have."

Her voice was oddly melodic, as though she were trying to hypnotize me or something.

"Thanks for the advice, but I'm managing just fine."

She smiled as if she knew my words were bullshit. "Whatever you say, dear." Then she turned on her heel and slowly walked inside her house.

I stared after her, a sense of dread spreading through me, though I couldn't say exactly why. But one thing was certain: Minnie was right to hate that woman.

VERONICA

When Owen told me about his run-in with the neighbor—after we'd picked up where we'd left off, of course—I was irritated, to say the least. Owen had enough on his plate without some old hag acting like she knew his business and giving him unsolicited advice.

With all that he was juggling, I wished I could be of more help to him. But my only means of helping was supporting him as best I could. He didn't want my family to know anything about what was going on—which I totally understood—but I didn't have much in the way of finances to contribute.

I still worked some hours at Safe Haven when they needed me and did some basic office work at the law firm I'd interned at a while back, but none of that was enough to make any real impact on Owen's financial situation.

But one thing I could help with was finding out everything about what we were up against. And since Mrs. Aberdeen was right next door, I decided to start with her.

When I'd called June, she'd been happy to hear from me and readily agreed to meet up. Despite Owen saying he didn't want to involve her when we'd talked about asking her if her family would supply snacks for the haunted house, I didn't see a way around it.

June had lived in this community all her life, and she'd grown up in the house we currently lived in. She probably had insight that could help us.

Though it was tempting, I decided not to keep my meeting with June a secret from Owen. I'd already been down that road, and we'd promised each other we'd be better about communicating.

It was clear he wanted to argue, but he also understood my reasoning. Ultimately, underneath all his feelings was embarrassment, and I wanted to be sensitive to that. He didn't want to tell the woman who'd gifted her childhood home to her lover that he was going to lose it.

But he also needed to understand that this whole ordeal had been set in motion long before he'd inherited the house. He was being punished for Minnie's mismanagement, and as such, he shouldn't be so hard on himself.

Easier said than done, but at least he agreed to let me talk to June. I asked if he wanted to come with me, but he said no. I don't think he wanted to face her, and I was fine with that. I wanted to be able to handle *something* for him, even if it was a simple conversation with a sweet old woman.

I walked into the same café we'd met in last time and again found June waiting for me. She picked at a muffin, a look of distaste on her face. When she saw me approach, she smiled broadly, and then gestured at the muffin.

"Skip the cranberry. Something tastes off with the baking soda."

"Will do. Can I get you anything else?"

She waved me off. "I'm fine with my tea."

"I'll be right back, then." Walking to the cashier, I placed my order and collected it before returning to sit with June.

"So, to what do I owe this pleasure?" she asked.

"Maybe I just wanted to see you."

Her smile turned a bit slyer. "Maybe." She stared at me for a moment longer before I caved.

"I need some intel."

Her smile was very self-satisfied.

"But I *did* also want to see you."

She patted my hand. "I know. And I'm glad. Now what can I help you with?"

I gave her the abridged version of the tax issue, the talk with the developer, and finally about Mrs. Aberdeen. As soon as I mentioned the woman's name, June's face grew stormy.

"I could never stand that woman. She didn't live there until a few years after we'd signed the house over to Minnie, but she used to go to my church. Always up in everyone's business and *very* opinionated. She and her husband left the congregation when their . . . let's say *narrow* worldviews weren't supported by our pastor."

"I don't like that she was spying on us. I mean, I understand, ultimately, there's not much she can do to hurt us or anything. But with so many things working against us right now, I don't like having another one living next door." I sighed. "I'm probably just being paranoid."

She hummed. "Perhaps. Or maybe your intuition is telling you something. Either way, I think it's smart to be on your guard. Janice—that's her first name—is a pot-stirrer. After she somehow caught wind of the rumors swirling about us and Minnie, she bad-mouthed us to anyone who'd listen. Came into my bakery and complained that goods were stale or the service was poor. Whatever she could think of. And remember, this was years *after* everything had already ended. There was no reason for her to involve herself other than good old-fashioned boredom and ill will. So I wouldn't put anything past her."

"But what could she even do? Now that I'm saying it all out loud, I feel like I'm overreacting."

"I don't know. But I'm sure if she wanted to, she could find a way to make things more difficult for you. It seems to be a personality trait of hers. Even if she's just a plain old pain in the ass, it's still added stress onto an already tense situation."

I sighed. "It all seems so surreal. I thought the biggest problem I'd have would be acclimating to law school. But now we have all this real-life adult stuff going on, and I'm not sure how to best go about handling it."

"We never know how to handle things before we come up against them. You just have to keep fighting."

I took a sip of my iced coffee. "I guess that's true."

"And I'll help you any way I can. I can't be much help financially—"

"Oh no, we would never ask that of you." I was horrified that she might think I came here with an ulterior motive of squeezing her for cash.

She smiled kindly. "I know you wouldn't. But I'd give it anyway if I had it to give. I can, however, offer you support."

"Thank you. We were a little worried you'd be disappointed."

She looked perplexed. "At what?"

"That we're in this situation. That your childhood home might go to some sleazy builder because we didn't do our homework."

"Don't take any of that on yourselves. Like I said, we don't learn how to handle things until we're faced with them. You can only control your response to it. And even if you do everything you can, and it still doesn't go your way, that'll be okay, Vee. It's just a house. It's the people inside that make it a home."

Even though I'd known that, I was thankful for the reminder. No matter what happened, Owen and I would face it together. And if we lost, at least we'd still have each other.

And as long as that was the case, maybe we couldn't ever truly lose at all.

Chapter Fifteen

OWEN

Things were hectic. We were all busy trying to get things ready to open the haunted house with a couple of weekends left in September, I still had work and school, and there was the added bonus of worrying nonstop about the house.

The fact that Mrs. Aberdeen seemed to be hovering around our property wasn't helping.

Vee told me about her conversation with June, and it did nothing to quell my steadily rising anxiety. I was probably doing untold damage to my blood pressure.

But whenever I asked for help, I received it.

Xander, who still had a few weeks until he started his new job, had been especially helpful in planning out the haunted house and rigging things to move, shake, steam, or glow for added effect. We'd decided that we should market the room Wynter had stayed in as a legitimate haunted room. It would be our pièce de résistance, so to speak. While the whole house would have an added spooky element, that room would be our focus.

Cody had suggested we offer late-night challenges to see who could spend more than half an hour in the room. We could charge people for the experience, and Xander said he could add some elements to make it even creepier. But ultimately, he said, it would be the psychological effect that would be most important, so he and Cody set about spreading word on social media about the "presence" that inhabited the room.

We even ordered some T-shirts for people who made it to the half-hour mark. Vee's cousin Adrien knew a guy who could get them cheap. Who knew where they'd come from or how high quality they'd be, but that was a worry for another day.

Today, my only worry was passing my first accounting test and then meeting up with Jagger and Brae to practice for our concert. At least Professor Ted hadn't given us a hard time when we'd told him we'd only have three in our group since Xander had left.

He knew it wasn't our fault and said that it would be a good lesson for us since most famous bands have at least one member who dies young from a drug overdose or other unnatural causes. I didn't think our situation was quite the same, but I kept that to myself since Ted was letting us off the hook for one of the requirements. I would've hated for each of us to have had to join other bands that were already established.

They were excited to play "scary" music for the haunted house, which honestly worried me a bit. When the idea popped in my head, it seemed like a way to kill two birds with one stone, while also not expecting us to learn full songs. Just some horror anthems would suffice.

But Brae and Jagger might have had other ideas. Where I was imagining the theme from *Jaws*, I was beginning to get the impression they were thinking something more like that classical song from *The Omen.* They'd been sending links and sheet music to our group chat—even though only one of us could read it.

As I trudged across campus to the music building after hopefully acing a test, I tried to think of ways to rein them in if they got out of hand. Damn Xander for abandoning me with them. He was better at being a dick than I was.

When I arrived at Fellerman Hall, home to the music department, I wandered around trying to find the rehearsal rooms. Professor Ted had offered to reserve rooms for anyone who needed them, and Brae and Jagger had jumped on the opportunity like they were being offered a chance to audition for Aerosmith or something.

Finally, I saw Ted standing at the end of a hallway and headed for him.

"Hey, Prof . . . uh . . . Ted." *God, that was weird.* "I can't find the rehearsal rooms. Can you point me in the right direction?"

He smiled a cheesy grin. "You found 'em. Brae and Jagger are already in there doing a little jam session." He deepened his voice on the word *jam* and gestured like he was playing an air guitar.

At least one of us was excited by what was happening in that room.

"Thanks." I slipped past him and saw Brae and Jagger. Brae was strumming his guitar and Jagger had some kind of . . . wood . . . thing.

"Hey, how's it going?" I asked.

"Pretty good," Jagger replied.

"What's that?" I asked, pointing to the instrument in her hand.

She looked down at it as if she had to remind herself what she was holding. "It's a pan flute. I found it at a thrift store."

I had to quash the urge to throw up at the fact she was putting her mouth on something she bought from a thrift store.

"I thought you were gonna sing."

She shrugged. "Most of the songs we found don't have a lot of singing. I don't want to lose points for not contributing."

"What did you decide on?" Brae asked me.

I opened my schoolbag and pulled out my instrument with a flourish. "Ta-da!"

"Is that a kid's keyboard?" Brae asked disparagingly.

I looked down at my instrument. "No. It's an adult's mini keyboard. My friend Roddie had it sitting at his parents' house and offered to let me borrow it."

Roddie had heard me telling Vee that a lot of the theme songs I'd listened to had seemed like they relied on a piano, and he'd graciously offered his small keyboard. He supposedly had a full-size one as well, but that was too hard to cart around. He'd even told me that while he couldn't really read sheet music, he was pretty good at replicating sounds he heard and therefore might be able to help me learn how to play a few.

If I'd ever questioned my decision to let Roddie move in, I now knew better. The guy was a godsend. He was a jack-of-all-trades, and I couldn't give a shit less if he was a master of none of them.

Brae and Jagger looked less enthused.

"You're going to make us look like kids," she said.

"Says the girl blowing through sticks," I shot back before I could catch myself. Not that I wanted to catch myself, because honestly, who was she kidding? At least I hadn't mentioned that she was practically the *size* of a child.

"It's a pan flute," she said through gritted teeth.

"Uh, hey, guys. And girl."

We all whipped our heads in the direction of the soft, placating voice that had come from behind us.

Professor Ted stood there with outstretched hands.

"I love seeing the passion you all have—"

Passion? Where was he seeing passion? The only thing I was feeling passionate about was leaving the music building and never returning.

"But I think you need to look at the bigger picture."

I couldn't wait to hear this.

"Imagine you're on a cloud. And that cloud is like a cloud, but it's also like an instrument. Like those instruments that you're holding. And you're all like, *Yeah, this is awesome. I'm on my own music cloud.* But sometimes, those clouds are going to come together and form new, bigger clouds. And you can't be all, *Hey, bro, get off my cloud.* You need to *share* the cloud. You get what I'm saying?"

Fuck no.

"Wow, you're so deep, Ted," Jagger said dreamily.

"Yeah, man. I get it. We're all on this one cloud together." Brae was nodding avidly like he'd just been told he'd see Jesus if he just drank the Kool-Aid.

Three pairs of eyes turned to me expectantly.

"Yeah, one band, one cloud. Got it."

Kill me.

"Right on," Ted said, nodding like a hippie high on peyote. "What type of music are you playing?"

And that was how I ended up being taught to play the score to *Halloween* on a mini keyboard with bamboo stalks as accompaniment by a well-intentioned imbecile.

VERONICA

I loved learning about the law. Always had. What I didn't necessarily love were law students. To say my fellow first-year classmates were competitive was an understatement. Some of them were downright cutthroat.

When word had gotten out—because I hadn't thought admitting it would be a big deal—that I'd interned at a prestigious law firm in town last summer, people instantly began looking at me differently. Like I somehow cheated my way to having an edge over them or something. And the fact that I had a job in a law firm currently, even though it was only doing basic office work that had nothing to do with the law, they still felt like that was me trying too hard.

It didn't make any sense, and it made interactions that had been previously smooth now stilted and awkward. Especially with my study group, though I believed that was down to a single girl with a flair for the dramatic.

Bethany.

Bethany constantly looked like she smelled something bad. She sucked up to professors and tossed catty glares at any student who got their attention. It appeared like everything was a personal affront to her.

Someone else was called on to answer a question? That person was trying to show her up.

Someone challenged her on her interpretation of a statute? They must be jealous of her superior intellect.

Someone got a higher grade than her? They must've cheated.

Someone worked their ass off to earn an internship, and then used those contacts to secure a mundane job that didn't even require a college degree? Well, that person must've slept with every boss she'd ever had to get those kinds of opportunities.

But once she'd put it in people's heads that I didn't play by the rules, the rest took it to heart because it was easier to believe something negative about me than it was to face their own shortcomings.

Well, screw Bethany and screw all the rest of them too. Who needed friends at school? Not me, thank you very much.

I had all I needed at home.

"What's your problem?"

I turned around to glare at Nattie. "Nothing." Maybe I'd been slamming drawers and cupboards a little too hard. I lived here—I could do whatever I wanted.

She gave me a disbelieving look. "If you say so."

"I do."

Nattie grabbed a bottle of water from the fridge and then eyed me as she took a gulp. "What happened? The other law students not playing nice with you or something?"

Seriously, how did she even guess that?

I rolled my eyes and kept slamming cabinets as I looked for something unhealthy to snack on. Finally finding a bag of Oreos hiding behind granola bars, I took them out and dug in.

"Wait," Nattie said. "Is that really happening? Because I will cut a bitch if I need to, lawyer or not."

I couldn't help the laugh that bubbled out of me. She'd started off mocking me and now was offering to commit an assault on my behalf. Stepping closer and without bothering to put down my cookies, I pulled Nattie into a hug.

She patted my back awkwardly. "Um, why is this happening?"

"I just appreciate you having my back."

We broke apart, and she ran a hand down her clothes as if to smooth any wrinkles I might have caused.

"Oh. Well, yeah, of course. Anytime." She looked at me curiously for a second. "Do you wanna talk about it?"

"Nah," I replied, even though I did. Just not to her.

While I had no doubts Nattie had my back, I needed someone with a larger emotional range. I needed Owen. But he wouldn't be home from work for another hour.

I wondered how many cookies I'd be able to down by then.

The answer was all of them, and if I was supposed to feel shame for it, I'd have to disappoint.

When Owen walked in, he found me in a ratty tank top and shorts, clutching an empty package of Oreos and watching *Judge Judy.*

"Hey," he said haltingly. "How was your day?"

"Shitty."

He dropped his bag and sat beside me. "What happened?"

I sighed. "It's basically the law-school equivalent of no one playing with me at recess because they all thought I sucked up to the principal. Or something like that. I didn't workshop that metaphor enough."

"Do you maybe want to start from the beginning?" he asked.

I let the Oreo package fall to the floor so I could shift and cuddle into Owen.

"Not really." And I then unloaded the whole story on him like he was my personal Dr. Phil. "It's not even a big deal," I said when I finished talking about Bethany. "I probably won't even care tomorrow. It's just making me sad today."

"You're entitled to feel how you feel for as long as you feel it."

"I know, but it's such a waste of energy."

He pulled me even tighter to him. "How can I help?"

I shifted so I could turn my face toward him. "You can make me forget."

And he did. After leading me upstairs and undressing me with a level of reverence I wasn't sure what I'd done to deserve, he slowly took me apart until I was a bundle of nerves beneath him.

When I broke apart, climaxing with an intensity I had never felt before, Owen held me until I was fully put back together again.

Who needed friends when I had an Owen?

Chapter Sixteen

VERONICA

Aamee and Brody decided to move their joint bachelor/bachelorette party up a couple of weeks so that we could all attend without the haunted house getting in the way. It was more thoughtful than I would've expected Aamee to be, but it was also one time I wished she would've been less accommodating.

I *really* didn't feel like going. Which probably made me a bad person, but it was what it was.

We had so much going on, and life was so crazy, I wanted all my downtime to be exactly that. Not to mention the fact that we didn't have the best track record at parties. Though I guessed Xander's had gone well, so maybe the tide was turning.

One thing was for sure—no one was getting married on my watch.

I was at least partially relieved that they were having a joint party. Supposedly, Aamee didn't trust Brody not to get arrested or abducted or whatever else. The possibilities truly were endless.

Sophia suspected that Aamee's real reason was that she didn't want to have to split up the group. We were all friends and should therefore stay together. But that was too sentimental for Aamee to admit out loud, so Brody's idiocy was a safe excuse.

They'd also only invited the core group of friends to keep things manageable. Sophia and Drew were there of course, as well as Taylor and Ransom, Carter and Toby, Xander, Aniyah, and Owen and I rounded out the group. It had been nice for Aniyah to come down, especially because it meant Xander didn't feel like an eleventh wheel.

Because money was a concern in light of recent events, they'd decided to skip having everyone meet for dinner, so we'd all meet up later in the evening for drinks. I felt bad that they were changing their plans to accommodate us, but I also appreciated it. Which was why I plastered a smile on my face and behaved as if I was thrilled to be there.

They'd chosen a burlesque bar that had both cis women and drag performers. The place was crowded, but Aamee and Brody had reserved a giant booth along one side of the large, open room. The section of booths was raised slightly, so we still had a good view of the stage, which dominated the entire front of the venue.

Lights flashed as a dancer worked with silks in a way that should have been rendered impossible by the laws of physics.

Since we were slightly off to the side, it wasn't quite as loud, so we wouldn't have to shout all night. A server dressed like a 1920s flapper kept the drinks and appetizers coming, and I began to relax into the evening. If I had to be out of my bed, this was as good a place to be as any.

Carter, who was sitting to one side of me, was staring intently at the stage.

Toby leaned into him. "What's wrong?"

Carter startled. "Oh, uh, nothing."

Toby gave him an incredulous look.

Carter looked unsure for a second before saying, "I've never seen drag queens before."

"Okay," Toby said, a question in his tone.

"It just occurred to me that I've never done a lot of things other gay guys might have done."

Toby held up a hand. "Okay, there's a lot to unpack there. First of all, you're not a gay man. You're a bisexual man who's on his own unique journey. There's no scorecard someone's keeping that you have to complete before you can date men."

Carter didn't reply immediately, but his eyes strayed to a table closer to the stage.

I followed his gaze, as did Toby. I almost felt bad for it, since this conversation had nothing to do with me, but I couldn't help it. Curiosity was always going to get the better of me.

Carter was looking at two men who were holding hands and watching the show with rapt attention.

"I don't feel like we look like them," he said.

Toby's brow furrowed. "How do we look?"

Carter shrugged. "Most people probably just think we're buddies. Am I . . . am I doing things wrong?"

Toby melted a little, but Carter continued before he could say anything.

"Because if you wanna do all that relationshippy stuff, like holding hands, I can do that. I never really did it with girls either, so it's not just because you're a guy. But I never told you that, so maybe you thought it was?"

Carter didn't give Toby time to answer. It was as if a

floodgate had opened, and everything had to come out before he could close it again.

"I don't mind being more... affectionate. In public. If you want to, that is. But you're going to have to tell me if I'm not doing things right, because I won't know otherwise. And I *want* to know because I don't want you to get tired of me or anything. So, yeah, I don't know how to stop talking because I feel like I'm not saying things right, but I love you and I wanna keep you, so just... tell me what to do to make that happen."

Toby smiled and reached out to cup Carter's jaw. "You are the best thing that ever happened to me."

"Oh. That's... good. You too. For me. You're the best."

They stared at each other sappily for a second, and I forced myself to stop intruding on their moment and looked away.

"Did you guys hear the good news?" Brody asked the table, loud enough for us all to hear. When none of us responded, he added, "Aamee said I could make the cake. The *only* cake. Gonna bake the shit outta that thing."

"I really hope he's not being literal," Owen whispered to me.

"Well, I hope he doesn't leave it in there," I countered.

Owen snorted. "True."

We ate, drank, talked, and laughed. By an hour into the evening, I was glad I'd gone. There was something stress-relieving about being with people who accepted and liked me for who I was.

"Ladies and gentlemen, whores and perverts, can I have your attention, please?"

All of our attention shot to the stage where a drag queen, wearing a long blue sparkly gown and a blond wig, stood in heels that would've made a lesser person cry out in pain.

"My name is Ivanna Bangbang, and I want to welcome you to Tailfeathers Cabaret. Are you all having a good time?"

The crowd clapped and hollered their assent, but Ivanna wasn't satisfied.

"That was more pathetic than my third husband. I said, are you having a good time?"

Our response was more raucous that time, and she seemed pleased.

"That's more like it. Now, I was asked to come out here and welcome some very special guests. It seems we have a couple here on their joint bachelor and bachelorette party tonight. Can you imagine?" She put her hand next to her mouth as if she was imparting a secret. "Sounds pretty fucking lame to me, but who am I to judge?"

Everyone laughed, including Brody, who leaned toward Aamee and yelled, "Can you believe another couple is here for their bachelor party?"

She turned her head toward him so slowly, I almost expected to hear her neck creak with the movement.

"She's talking about us."

He somehow looked even more gleeful. "Really? Awesome."

Aamee shook her head slightly before we all turned our attention back to the stage.

"Anyway, we're nothing if not hospitable at Tailfeathers, so we want to invite the happy couple up and congratulate them personally. Where are you, Aamee and Brody?" Ivanna held her hand up over her eyes and scanned the crowd.

Aamee slumped in her seat as Brody began waving.

When Ivanna's gaze settled on them, she smirked a

predatory smile. “Get up here, you two,” she yelled, waving them toward the stage.

“Hell, yeah, we’re gonna be famous,” Brody said as he attempted to slide out of the booth.

But Aamee hadn’t budged. “I’m not going up there. I specifically told them I didn’t want any special attention.”

“Well, that pretty much sealed your fate,” Aniyah quipped.

Drew and Sophia, who were sitting on one end of the booth, blocking Aamee and Brody’s exit, stood.

“Come on, Aam,” Brody said, trying to gently push her out of the booth.

“No.”

“But you love attention,” Brody practically whined. “This should be right up your alley.”

She glared at him. “I do *not* love attention. I love minding my own business.”

Taylor snorted, but when Aamee turned a steely gaze on her, Taylor refused to wilt.

“You have literally *never* minded your own business. And now this is fate paying you back. So quit being such a little diva and get up there.” Taylor smiled. “Unless you’re too scared.”

Aamee scoffed. “What would I be scared of?”

Taylor shrugged. “You tell me. You’re the one white-knuckling the table.”

Aamee looked down at her hands, which were, in fact, white-knuckling the table, and quickly moved them into her lap. “I’m not scared.”

“Prove it.”

Ivanna called Aamee and Brody again and then threatened that someone named Boris would come get them if they didn't get a move on.

Taylor quirked an eyebrow at Aamee as if daring her to get up.

It worked. Aamee got up with a huff and smoothed down her white, strapless summer dress.

"You owe me for this," she said to Brody.

He nodded eagerly, as if he'd give her anything as long as it meant he got to get up on the stage. Brody took her hand in his and led her to the front.

And we all sat back and readied ourselves for the carnage.

OWEN

Watching Brody and Aamee play a variation of *The Dating Game* was not what I'd envisioned when they'd been invited to go onstage. Ivanna had immediately latched on to Brody, rubbing her hands all over his chest as a tech took Aamee behind a free-standing curtain they'd brought out. She was soon joined by two drag queens.

While backstage workers got them settled in chairs and mic'd up, Ivanna interviewed Brody about his gym regime and if he was open to adding a third to their relationship. She also asked him more mundane things like how long he and Aamee had been together and what they did for a living.

Brody grinned through the whole ordeal, playing into Ivanna's flirty banter, which only made Aamee's face grow darker and darker until she looked like a thin, blond storm cloud.

"Okay, Brody, let me tell you what we're going to do. Aamee is on the other side of that curtain with a couple of my friends, Kitty Beaverhausen and Ophelia Butte."

Each woman waved when she was announced.

"We're going to ask a question, and then each girl is going to respond, and you're going to guess which one is Aamee. But if you think you'll be able to tell from the voice, think again. Each of their mics have synthesizers on them, so you'll have to really listen for their responses. Got it?"

"Yup."

"How confident are you that you'll choose correctly?"

"Pretty confident."

"Then let's get started," Ivanna said. "We'll start with something simple. Aamee, tell us your favorite color?"

There was a tech onstage who pointed at Kitty Beaverhausen in the first chair. I assumed he was going to direct them to answer each question in a different order so Brody couldn't anticipate which would be Aamee.

Kitty spoke into the mic and said, "Blue, like the oceans where I hope we'll one day get to vacation together."

Brody's face screwed up in what almost appeared to be disgust.

"Not a response Aamee would give?" Ivanna asked him.

"Definitely not."

The tech pointed to Ophelia Butte, who looked a bit sassier than Kitty.

She said, "Red, like the blood of the people who made me come up here."

Brody tilted his head as if considering the answer, and Aamee's head snapped toward the drag queen. Her face held what appeared to be respect.

"And Aamee Number Three?" Ivanna said.

"Purple, like the invitations for our wedding," real Aamee

said. She looked smug, as if she'd given Brody a major clue, but he looked alarmed.

Ivanna grinned. "Do you know what color your invitations are, Brody?"

"Uh, well . . . purple?"

Ivanna hummed. "Maybe. Or maybe one of my girls took a chance that you wouldn't know what color they were and just guessed anything."

Brody looked terrified. He was clearly racking his brain to see if he could remember what the invitations looked like.

Then, all of the sudden, he brightened. "They're purple."

"Are you sure?"

"Yeah, because Aamee said I could make our wedding cake as long as I incorporated purple."

Ivanna looked stunned. "*You're* making the wedding cake?"

Brody nodded happily.

Ivanna took a few steps forward and looked around the curtain. "Girl, we're gonna have to talk," she said to Aamee, who was smirking victoriously.

The game continued, and to our shock and the audience's obvious disappointment, Brody got all of them correct.

"Okay, last question," Ivanna said. "Aamee, what would Brody say is your worst trait?"

The tech pointed at Ophelia to go first. "I can be a little . . . judgy from time to time."

That was a really good answer, and I could tell Brody was considering it. I wasn't sure how Ophelia had read Aamee so well, but almost all her answers had been things Aamee would say. It had only been some kind of miracle that had kept Brody from picking her during any of the previous rounds.

If I were honest, it was surprising how well Brody clearly knew Aamee. It's not that I doubted they loved each other, but I had maybe doubted how well they knew each other.

Aamee was a hard nut to crack, and even after knowing her for over a year, what I knew about her could fit on a Post-it. I wasn't marrying her, but still. I couldn't help but be surprised how well Brody was doing. He'd never struck me as someone who paid a lot of attention.

Kitty went next, and while she'd mostly kept giving sweeter answers that weren't even remotely things Aamee would ever say, she looked determined for this one.

"I'm a control freak. I need things done my way, or I lose my shit."

Damn, another good answer. These women came to play.

Brody was starting to look a little worried.

The tech pointed at Aamee, who crossed her arms over her chest and leaned back in the chair.

"Nothing."

Ivanna startled. "I'm sorry, did you say 'nothing'?"

"Yeah, nothing."

Ivanna laughed. "I guess this Aamee thinks she's perfect."

But Aamee didn't laugh. "I didn't say I didn't have bad traits. Everyone who's ever met me knows I do. But Brody... he doesn't see those things. To him, I'm just Aamee. I've never had anyone accept me as completely as he does."

I whipped my face toward Brody, who was smiling widely.

He looked over at Ivanna. "That's my girl."

"You two are so sweet it's sickening. Come on over, Aamee, and hug your man."

When Aamee came around the curtain, Ivanna smiled at her. "You got a good one, honey."

This time, Aamee smiled too. “I know.”

Vee rested her head on my shoulder as we watched Brody dip Aamee and kiss her deeply. Even from a distance, I could tell Aamee was smiling.

Chapter Seventeen

OWEN

Once the game was over, Aamee and Brody were given a gift certificate to come back to Tailfeathers. But they weren't just handed it, as one might expect. They were told to sit in two chairs and gyrated on until the longest version of Jagged Edge's "Let's Get Married" ended. The place erupted in applause when it was all over and Aamee and Brody returned to the booth.

We received a round of complimentary drinks and a tray of assorted desserts for their participation—not that they'd been given much choice. Still, we enjoyed them.

I was laughing at a ridiculous story Drew was telling about a time Carter kissed him when I felt Vee shift beside me.

She'd pulled out her phone and was looking at the screen.

"Everything okay?" I asked.

"I don't know. Hello?"

I watched as her brow furrowed as whoever was on the other end of the line spoke.

"Okay, okay, we're on our way," she said before hanging

up. "We gotta go," she said, pushing at me to get me to move.

Ransom and Taylor slid out so we could exit the booth.

"What's going on?" Taylor asked.

I turned to see everyone at the table studying us, their faces etched with concern.

"I just got a call from Inez," Vee said, her voice bordering on frantic. "She said Nattie's in a lot of pain, but she won't go to the hospital."

"Pain from what?" Sophia asked.

"I don't know. I'm sorry," she said to Aamee and Brody, "but we have to go."

"Of course," Aamee said.

"Do you need us to come with you?" Brody offered.

"No, please, enjoy the rest of your night. We'll text you when we know what's going on."

They all looked unsure about not coming with us, but Vee didn't give them time to reconsider. She took off toward the exit. I almost had to sprint to catch up. After practically running to the car, I got us home as quickly as I could.

Vee burst into the house and yelled for Nattie.

"Upstairs," Inez called back.

We raced to Natalia's room and saw her in the fetal position on her bed, groaning.

"What happened?" Vee asked as she knelt by Natalia's bed and pushed her hair back off her face.

"I don't really know," Inez answered when it didn't appear Nattie was going to. "I was in the kitchen when she came home. She said she wasn't feeling well and was going to go to bed. I came up about an hour later to see if she wanted some soup or anything and found her like this."

Concern and fear radiated off Vee, but she kept her voice

steady when she spoke. “Nattie, what happened?”

“I don’t know. I had, like, a cramp all day. I just tried to ignore it. But then a few of us went out after work, and I started to feel sick to my stomach, so I came home.” Natalia groaned again, and Vee looked terrified.

“We need to go to the hospital,” I said.

“No, it’s probably just something I ate. I’m sure I’ll be fine,” Natalia argued weakly.

Vee looked up at me, clearly unsure of what to do.

“We have to go,” I said firmly. “There could be something really wrong.”

“Okay,” Vee said. “Nattie, we’re going. Can you get up?”

“Yeah, I—” She tried to push herself up, but her arms gave out as she clutched her stomach again.

“Move back,” I told Vee, who instantly did as I asked. I stepped forward and scooped Natalia into my arms and began carrying her from the room.

“Maybe we should call an ambulance?” Vee said as she followed after me.

“The hospital is ten minutes away. I can get her there quicker than if we had to wait for an ambulance to come.”

Once outside, Vee hurried ahead to open the door to my truck. I placed Natalia in the back and Vee climbed in next to her. I ran around to the driver side and started the car, yelling to Inez that we’d text her when we knew something.

Then I drove like a bat out of hell to the hospital, skidding to a stop outside the emergency room and carrying Natalia inside.

They thankfully took her right back, asking me to lower her into a wheelchair. Vee went back with her while I went out to move my car. By the time I got back inside, Vee was waiting for me.

"What happened?" I asked, putting my hands on her arms and drawing her to me.

Tears streamed down Vee's face. "They rushed her to imaging. The nurse said depending on what they found, they might take her straight to surgery, so I should wait out here until someone comes to update me."

"Jesus," I breathed.

She sniffled and then buried her face in my chest. "I need to call my aunt," she said, though her voice was muffled.

"Okay, let's find a seat, and then we'll call her." I led Vee to some open chairs in the corner.

She called her aunt and relayed everything she knew. I could hear her aunt's panicked voice through the phone. After a minute, Vee hung up.

"They're on their way," she told me.

I shot some texts off to Inez and the group chat with everyone else to let them know what was going on. They all offered to come keep us company, but I told them there was no reason for us all to camp out in the waiting room. I did appreciate their offers, though.

After a while, a nurse came out and looked around. "Family of Natalia Vargas?"

Vee's head shot up. "Here," she called.

The nurse approached and took a seat beside Vee. "What's your relationship with Miss Vargas?"

"We're cousins."

The woman nodded and made a note on the tablet in her hand. "Does she have any other family in the area?"

"No, but they're on their way from New York. Hopefully, they'll be here in two hours or so."

The nurse made another note.

"Is she okay?" Vee asked, and I hated how small her voice sounded.

The nurse looked up. "Tests came back indicating acute appendicitis. The doctors took her up to surgery."

"Oh my God," Vee said, beginning to cry again. "Is she going to be okay?"

The nurse offered a small smile. "From the ultrasound, it looks like you got her here before it ruptured. The doctor will be able to give you more details once he's removed it. For now, you can both go up to the third floor and wait in the surgical waiting room. A receptionist there will explain how you'll get updates and such."

Vee and I stood, and the nurse directed us to the elevators. Once we were on our way up, Vee huddled close to me.

"I can't believe this is happening," she said.

I pressed a kiss to her head. "I'm sure she'll be fine."

She hugged me tighter. "Thank you for being here with me."

"There's nowhere else I'd ever be." I hoped she knew how true that was.

VERONICA

A little over an hour later, our name was called, and we were told to go to a bank of phones and pick up the first receiver.

The doctor informed me that all had gone well. They'd been able to remove Nattie's appendix laparoscopically, which would cut down her healing time. Once she woke up and was moved to a room, someone would let us know where we could go to visit her.

My aunt, uncle, and Adrien were all there before that information came. The nurse said only two people could see her because visiting hours were over, and obviously Owen and I would not be those two people, which upset me more than I let on. I wanted to set eyes on Nattie, see for myself that she was okay.

But that would have to wait until the next day. My aunt and uncle hadn't made any arrangements for where they were going to sleep, but they said they'd figure it out. We offered to let them to stay at our place, but my aunt wasn't too keen on leaving the hospital anytime soon. Adrien also elected to stay behind. He looked more rattled than I'd ever seen him, and he said he was happy to hang out in the waiting room.

Even though it felt wrong to leave, my aunt insisted we get some rest. Owen led me out of the hospital and into his truck. It was late, probably close to two in the morning, but I felt wired.

Inez was asleep on the couch when we got home, and Roddie was sitting in a nearby chair watching TV. When he noticed us, he grabbed the remote and turned the TV off before giving Inez a gentle shake.

"How is she?" Inez asked groggily.

"The doctor said she'd be okay," I answered. "Her parents showed up, so we didn't get to see her."

"Well, I'm glad she's okay."

"Me too," Roddie added.

I went over and sat beside Inez. "Thank you for checking on her tonight. I don't even want to think about what might've happened if you hadn't."

Inez smiled. "Of course. I'm just happy I was here."

We talked for another couple of minutes before we all

headed to bed. Even though my mind was still reeling, my body was exhausted. I quickly undressed before collapsing into bed, allowing Owen to pull me close.

"Tired?" he asked.

I hummed. "Yes and no."

"Try to get some sleep, and we can head back to the hospital when we wake up."

I scooted back a little so I could look up at him. "Why are you so wonderful?"

He smiled. "It's easy to be wonderful to you."

Returning his smile, I said, "Think Ivanna would say we're sickeningly sweet too?"

He rested his head against mine and said, "Definitely."

His embrace was so warm and safe that I slept more solidly than I'd expected. When my phone went off the next morning, I was jerked out of a deep sleep. I reached for my phone and saw my Aunt Ana's name.

"Hello?"

"I would've preferred you let me die than call my mother, Vee."

I bolted upright at Nattie's voice.

"Hey. How are you feeling?"

"Well, let's see, I had a hole dug into my stomach, and then I woke up to my mom standing above me, holding a rosary, and performing what sounded a lot like the last rites."

"How do you know what last rites sound like?"

"You're missing the point. How could you do this?"

"Do what? Tell your parents that their only daughter was having emergency surgery? God, I'm such a monster."

"At least you admit it."

"I'm assuming you're feeling fine if you can be such a pain in the ass."

"Pain meds are the glue holding my fragile life together. So what time are you coming to pick me up?"

"Pick you up?"

Owen shifted behind me, and I turned to give him a look that I hoped conveyed I was on the phone with a crazy person.

"Yeah, you gotta come get me," Nattie said, her voice a whisper.

"They're releasing you already?"

She'd just had surgery hours ago. What kind of operation were they running over there?

Ha. Operation.

"I don't know when they're letting me leave, but Mom is making plans to move me back in with her. There is no way in hell I'm staying with her."

"She loves you and wants to take care of you. There are worse things."

Nattie groaned. "Please don't get sentimental on me. I know with your mom not here anymore, all of this smothering seems sweet, but it isn't. At all. Not to mention, the last thing I want to do is sit in the car for two hours while my parents bicker over whose genetics contributed to my bad appendix while Adrien grills me about organ removal."

I scrunched my face up. "Why would he ask about organ removal?"

"Because my appendix probably gave him ideas about black market organ donations. I don't know, Vee. It was supposed to be a joke." She was getting exasperated with me, which she had a hell of a lot of nerve to do after all she'd put me through. "You have to come save me."

"I already did that once in the last twenty-four hours."

"Shut up," she whined. "I'm serious."

"How am I supposed to save you?"

"Insist that you can take care of me," Nattie pleaded.

"But I *can't* take care of you. We all have classes and work. None of us can be around twenty-four seven to look after you."

Nattie sniffed. "I'd call out sick of my job if you needed me to take care of you."

"Yeah, I'm sure there'd be a lot of arm twisting to get you to not work," I replied drolly.

She gasped in afront. "I haven't missed a single day since I started."

I rolled my eyes. "I'm not sure what I can do, Nattie."

"Just try. Please. Just come and talk to my mom. She trusts you. If you say you'll look after me, she'll believe it."

"But I just told you that I can't look after you. At least not all the time."

"What she doesn't know won't kill her."

"No, but it might kill you! What if something happens and no one's here?"

"What's going to happen? My appendix is going to rupture? It's already gone."

I opened my mouth to argue because the safest place for her *was* with my aunt and uncle. I'd do what I could to help her, but with classes and the haunted house teaser coming up, I couldn't spend every moment of my day with her. And honestly, after seeing doctors and nurses rush around her in a panic in the ER, I was terrified something was going to happen to her. But before I could say any of that, she continued.

"Just . . . come. Please. I understand if it's not going to work out, but let's at least talk about it. I hate having everyone else making decisions for me. I may not be the most functional adult in the world, but I'm not a child either."

I sighed. When had I become such a pushover? “Okay, Nattie. We’ll be there as soon as we can.”

She squealed in delight, and I tried to figure out how it was that she always got what she wanted. It was truly a gift.

Chapter Eighteen

VERONICA

As expected, Aunt Ana put up quite a fight, and I couldn't argue with most of her points. She could dedicate her time to being there for Nattie and making sure she healed the way she needed. I couldn't make those promises.

But then Adrien spoke up that he could stay and help Nattie until she was feeling better, and the tide turned. With Nattie refusing to go back to New York, a caretaker in place—though what kind of caretaker Adrien would turn out to be remained to be seen—and the fact that making Nattie sit in a car for two hours wasn't ideal, my aunt and uncle had to admit defeat.

And when Adrien pulled out a box of the T-shirts he'd arranged to have fall off the back of a truck for Owen's haunted house, they hadn't asked any questions. I think they were well aware of the benefits of plausible deniability when it came to Adrien.

After another day in the hospital, my aunt and uncle brought Nattie home, helped her settle in, and then hit the road. We invited them to stay, but they could obviously tell space was limited—I think I overheard Aunt Ana referring to our place as a halfway house—and Nattie wasn't exactly a star patient.

Secretly, Aunt Ana was probably glad to not have to care for her after a day of doing so. Nattie was a nightmare. She fluctuated from saying she was fine and didn't need help to whimpering like a puppy and requesting all kinds of things. She'd even asked if those hot water *things* people put on injuries in old movies were still a thing.

It turned out they were, and she ordered one online.

But Adrien, to his credit, never lost patience with her. He ignored her from time to time, and we had to listen to her yelling for him from her bedroom, but he always made sure she had what she needed and didn't seem at all bothered by Nattie being Nattie.

Guess he was used to it.

The rest of us were insanely busy. We had classes and work, and we had to finish preparing for the opening of our haunted house the coming weekend.

We were doing what Xander called a soft open—only running the haunted house Saturday night for two hours. Cody put up a link where people could preorder their tickets and that he'd marketed it like people were missing out if they didn't come to the opening.

It wasn't true because there was absolutely nothing special happening, but he argued that people didn't know that. Some people simply liked being first, and that would be enough of a draw.

I hoped he was right. But when Thursday rolled around, he texted that we'd sold out of tickets, which floored both Owen and me. Granted, we hadn't offered that many, not wanting to be overwhelmed our first time out, but still. The fact that *anyone* wanted to come was crazy enough.

I hoped that the soft open wouldn't have the opposite effect of causing people to spread the word that it wasn't worth the money, but at least we'd have time to tweak anything that didn't go over well before the real opening night.

On Friday night, Roddie made sure the yard was clean of anything dog related, Drew and Brody came over to set up their makeshift bar as well as some promotional stuff they were going to give away, and Xander rigged up some more devices that would make noise, cause furniture to shake, or create mist. Everyone else who was available helped us decorate.

We put caution tape to keep people out of the occupied bedrooms, and at Cody's suggestion, we roped off the "haunted" room but left the door open. He said allowing people to see it but not go in might entice them to come back and try their luck at lasting thirty minutes inside.

We put a freestanding mirror that Minnie had in the attic in there with a sheet over it, and Xander recorded Gimli's nails clacking and scraping against the hardwood and set up a speaker to play it in that room, so it sounded like an animal was scurrying around in there.

I thought Xander missed his calling and should look into getting a job making horror movies.

It was a little stressful for me that people would be wandering all over our house, but I was trying not to show it. Ideally, we'd keep people out of the second floor, but that was where the "presence" was that Wynter had claimed to witness. Cody had even somehow tracked her down and interviewed her about her experience in the room so he could post it to Instagram. He said it had gotten a lot of traction, and when I looked, it did have a ton of likes and comments.

But looking at all that made both Owen and I almost sprout hives because it added pressure to make the house fun for people. We decided to let Cody do his thing and stay off social media in order to retain our sanity.

When Saturday finally rolled around, I was so nervous, I was shaking. What the hell were we thinking? We couldn't pull this off. We had no experience running anything.

I was in our bedroom, approaching a full-on meltdown, when Owen appeared.

"Hey, what's wrong?" he asked gently, guiding me away from the closet where I'd been spiraling and leading me to sit on the bed.

"What if we can't do this? What if no one shows up and we don't raise any money? What if *I* screw up somehow and ruin the whole thing? What if—"

"Stop," he said firmly but not unkindly. "None of this comes down to you. You and everyone else are helping me, but in the end, we can only do our best. Maybe it'll be enough and maybe it won't. But that's all beyond our control now. What's important is that we tried."

"I just... You don't deserve what's happening."

He smiled. "None of us do. This is your home too, Vee. I don't want any of us to lose it. But if we do"—he shrugged—"then we'll deal with that the way we've dealt with everything else."

"Like lunatics?"

Laughing, he said, "No. Together."

"Oh. Yeah, that's a better answer."

"We're going to be okay, Vee. Whatever happens, we'll always be okay."

I took a deep breath and nodded. "You're right."

He smiled a roguish grin. "Say that again."

I pushed him lightly. "Shut up."

He stood up from where he'd been crouching in front of me and extended his hand. "You ready to scare the shit out of some people?"

Putting my hand in his, I let him pull me to him. "Yup. Let's do this."

OWEN

As it turned out, scaring people was a lot of fun.

Xander had set up scary music to play throughout the house using speakers he had—not sure why he had a bunch of speakers, but I wasn't going to look a gift horse in the mouth—and I was thankful because our band was definitely not stage-ready. I didn't think we'd ever really be.

I'd convinced Brae and Jagger that it'd be better to have us play Halloween weekend. That gave us a little more time to practice. They initially weren't happy with having to wait, but I told them we could advertise us as the headlining act that would draw the big crowds for the final weekend, and they were appeased.

We were actually more likely to keep people away than draw them in, but that was something I'd have to worry about when it got closer. For now, we still had a month until Halloween.

I did a final walk-through before we opened the doors,

and I couldn't believe how much we'd accomplished. The place was honestly terrifying, and if I hadn't been part of the setup, I probably would've been scared to walk through it.

Cobwebs were strewn about, but not the cheap-looking white ones. I didn't know who'd found these, but they looked like they'd been spun by the spiders in *Arachnophobia*. A lot of our friends had clearly grown up in families that loved Halloween, because we had skeletons littered around, a creepy head in a crystal ball that spoke as people walked past it, some kind of witch that moved and had a cauldron that steam floated up from. There were also sliced-off appendages all over the place, spiders that jumped out when people walked past, strobe lights, creepy music, and all kinds of other things that startled the shit out of me when I passed it even though I knew it was there.

Xander had somehow made a lot of our furniture move. Some were attached to devices that caused them to slide across the floor, and others shook or vibrated. I had no idea how he did it, and I hoped he planned to be at all the nights we were open because I had no idea how to fix anything if it broke.

Add all this to the fact that some of us were going to be hiding around the house and jumping out at people, and I felt like we had the makings of an epic Halloween attraction.

All of our friends had come out to help with our dry run. Taylor and Sophia were taking care of tickets. Vee, Carter, Roddie, Toby, and Ransom were hiding in various places to scare people. Cody was taking pictures. Inez and Aamee were acting as guides throughout the house, answering questions and directing people on where to go. Xander was making sure everything stayed running. And Brody and Drew dealt with the cocktails they'd created.

Natalia and Adrien hung out in her room. She wanted to come down and help, but she was still recovering and shouldn't be moving around too much. Adrien was making sure no one accidentally went into her room. Gimli hung out with them so we didn't have to worry about something happening to him.

And I was running around filling in wherever I was needed. Though mostly I felt as if I was just running in circles. I did try to talk to almost everyone once they went through the house and entered the backyard so I could encourage them to come back and try the Haunted Room Challenge that would open next weekend.

Overall, people were impressed with the house, and many said they'd come back to try spending thirty minutes alone in the room. We talked about lowering the time to fifteen minutes to accommodate more people, but Drew had argued that people were more likely to get bored before the thirty minutes were up and leave without us having to give them a T-shirt. I didn't think people not winning because they were bored was the right way to go about it.

Carter suggested doing a more random number like twenty-three, which he said was a weird number, though he had no explanation as to why. Cody jumped at that, saying we could tell people the presence made itself known slowly but was in full poltergeist mode by minute twenty-two. That way, he explained, people were more likely to psych themselves out.

He said he'd come by the next week and film a kind of *Blair Witch* video in the room to drum up interest. He seemed excited about it, and there was no way I was going to turn down anything that could get more people to come out.

The night was going smoothly. To say I was shocked we

were pulling it off was an understatement. The quiet night was filled with sudden screams followed by bursts of laughter—a good indicator of a solid haunted house.

I was checking in to see if Drew and Brody needed anything as they mixed cocktails for a group that had just exited the house when I heard screaming again. I chuckled at someone else getting spooked by one of my friends, but then I heard a loud crash and the sound of feet thundering on the hardwood.

People were running, and the screams continued.

What the hell?

I rushed into the house through the back door and almost ran into a couple wide-eyed teenage girls.

"You okay?"

"How do we get out of here?" one asked, her voice shrill.

I pointed behind me, and they tore ass through the door, knocking into me in their panic. Following them, I saw them all huddle together next to the bar where Drew and Brody looked at them in concern.

"What happened?" I asked the girls as I approached.

They were probably about thirteen or so and looked shaken.

"There's a ghost in there," one said, sounding close to tears. "I wanna go home. Is your mom on her way?" she asked one of the other girls.

"I don't know. She's not answering my texts."

"Oh my God, did she *abandon* us here?"

The drama level was reaching tantrum levels.

"It's okay," I placated.

I wasn't sure what else to say. I didn't want to tell them there were no ghosts in the house, because that was kind of our whole schtick. I also wasn't fully on board with the *Wynter is a quack* crowd. For all I knew, there really was a ghost inside.

"It's a haunted house," I said. "I'm sure you just got a little spooked."

"No, I never get scared at these things. But you have a real ghost!"

Cody came running over. "Would you be willing to say that again on camera?"

The girls all exchanged a look, and then quickly nodded and all began talking at once. Guess a little fear was no match for an Instagram appearance.

"Is this going to be on the official Insta page?" one of them asked.

"Sure is," Cody replied.

They looked thrilled at that and began recounting their adventure.

"We were upstairs, and we heard claws on the floor of the room that's roped off. But we just figured it was a sound system or something. But then we heard a door creak behind us."

"And we saw a shadow on the wall," another one interjected. "It moved down the hallway."

"That's when we started to get creeped out."

"But we weren't, like, *scared* scared. It was just weird."

My, how attitudes change.

Seconds ago, they were running terrified through my house. Then a camera came out and they're too cool for any of it.

"We decided to go back downstairs, but then we heard whimpering from one of the rooms. It sounded like a dog."

Gimli.

Another girl added, "And I'm an animal lover, so I couldn't

leave without checking to make sure everything was okay."

"So we opened the door and peeked inside and found a dog. He seemed okay, but we weren't sure what to do with him. Like, did you guys lock your poor dog in a room on purpose?"

There was a lot of judgment in that statement, and I figured it best not to answer. Good thing these girls didn't know about Roddie's doggie day care.

"But then we heard it."

"It?" Cody asked.

"A moan. We looked around the room, and that's when we saw her."

Oh God. I had a feeling I knew where this was going.

"A ghost was lying on the bed. She was facing the other way, but she started to turn and said, 'Adrien.' We slammed the door shut and got the hell out of there."

"Sorry for leaving your dog with a ghost. You may want to get a priest over here or something so you can get him back."

I gave them a half smile. "I'll do that."

Cody kept asking them questions as I excused myself and went into the house. I ran into Vee, who asked what happened.

"I think the girls went into Natalia's room and thought she was a ghost. I'm gonna go up and check on her."

The event was almost over for the night, but there were a few people still milling around. I hurried upstairs, Vee behind me, and knocked on Natalia's door.

It swung open, and Adrien stood there with Gimli at his feet.

"Hey, we were just checking that everything was okay. A couple of girls wandered in here by accident," I explained.

"Is that what all the screaming was? I stepped out to use the bathroom, and next thing I know, there's screaming in the hallway and people running."

"Yeah, I guess they heard Gimli and poked their heads in to make sure he was okay. Then they saw Natalia and thought she was a ghost."

Adrien looked at me for a second before dissolving into a fit of laughter. "Hear that, Nat? You look so good, people thought you were dead."

Natalia scowled at him. "*You* have an organ removed and see how you look."

"Oh, please. They took that thing out a week ago through a hole the size of a penny. You're fine."

"First of all, it's bigger than a penny. I think. And it was a major surgery. The doctor said it could take me weeks to feel normal again."

Adrien scoffed. "You were never normal before, so I wouldn't hold your breath for that one."

"You know what, dickhead? I'm going to tell—"

I pulled the door shut, muffling the rest of their argument.

"Wanna do a sweep and see if anyone's still here?" I asked Vee.

"Sure."

We descended the stairs, the sound of Adrien and Natalia echoing behind us. There was no one left in the house, but a few were still having drinks in the backyard.

We all gathered there too, Brody and Drew fixing each of us a drink.

"Pulled in about a hundred and twenty bucks tonight," Drew said. "Not bad for only two hours."

"You guys need to take at least half of that," I told them.

They'd originally offered to donate the drinks since it was a marketing opportunity for them, but they'd both made drinks all night. There was no way I could keep all that money.

Drew studied me for a second, and whatever he saw had him say, "We'll keep the money that was left as a tip. How about that?"

I eyed him skeptically. "That doesn't seem like enough for all the work you did."

He shrugged. "You had a good turnout, and it'll only get better. We were able to hand out a ton of info on the bar opening, so it's not like we're not getting anything out of this arrangement."

"If you're sure," I said.

He smiled. "Hundred percent."

The rest of the guests filtered out, leaving only us Scoobies. And as I looked around at them as they bragged about how great the house was, I was filled with hope.

Maybe, with all of us working together, we really would pull this off.

Chapter Nineteen

OWEN

The morning after the haunted house opened was slow moving. Vee and I had finally pulled ourselves out of bed when the growling of our stomachs couldn't be ignored anymore.

I had no idea why, but my body was sore. Vee said it was a combination of stress and moving and hanging things all day that had done it, and she was probably right. Either way, I felt like I'd been hit by a bus, and I didn't want to do much of anything besides eat, sleep, and hang out with Vee—preferably naked.

We went to the kitchen and scavenged around for whatever we could eat that didn't need to be cooked. As I poured cereal into bowls and Vee put a container of fruit on the table, the doorbell chimed.

Vee looked over at me. "Who could that be?"

I shrugged, handed her the cereal, and made my way to the door. When I swung it open, I had to bite back a groan.

"Mrs. Aberdeen. How are you?"

For Christ's sake, what does she want?

"I'd be better if my inconsiderate neighbors hadn't decided to throw a party all night long," she sniped.

"All night? Everyone was gone by ten thirty."

She huffed. "Maybe that's not late to a bunch of college kids, but this is a neighborhood of *families*. And some of those families have young children who go to bed early."

"No one complained."

"Not to you," she huffed. "They probably don't want to run the risk of having you and all the people you have living here retaliate."

"Retaliate? What have I ever done to give anyone the impression that I'd do something like that?"

She waggled a finger at me. "Don't act like you're innocent. I've seen what's been going on over here. Got all kinds of people coming and going, and I bet that one young man is running some kind of... dog business out of your house. Do you have a license for that kind of thing?"

No, we did not. Roddie had promised to keep it small so we could avoid the added hassle and cost. But we hadn't banked on a nosy neighbor exposing us.

A hand rubbed across my back, and I looked to see Vee sidle up beside me.

"What's going on?" she asked.

"Mrs. Aberdeen came over with a few... grievances."

"Oh, yeah?" Vee's voice held concern, but from the way her hand pressed into my back, I could tell the sentiment wasn't genuine. At least not in regard to our pain-in-the-ass neighbor.

The presence of Vee seemed to change Mrs. Aberdeen's demeanor slightly. I wasn't sure if it was because another woman was involved or if Vee just intimidated her for some reason, but Mrs. Aberdeen fiddled with the hem of her shirt and cleared her throat.

"Yes," she said, her voice firm even though her eyes darted around a bit. "I just don't think you all are suited for living in a neighborhood such as this one."

Vee cocked her head. "Why is that?"

"You're all just a little . . . wild for this area. The parties, the dogs, all the people living here. This isn't a frat house, you know? This is a quiet, suburban neighborhood where people are trying to live their lives in peace."

Vee seemed to think about Mrs. Aberdeen's words before replying. "So no one else in this neighborhood ever has parties? Because I seem to remember you having a pretty big event at your house for the Fourth of July."

Mrs. Aberdeen scoffed and brought a hand to her chest. "That was a special occasion. It's a celebration of this great nation's independence from tyranny."

"A special occasion that involved someone setting off fireworks if I remember correctly. Isn't that illegal?" Vee asked me.

"Pretty sure it is," I answered happily.

"Hmm. And I'm not sure how someone doing some friends a favor by watching their pets is an issue."

"It's an issue when he's being paid to do it," she spat.

"Have you seen money exchange hands?" Vee asked.

I tensed because Roddie *was* accepting money for this business. I knew Vee was attempting to point out that Mrs. Aberdeen didn't have any proof, but if she were so inclined, she could probably find it.

"No, but I know it's happening. You kids probably trade bite coins or whatever they're called. There's no way that boy watches all those dogs every day out of the goodness of his heart."

"How do you know? Have you ever even spoken to 'that boy'?"

"He looks like common riffraff. He wouldn't be able to pay whatever rent you're charging him if he wasn't babysitting those dogs. And if you tell me you're letting him live here for free, well, you're either stupid or liars."

Mrs. Aberdeen had gotten herself all worked up. Her face was nearly purple by the end of her tirade, and she looked shocked that half of what she'd said had actually come out of her mouth.

Vee moved past me, stepping just outside the door so she was closer to Mrs. Aberdeen. "Let me make something clear to you. You will never again come onto our property and hurl accusations and insults at us. If you do, we'll have you cited for trespassing. What we do on our property is our business. We're not hurting you or anyone else. So mind your business and stay on your side of the fence."

Mrs. Aberdeen looked apoplectic. Her mouth moved silently with words she wanted to say, but none left her mouth before Vee had stormed back inside and slammed the door in her face.

Vee stood there huffing for a second, and I eyed her cautiously.

"Do you think making an enemy of her was a good idea?" I finally asked, not to be annoying but because I genuinely wanted to know.

"She made herself an enemy. We just need to show her we won't back down."

"What if she reports us to the township or whoever? We

are doing things we could get in trouble for."

Vee looked up at me. "I don't know, Owen. I just... We can't let her intimidate us. Because if we do manage to pay off the bill and keep the house, we'll have to keep living next to her until she dies. And with the amount of evil in that woman, she'll probably live forever. We can't show her that we're easy for her to manipulate, because she'll never stop."

These were all good points, but they didn't do much to make me feel better. Because keeping the house was a big *if*, and Mrs. Aberdeen had shown she wasn't going to make that process any easier.

But no good would come out of harping on that. So I pulled Vee into a hug instead and said, "Thanks for sticking up for me."

She wrapped her arms around me in return. "Always."

VERONICA

There was a very real chance I was going to become a homicidal maniac by the time all this was over. And then Owen would have this big house all to himself because I'd be in prison for murdering first Mrs. Aberdeen and then Nattie. And maybe I'd do Bethany in to round it out at three.

But I was trying not to let Bethany get to me. Things had calmed down at school, people having found other things to focus on. She still shot me irritated looks in class and during study group, but I ignored her. Letting her get to me wasn't worth the jail time.

Mrs. Aberdeen, on the other hand, definitely was.

She'd been spending a lot more time outside her house, and I'd seen her snapping pictures with her phone. She tried to be covert about it, but her having to hold the phone two inches from her face and pecking at it like a chicken searching for corn was a dead giveaway.

Then there was Nattie, who should've been close to fully recovered from her surgery but acted as if she'd just been probed by aliens an hour ago. She also behaved as if she'd donated a kidney to someone on their deathbed rather than had an organ up and quit on her. The way she walked gingerly around the house and insisted on sitting on pillows was only made more annoying by her lectures on the fragility of life and how we had to live each day to the fullest.

It was like Socrates had merged with the Queen of England.

Someone had also given her a bell, which she rang at varying intervals whenever she needed attention. Thank God Adrien dealt with her for the most part. I wasn't sure how he hadn't smothered her yet. He had to be approaching his breaking point. Any day, we were going to find Nattie impaled by that damn bell, and Adrien would be in the wind.

I'd even let him have a head start before reporting it. What were cousins for, after all?

After leaving work a little later than normal due to a brief having gone missing and the bosses calling an all-hands-on deck to locate it, I was exhausted. So when I walked into a house full of mechanics from the shop Nattie worked at, I wanted to cry.

"Hey," Nattie called. "The guys came to see me. Wasn't that nice?"

I bit back a whimper. "Yeah. So nice."

Pizza boxes, wing containers, and cans were littered about. Nattie was sitting on the couch, and four guys and a woman were in various places around the room.

I'd met her coworkers briefly before, but at the moment, I couldn't remember any of their names. While I was happy Nattie had made friends in town, I desperately wanted the mess and company to go away.

"You hungry?" one of the men asked me. "Help yourself."

I offered him a small smile. "I'm good, thanks." I looked at Nattie. "Is Owen here?"

"Uh, yeah, I think he went upstairs."

I smiled again. "Have a good night, everybody."

They all murmured their goodbyes, and I booked it upstairs. I found Owen lying on our bed, reading.

He dropped the book on his chest when I came in. "Hey. Didn't want to join the party downstairs?"

I laughed. "Not really." Climbing into bed beside him, I tucked myself against him.

"Everything okay?"

I sighed. "Yeah. I'm just... in a mood. I'm hungry but don't feel like making anything, and I don't feel social enough to hang out with Nattie and her friends."

Owen was quiet for a second before he said, "Let's go out to eat."

I burrowed into him more because I *really* wanted to do that. But... "We need to save all the money we can."

"One meal isn't going to make or break us. It'll be good for us to get out for a night."

"Really?" I asked, unable to hide the hope from my voice.

Owen's brow furrowed as he studied me. "I'm sorry if I made it feel like you couldn't do things you enjoy because it might cost money."

I sat up. "You didn't."

"It kinda sounds like I did. You sound like I offered you

a trip to Paris rather than dinner out. I didn't mean to make things feel so . . . dire."

I grabbed his chin. "You aren't making me feel any kind of way. I *want* to save money because I want us to keep the house. Not wasting money on things I don't need is a choice I'm making."

"But you're only making it because of me."

"No, I'm doing it for both of us. I live here too. And I love this house. I don't want to have to move. I'm happy to make some small sacrifices now if it gets me what I want in the long run."

He was quiet for a moment while he seemed to contemplate my words.

"Still. I'd like to take you out to dinner. One night where things are a little more normal."

Part of me wanted to say no. It felt frivolous. But I could also see that Owen wanted to go, and I couldn't deny that *I* wanted to go too. Maybe a break from reality would do us good.

"Okay."

He beamed. "Great. Just let me change."

We both hurried to get ready and were out of the house fifteen minutes later, saying quick goodbyes to Nattie and her friends.

"Where do you want to go?" I asked Owen as I buckled my seat belt.

"I was thinking that little café on Holt Street? I walked by there last week, and it looked good."

"Sounds perfect to me."

Owen put his hand on the center console, and I threaded my fingers through his. It felt good to be out with him like this. Just the two of us with no set agenda other than sharing a meal. I was really feeling it, and it made me long for all the drama in our lives to settle down so we could get back to this.

We pulled up near the restaurant and pulled into an open spot. There were a lot of people about, probably enjoying the temperate weather. We walked hand in hand toward the café. Thankfully, it wasn't too crowded, and we could sit at a table out front and enjoy the night.

The server took our drinks and appetizer order, and then we relaxed into conversation.

"How are your classes going? Any more Professor Ted stories?" I asked as I broke off a piece of bread before popping it in my mouth.

"Eh, not really. I think I've become desensitized to how whacked out he is. And my other classes are fine. It's been a little hard to get into them with everything going on, but I'm keeping up with stuff. What about you?"

"It's a lot," I said with a laugh. "I always heard how difficult law school was, so I thought I was prepared, but I was not. I mean, it's fine. I'm adjusting, but it *was* an adjustment."

"Any more issues with that girl who was being an asshole?"

"Bethany? Nah. She clearly doesn't like me, and I have no idea why, but I can't spend any energy worrying about it."

We were interrupted by the server bringing our drinks, and then our conversation strayed to Nattie's recovery, Aamee and Brody's upcoming wedding, and how well Roddie had melded into living with us. When our dinner came, all talking stopped as we devoured our food.

Afterward, we walked around town a little before sleepiness called us home. The house was quiet when we got there, and Owen let Gimli out as I went up and got ready for bed.

When Owen joined me a short time later, he disappeared into the bathroom before sliding into bed beside me and pulling me close.

"Have I told you lately how much I love you?" he whispered into the darkness.

He had. He told me every day. But I never got tired of hearing it, and I told him so.

"I love you too. So much."

He pressed kisses down my face before arriving at my lips. His tongue slipped inside and tangled with mine as he shifted so he could blanket my body with his.

I began to writhe beneath him, wanting to be closer, to feel his hardness against me, to know how much I turned him on.

We filled the room with moans of pleasure as we slowly stripped each other of the few pieces of clothing we wore. When he finally pushed inside me, I arched my back and gasped.

This was what home was. Feeling this intimacy and contentment with another person who accepted me with all my flaws. Who loved me in spite of them and, maybe in some cases, even because of them.

There was no one in this world like Owen Parrish. And I would forever be thankful he was mine.

Chapter Twenty

OWEN

"What do you think?"

I turned toward where Roddie was standing with two dogs in the yard. The large white one was wearing a top hat and collar with a bowtie, and the other smaller brown and black one had on a tutu.

"I think you have too much time on your hands. Also, aren't they both boys?"

"Yeah, but I only bought one girl and one boy outfit. And my followers won't know Bruno's a boy." He backed up slowly, holding a closed fist around the treats he'd just grabbed from a pouch on his waist.

I wasn't sure who looked more ridiculous—Bruno or Roddie. I'd rarely seen him lately without his fanny pack, complete with treats, a clicker he used to train the dogs, and a container of poop bags attached to a clip. It was like a tool belt for dog dads.

Roddie stopped and knelt down in the grass. Then he removed his phone from his fanny pack and tried to get Bruno and Donner in frame.

I watched him for a moment before going back to my latest project: patching up part of the shed that another dog had chewed off a few days ago. I didn't replace the wood completely because chances were that he would chew it again, but I wanted to at least nail a board back to the outside for now.

Roddie had recently started an Instagram account for his doggie day care and was trying to increase his followers to get the word out. He had a good number of customers, but they tended to alternate days, so he didn't usually have more than three dogs at a time.

I had to hand it to him. He put the effort in to get clients instead of hoping clients would just come to him. It did worry me slightly that Roddie was being so public about his business, but I doubted Mrs. Aberdeen trolled Instagram often, so we were probably safe as far as that was concerned.

"I'm gonna tag the café where Hudson works because the treats are from there. I'll include some pictures of the dogs eating them. Maybe I'll get some cross promotion that way."

"What is it you're promoting exactly?" I heard Mrs. Aberdeen ask from the other side of the bushes that lined her yard.

"None of your business, Mrs. Aberdeen," Roddie called. "Now go back to bathing your birds or whatever you're doing over there." He snapped some more pictures of the animals.

I saw the bushes move before I saw Mrs. Aberdeen, causing them to look like some sort of invisible presence had moved them. A moment later, the woman appeared, a few leaves sticking to her white hair. She wore a pair of gardening gloves, a long-sleeve shirt, and tan linen pants.

"See," she said with angry enthusiasm as she pointed at Roddie. "He's got some sort of business going on out of this house."

It took me longer than it should have to realize she'd been speaking to someone other than me. At first I thought she'd forgotten we'd already had this discussion, but when I saw the trees move again and a man with a clipboard appear next to her, it didn't take me any time at all to see the situation for what it was—my nosy neighbor had ratted us out. But to whom exactly, I wasn't sure.

"Listen, Mrs. Aberdeen," I said as calmly as I could manage.

"It's *Mizz*," she said, emphasizing the end sound.

I had no idea if she was married, single, widowed, or divorced, and I cared even less. This woman was making an already difficult situation harder for no good reason.

"Sorry. *Mizz* Aberdeen. I'm confused because we've already been through this. Roddie's a friend, and he has some friends' dogs staying here." I turned toward the man with the clipboard who'd been looking back and forth between us. I wondered if he'd seen Aberdeen rolling her eyes at me. I could only hope he thought she was as crazy as I did.

"So you say." She rolled her eyes again, and I noticed the man write something down.

"I'm sorry, who are you?" I asked him.

"My apologies," he said. "I should've introduced myself. I'm Jeremy Henderson. I work for the township. Janice called me about some concerns she had, so I'm just here to find out what's going on. If it's nothing, it's nothing. But I wouldn't be doing my job if I didn't investigate the complaints that come in."

I assumed all the complaints were from the bitter old woman standing next to him, but I knew better than to voice that. It would only make me seem defensive. Deciding quickly it would serve me better to be my jovial, likable self, I reached my hand over the fence to shake Jeremy's.

"Owen Parrish. But you probably already know that."

Jeremy nodded. "I do. But it's nice to meet you formally. So the dogs belong to your friend's friends?"

"Yeah, my friend Roddie." I pointed behind me to where he was likely still using my yard as a canine runway.

When I turned around fully to see him, he was holding a hula hoop with one hand and a box of Cheerios in the other as he tried to get Gimli to jump through. He tossed a couple pieces of cereal through the hoop, but all the dogs went around it instead of through and gobbled up the snacks before sitting in front of Roddie to beg for more.

Jeremy wrote something down on his notepad again. "And all three dogs are Roddie's friends' dogs?"

I heard the skepticism in his voice, like the possibility was completely improbable. It wasn't. But it wasn't true either.

"Well, Gimli's mine. He's the one with the green collar. I'm not sure who the other two belong to. Roddie knows them." As soon as the words left my lips, I realized my mistake. And it was too late to correct it.

"I'll need to speak with Roddie, then," Jeremy said. Then he called Roddie's name loudly and waved him over.

Not surprisingly, Roddie looked excited to be included in whatever was happening. He looked like a kid who'd just been told there was a new bike for him in his dad's truck. The FOMO was strong in this one.

"What's up?" Roddie asked when he made it to the fence, followed by the three dogs. They were either super attached to him or they had a serious case of FOMO too. I kind of thought it was a combination of the two.

Roddie stood tall with a wide smile on his face, his hands on his hips and his elbows out to the side. He looked like he should've had a red cape blowing in the breeze behind him.

"I'm Roddie," he said to Mrs. Aberdeen and Jeremy. "But I guess you already know that." He laughed at himself and then pulled his shirt up over his face to wipe some sweat away like a turtle retreating into its shell. "Sorry, I'm a little delirious from the heat." He laughed again.

Early fall weather in Pennsylvania was about as predictable as a blackjack hand.

"You've been out here a while?" Jeremy asked.

"Yeah, man. Off and on for most of the day. Can't leave these guys out here too long, but they've sure got some energy to burn."

"They're cute," Jeremy said. "They yours?"

Shit. Here it comes.

I tried to make eye contact with Roddie, but I could tell he was oblivious to anything other than what was in his own mind at that moment. And even if I'd been able to catch his gaze, he likely wouldn't have been able to decipher what he was supposed to say. How could he?

"That guy's Owen's dog." He pointed to Gimli. "The other two I'm watching."

Jeremy went back to his clipboard.

"I'm sorry, I know you have my name," Roddie said, "but I didn't catch yours."

"Jeremy."

"Whatcha writin' down, Jeremy?" Roddie asked.

Jeremy waited until he was done writing and then looked up at Roddie. "I'm from the township. We've been getting some complaints about this property lately, so it's my job to come check it out."

He sounded casual, almost like all of this was a formality that he had no interest in taking part in. But I had a feeling he was doing more than simply going through the motions.

"Well, you can tell your supervisor that you've checked it out and the case can be closed," Roddie said.

Suddenly all three dogs were beside him, panting and smelling the treats that were hanging off his hip. He pulled a few out and kept his hand closed until the dogs calmed down and sat. Then he opened his hand to give one to each.

"I'm sure you guys have better things to spend residents' tax money on than asking questions about me and a couple of dogs. I'd understand it if they barked constantly or something, or of course if they bit another animal or a person, but these guys are as sweet as your grandmother's tea."

Roddie definitely had an interesting way with words.

"My grandmother died a few years ago," Jeremy said dryly.

"Oh. I'm so sorry for your loss. And also for the terrible analogy." Then Roddie's face crinkled a little. "Both grandmothers are dead?"

"Both."

Roddie nodded slowly before shoving his hands in his pockets and hanging his head for a few seconds.

"Again, my condolences."

"Anyway," Jeremy continued, "the complaints weren't regarding the dogs' behavior. We've received some calls about you possibly running some kind of doggie day care or training classes out of this home."

Roddie let out an exaggerated laugh. "That's a ridiculous accusation. Do I look like the type of person you'd *pay* to watch your dog, let alone train them? I'm just keeping an eye on them for some of my buddies. They work nine-to-fives, and they didn't wanna crate them all day. I'm home, so I said it's fine for them to drop 'em off. We have a big fenced yard, so why not, ya know?"

"Right," Jeremy said.

I didn't know if he believed anything we'd said, but he put his pen back in his pocket and allowed his arm that was holding the clipboard to relax at his side.

"He's lying," Mrs. Aberdeen called out abruptly.

She must've also sensed that Jeremy wasn't getting anywhere with his questions and was wrapping things up.

"I've *seen* people come and go. *Different* people. Different *dogs*!"

"So?" Roddie said. "So what if there are different people and different dogs? That doesn't mean anything other than I like animals and have a lot of friends."

As Roddie spoke, I saw Mrs. Aberdeen's face transform into a shade of red that looked like it should've hurt. Roddie's tight smirk told me it was exactly the response he'd been hoping for.

Mrs. Aberdeen moved closer to the fence, pointing at Roddie with a gloved finger. "We'll see how many *friends* you have when your little pet project gets shut down!"

"Okay, okay," I said. "Let's not make this more than it needs to be." I did my best to stay calm. "Jeremy asked his questions, and I believe we answered them. Right?" I asked him quietly, respectfully.

"You did. I can't promise that this will be the last you'll see of me, but for now I think I've done everything I can do." He looked at Mrs. Aberdeen. "Rest assured that if you have any other problems with Mr. Parrish or his friends or you bring anything else to my attention, I'm happy to come back out."

"Oh, I'm sure you'll be hearing from me." She turned away without a word and went back to whatever yard work she'd been doing before all of this had begun.

Jeremy thanked us again before saying goodbye and heading through the gate that led to her driveway.

Once he was in his car, Roddie yelled, "You have no idea what you started, Aberdeen!"

"Oh, I do indeed." She looked up slowly from her flower bed. "And I damn well intend to finish it."

As it turned out, Robert Frost was wrong; good fences don't make good neighbors.

VERONICA

"Hold on a second. Slow down. Go back to the beginning." I was holding both hands up in an attempt to stop Roddie from speaking so quickly. Or at all.

Unfortunately, it didn't work, and Roddie continued firing words like he was trying to mow me down with them.

"And this guy might be back if she says anything else to him, but I have to keep my business going. I also don't wanna cause any more problems for you guys and, oh my God... I'm so sorry, Owen, you let me stay here, and now this lady's all over you for something *I'm* doing and—"

"It's fine," Owen said, putting a hand on his shoulder. "Or maybe not." He laughed. "But it will be."

Roddie took a breath and blew it out slowly. If we had a paper bag around, I would've handed it to him to breathe into.

I felt bad for the guy. Ultimately Owen had allowed Roddie to run his business here, so it wasn't entirely Roddie's fault. Not to mention, Mrs. Aberdeen had already complained about the excessive noise coming from our house that night.

"Owen's right. We'll figure it out. I'm sure when her complaints don't get anywhere, she'll give up anyway."

"Let's egg her house on Mischief Night!" The suggestion came from Nattie, who I hadn't realized was standing behind me in the kitchen.

"We're not egging her house," I said.

"Why not?" she whined.

"Because we're not in middle school."

"I think it's a solid idea," Inez said.

"You've gotta be kidding me." My eyes opened wide at the two of them.

"I'm not," Inez said. "Gotta fight fire with fire."

"An eye for an eye," Roddie chimed in. "I like it."

"Just because there's an aphorism that has a nice ring to it doesn't mean egging an elderly woman's home—an elderly woman who already can't stand us—is a good idea."

"Why not?" the three of them asked at once.

I looked to Owen for backup, but he just shrugged. "She probably doesn't have cameras or anything."

"But what's the point?" I argued. "If it's on Mischief Night, she won't know it's us, so it's not like she'll hesitate to bother us again. She'll probably just think it's some kids messing around. And if we make it known that it *is* us, she'll probably have us arrested or something. Plus, Mischief Night is over two weeks away."

"But we'll get to watch her scrape egg off her door, so it'll be worth it." Roddie sounded more excited than he should have talking about tossing dairy products onto our elderly neighbor's porch.

Though, I had to admit, the image made me smile—at least internally.

"Vee," he continued, "isn't there something you can do about her? Legally, I mean."

"I'm not a lawyer yet. And she hasn't done anything wrong. She's just annoying. It's not like that's illegal."

"It should be," Owen said. "We have enough on our plates without having to deal with Mrs. Blabberdeen."

"That's a fantastic name," I said. "Blabberdeen."

"Thanks. It sounded even funnier when I said it out loud."

"So there's really nothing we can do but sit back and wait to see if we get in trouble?" Roddie was usually so carefree and happy, but the last few minutes, he looked like a kid who'd just found his goldfish napping on the surface of the water.

"I doubt it," Owen said. "We'll just try to lie low for a little."

I had to laugh at that. Lying low wasn't exactly something any of our friends did well.

"Let's bad-mouth her on social media," Nattie suggested. "I bet she's in some of those town hall type groups where people bitch and complain about everything. We can call her out without saying it directly. Like just ask what someone would do if they had a neighbor who was being a huge pain in the ass about everything."

I was just thinking what a terrible idea that was when Roddie perked up.

He stood up a little taller and his eyes seemed to light up. "There's this one group I'm in that's exactly like what you're talking about," he said to Nattie. He pulled his phone out of his pocket. "I'm gonna look to see if she's a member. People ask all kinds of dumb questions in there. Like when someone sets off fireworks, there are always people posting to see if anyone heard gunshots. Then other people troll the threads. It's awesome!"

"Why are you in a group like that?" Owen asked.

"Originally I joined so I could post about my doggie day care every Tuesday when they let people share business info, but usually I forget. Now I'm just in for the entertainment."

"So you joined this group to post about a business you're not supposed to be running out of a residential home and now you're hoping that our neighbor—who wants to shut down that business and get us in trouble with the township for it—is also in that group so we can bitch about her to other people in the community?"

Roddie was quiet while he seemed to fully absorb all of what Owen had said. His mouth opened and closed a few times like he was preparing to say something, but no words came out.

Then his lips twisted thoughtfully. "Well, when you put it like that, the idea loses its appeal." He went back to his phone again. "What's Blabberdeen's first name? Her last doesn't come up, but I want to make sure she's not on Facebook under her first and middle name or something."

"Janice," I told him.

"Okay, I think we're safe. There are two Janices here, but looking at their profile pics, I think they're much younger."

"The pictures might be her daughter or something, though. That doesn't mean it's not her account," Owen said, moving over toward Roddie to look over his shoulder at the phone.

Roddie held the screen toward Owen's face. "Well, this Janice commented that she was shook when she found out Justin Bieber had to cancel some concerts because his face was, and I quote, *all fucked up.*"

"Okay, so I agree that one's probably not her," Owen said. "But maybe we're worried about the wrong person anyway. It's the township that can do something, not her specifically."

As everyone else began debating the best course of action, something occurred to me. Roddie had mentioned the legality of all of this, but maybe I'd been too quick to dismiss that. The more I thought about it, the more I thought he might actually be on to something. But I didn't want to speak too soon and get anyone's hopes up.

I'd said Mrs. Aberdeen hadn't been doing anything wrong that would warrant any legal action. Maybe it was time to give the township a call of my own.

Chapter Twenty-One

OWEN

"Don't tell Vee we're doing this," was the first thing I said when Cody suggested we look into the builder who wanted to buy the house.

I did plan to tell her at some point—most likely afterward, when it would be too late for her to tell us it was a horrible idea.

Which was exactly what I thought it was once Cody turned what should've been an extensive internet search with the help of Xander into a full-fledged stakeout.

"You realize we're not gonna be doing this all night, right?" I said when Cody returned to my truck from the store, holding bags full of soda, chips, beef jerky, and protein bars. "Also, this looks like a heart attack starter kit."

"They're SSR," he said, grabbing a two-liter bottle of Coke out of the bag.

I should've known better than to think Cody would explain what he was talking about without prompting.

"SSR? What's that? I'm guessing you don't mean sustained silent reading." I'd loved that time when I was in school. It was so quiet, so personal.

"Uh, no. I don't even think they do that anymore. This girl I was talkin' to last year had to do some observation hours in a third-grade class, and she said it was fuckin' crazy. Screaming, hitting, no down time when she could get any work done. I think she changed her major after that." He laughed to himself. "Guess they finally realized no one likes to read."

"So, SSR?" I asked as a reminder.

"Oh, right. Standard Stakeout Requirements."

I pulled out of the parking lot and onto the street. "I doubt that's a real term."

I could feel Cody looking at me, but I kept my eyes on the road.

"You know what I doubt?" he said. "That you're gonna be any fun. And this is supposed to be fun."

"No, it's not. This is strictly a recon mission." I regretted my strong choice of words immediately because the last thing Cody needed was to get even more pumped up because I made it sound like we were part of some covert military operation. I continued before Cody had a chance to respond. "What can we even find out about this Cappello guy from sitting in a car near his house?"

"All kinds of things. Who he lives with, what kind of cars he has, what his house looks like."

"Couldn't we have found those things out with a quick Google search? As easily as we found his address?" I knew the answer but found myself asking the question anyway.

"Yeah, probably. But that's not as fun. And you never know what we'll find when we go through his trash."

For fuck's sake.

"I'm not going through his trash."

"Your loss," Cody said before taking a long swig from his two liter.

As we drove the fifteen minutes to Rich Cappello's house, I contemplated my life's choices. I was renovating a house I soon might not own, renting rooms to eclectic strangers, allowing a potentially illegal business to be run out of my home, and playing in a band that sucked too badly to play anything other than eerie melodies for a haunted house we'd been promoting. And that was just in the last few weeks.

So if this lunatic next to me thought I was going to jump into a trash can and dig around like Oscar the Fucking Grouch, well, then . . . it kind of seemed par for the course. But if I could get out of that by letting Cody take one for our incredibly inept team, then that was what I was going to do.

Turning down Rich Cappello's street was like pulling into a world I didn't belong in. The home Minnie left me was big, but these were easily twice the size. I wondered if Cappello's Custom Homes had built this development too. It appeared to be relatively new, and I couldn't imagine the guy would've bought a house from another builder.

The houses displayed a variety of sidings—vertical board and batten paired with painted wood shingles, or horizontal vinyl with metal roofs and stone trim. As someone who was interested in renovation and design, I had to admit these homes were gorgeous. Sprinkler systems watered thick green lawns that looked more comfortable than the bed I'd slept on as a kid, and gardens showed off colorful manicured bushes with black mulch to contrast the bright pastels of the flowers.

"Which one's his?" Cody asked.

"I think it's up here at the end. The one with the Range Rover. Three sixty-nine."

Cody chuckled to himself. "Sixty-nine."

Jesus Christ.

"Yeah, this is it."

He pointed to a home that was currently under construction, though it didn't look like anyone had been working on it today.

"Okay, park over there so we won't look weird."

For some reason, I followed Cody's orders.

"Um, we definitely look weird. We're in an old pickup truck on a street that doesn't have any car that's worth less than like sixty grand."

"That's why I said to park here," he said. "We'll just look like two guys who are working on the house."

"Except we're just sitting in my truck and not working on anything."

"Uh, yeah. That's what dudes like that do. People will think we're on a break."

I doubted it but had no better ideas, so I pulled in and shut off the engine. "And what if Rich Cappello sees us?"

It was probably a question I should've asked before now, but since Cody probably had no answer for it that would make the situation better, I realized it was a moot point anyway. We were parked at the end of a street—*his* street—in the driveway of a house that was still under construction. Most likely by Cappello's company. If he saw us, there wasn't much we could say to spin the story.

Cody shoved some chips into his mouth and shrugged. "He bothers you, we bother him."

"This isn't like an eye for an eye type of thing," I said, thinking back to our conversation not too long ago.

Cody turned toward me, a seriousness rolling over his face that I hadn't seen before. "It can be," he said ominously.

"Maybe we should move to the street so we're at least on property that's not his."

"Shh," he said. "I see movement." He tossed a few more chips into his mouth and leaned closer to the windshield.

I leaned closer too but crouched down a bit, hoping my dashboard would hide me should anyone spot us. At least Rich Cappello didn't know who Cody was.

"Who is it? Man or woman?" I asked quickly.

"Man." Then there was a pause. "And a woman. A much . . . *older* woman."

"Is it safe to look?" I turned down the radio. There was no way they would've heard it, but silence seemed like the better option. Like turning down the radio when you're looking for a certain location.

"Doesn't look like either of them has a gun or anything. And why are you whispering? He's not Clark Kent."

"It just seems like a good idea to whisper," I whispered again.

"Shit, he just looked over."

"Fuck, fuck, fucking hell. He's probably gonna get us on trespassing or something. We should've moved to the street. Did he see you?"

"He's walking over here." Cody grabbed my arm, which was the only thing still currently on the seat since I'd somehow managed to wedge myself between the driver's seat and the pedals.

"Shit, what do we do?"

Cody burst out laughing. "I'm just fuckin' with ya. No one's here."

After I crawled out from under the steering wheel and stretched out on the seat again, I looked over to Cody. "I'm one step away from throwing you into a vat of concrete and making your body part of the basement floor."

He was still laughing when he smacked me on the arm. "Come on. You've got no sense of humor. That was funny."

It was, but I'd be damned if I admitted it. So I punched him in the gut instead. Not too hard, but enough to knock the wind out of him a little, which made it more difficult for him to continue laughing.

When he finally caught his breath enough to talk, he said, "You're really gonna have to work on your bedside manner if you're gonna be a gynecologist."

"I'm not gonna be a gynecologist. Where did you even get that?"

Cody seemed about as confused as I was. "Drew said you were learning how to deliver babies."

I stared at Cody for a moment, trying to figure out what the fuck he was talking about. "A doula?"

"Okay, whatever it's called. I don't know all the proper vag terms."

I didn't know why it mattered that I corrected him, but I found myself saying, "Doulas don't deliver babies. They're there more for moral and emotional support throughout the pregnancy and birth. They provide breathwork to help the mother calm down and focus."

"Cause you're super calming. You just stuffed yourself on the floor of your car."

"Shut up. Your career plan isn't all that impressive either. And I don't plan to go into the field anymore anyway."

It was a low blow to go after his lack of career prosects but also an accurate one, and I didn't regret it. I'd been stressed lately, and Cody was making it worse with his stakeouts and his loud chewing and his pranks and unwarranted judgments. Who needed it? Not me.

"You know what? This whole thing is stupid. I should've never let you convince—"

"Get down."

"Let's just leave and have Xander—"

"Get down!" he said again. This time he grabbed the back of my neck and shoulders and pushed.

"What the fuck, Cody?" I pushed his hand away.

"This time I'm serious. He just pulled into his driveway, and he looked right at us."

After glancing toward Rich's house to confirm that Cody wasn't messing with me, I ducked again. It probably made us look even more suspicious, but there wasn't anything I could do about it now.

"He's coming over," Cody said.

I could tell from how panicked he sounded that he wasn't fucking with me this time.

"Shit, what should we do? How close is he?"

"I don't know! You want me to get a fucking measuring tape?"

This fucking kid.

Maybe we could tell him we were considering his offer and we'd driven over to discuss it further. But we probably would've called if that were the case, not shown up at his private residence and waited for him to get home. And it also wouldn't explain why I'd parked at another house and had ducked down when I saw him.

The only thing I could hope for was that since Rich's agenda was to convince me to sell my house to him, he wouldn't be too much of a prick about the whole thing.

"Put your head on my lap," Cody said, reaching for his belt buckle and undoing that as well as the button on his jeans.

"What the—"

"Just do it!" He grabbed hold of my hair and pulled my face toward his crotch.

A few seconds later, there was a knock on Cody's window. He rolled it down a bit, his hand still on my head.

"'Sup, man. Can I help you? Kinda busy here." Cody still had my hair in his hand and was using it to steer my head around his lap. For the first time in my adult life, I wished I'd buzzed my head.

I thought I heard the gravel move under Rich's feet, and I hoped that meant he'd taken a step away from the truck so he couldn't see me anymore.

"Well, you and your boyfriend are gonna have to be *busy* somewhere else because this is private property. And I own it."

"Oh, wow, I thought people who owned several properties usually had them in different cities, but that's cool, though, to have them on the same street. It's like having a fort in your yard but for adults, ya know, and also—"

"Do you always talk this much?"

"I talk when I'm nervous," Cody said. "And turned on," he added quickly.

I pinched the inside of Cody's knee, causing him to jump. Facing Rich was starting to feel preferable to my current circumstance.

"Why don't you get your boyfriend's head off your dick and have him start the truck?" Rich sounded angry, uncomfortable.

"Okay. Yes. We'll get going." I could tell by how loudly Cody spoke that Rich must've been at least a few feet away. Still, Cody used his hand to move my head up and down over his lap while he moaned. Loudly.

"This is because he's a dude, though, right? Just be honest."

Oh my God.

"What?"

"I said it's because I'm with a guy that you have a problem. If you'd found me with a girl, this would've gone differently."

Rich was quiet for a long moment before he finally said, more calmly than I expected, "Get off my property before I get the cops to do it."

"Got it," Cody said. Then he let out a strange low grunt. "I'll zip up now, and we'll be on our way." I didn't hear Rich say anything, and Cody took his hand off my head.

When I sat up, I saw Rich walking back toward his house. I turned on the truck and hit the gas before Rich looked back and had the chance to recognize me.

When we got to the end of the street, Cody turned to me. "Okay, so maybe the stakeout wasn't such a great idea."

But I had to disagree because right as I was turning off Rich's road, Mrs. Aberdeen was turning onto it.

VERONICA

"Oh, I put a bat house on that big tree that's right outside the porch," Roddie said. He'd stated it so casually, I wondered if a bat house was something I should've known about.

Apparently Nattie did too. "Um, ew. Is a bat house like an actual house for bats? And if so, why do we have one?"

Roddie pulled off his sweat shirt and tossed it on the chair. "Yes. I figured it would be cool for the haunted house if people saw real bats around. Or at least thought they were in there.

We can decorate around it or something with that spider web stuff or whatever to make it creepier. Plus, it's near Aberdeen's fence, so I'm hoping it'll have the side effect of pissing her off."

"Why would it piss her off?" I asked.

I mean, I didn't want to have bats around our house either, especially when I sat outside by the fire pit Owen had made back in June. Now that it was getting colder, we'd probably be out there more—if we kept the house, that was—and I didn't exactly want bats swooping down and getting tangled in my hair because, of course, that was what I imagined happening. But I wasn't exactly pissed about it. Just more skeeved out if anything.

"Because it's her tree," Roddie said simply.

"Are you serious? You can't install something like that on someone else's property."

"Before Adrien left, I ran it by him. He said that technically whose property it is is up for debate since the tree leans over the fence line, and I put them up high on the part that leans over Owen's property. No way Mrs. Aberdeen can reach it to get it down. And bats can eat thousands of mosquitos a day, so no more insect repellent needed." Roddie put his arms out like he was about to be applauded for his ingenuity.

"Oh, well, if Adrien said it..." I said, rolling my eyes at how ridiculous following basically anything Adrien suggested was.

"I hope Blabberdeen loses her shit," Nattie said. "Maybe she won't care about the dogs once she realizes her tree doubles as the Bat Cave."

I heard the door open and Cody and Owen come barreling in. Cody didn't do much quietly, but Owen didn't usually sound so fired up.

"What's wrong with you guys?" I asked when Owen came in to join us.

"Your boyfriend is so uptight," Cody called from the foyer.

"And you're a terrible liar," Owen yelled back.

"Whatever. He definitely bought it."

"Oh yeah, I'm sure he did. Your climax was so convincing." Owen rolled his eyes. "You sounded like a dying T. rex."

What the hell?

"It's called acting," Cody replied. He appeared in the kitchen a moment later and grabbed a beer out of the fridge. Tossing the cap into the recycling, he looked to Owen. "Last time I try to help your ass."

These two sounded like brothers.

"Can one of you please explain what's going on?"

Cody pulled his phone out of his pocket and unlocked it. A few seconds later, I heard his and Owen's voices coming from the phone.

"You recorded it?" Owen turned a shade of red I hadn't seen on him before.

"Well . . . just a voice memo. It's not like I filmed it. I kept it as evidence in case he threatened us or something."

"Can you two shut the hell up so we can hear?" Nattie said over them.

For the next few minutes, we listened to the recording. I could tell all of us were dying to comment, but we waited until the end, not wanting to miss a moment of the disaster I was so happy Cody had thought to record.

"You did kinda sound like a dinosaur," Nattie told him. "I don't think that's what you'd sound like, though. I mean . . . I'd imagine. Not that I'd imagine that." She looked around at each of us. "Can someone else talk now?"

"Yes," Owen said. "I'm happy to. Cody convinced me to look into Rich Cappello. He's the builder who wants to buy the house," he explained to Roddie and Nattie. They'd heard about him, but I doubted they remembered the name. "Anyway..." He looked at Cody. "Somehow I agreed to do a stakeout and watch the guy, but it ended up as an incredibly awkward moment of him watching us instead."

"Of him watching you *blow* Cody," I said.

"Vee, Jesus. I didn't actually blow him. I just pretended."

"I still think if we went through his trash we'd find something," Cody said. "We should go back when—"

"We're not going back," Owen said abruptly. "If anything, we need to look into Janice Aberdeen. I saw her turning onto his street when we were leaving. There's gotta be some connection. It's a small neighborhood. Can't be coincidental."

"Um, why are you just telling me about this now?" Cody sounded legitimately offended. "We could've parked on another street and hid in the bushes or something."

"Or we can finally let Xander look into it," Owen offered. "It'll take him a couple of minutes probably, and we won't get arrested. I'm gonna give him a call and then shower and head to bed. It's been a long day, and we have the grand opening of the haunted house this weekend."

I wasn't exactly sure why that mattered right now, especially since Nattie and Cody had been marketing the hell out of it and all the attractions were ready to go. Plus, the soft opening had been a success. At ten dollars per ticket, we'd made almost eight hundred dollars.

There wasn't a whole lot to do until right before it opened, which really only involved last-minute staging and plugging in some of the attractions. So I figured Owen's early bedtime had more to do with mental and emotional exhaustion than it did physical.

"Mind if I join you?" I asked.

There had been plenty of times when I'd hopped in the shower with Owen with no warning at all, and to say he welcomed the company would've been an understatement. But I could tell he might have wanted to be alone right now.

I wanted to be close to him . . . show him I was here for him no matter how all this played out. But I didn't want to overstep or suffocate him.

Owen took my hand in his and rubbed his thumb over the top of mine.

"I'd mind more if you *didn't*."

Chapter Twenty-Two

OWEN

For some reason, it worried me when Xander and Cody were together. Like Xander's intelligence combined with Cody's recklessness was a combination that could be lethal. So when they came into the hardware store with broad smiles and a gleam in their eyes, I instantly felt my stomach tighten.

"What is it?"

"What do you mean *what is it*?" Cody asked. "Can't your friends just stop by your place of employment without you assuming we're up to something?"

"Nope." I looked at Xander.

"Okay. Fine. We're up to something. Or we were. But that something may be the exact medley of information you need right now."

I heard the bell on the door jingle, and I looked over to see Mr. Winston, a regular who came in to chat more than shop. He'd always end up purchasing something eventually, but usually it would be a small, insignificant item like a keychain or a box of nails.

Mark had told me early on that Mr. Winston had lost his wife a few years back and had been lonely ever since, so I usually spent time talking to him when he came into the store. But right now, I wanted to find out what Xander and Cody had come to tell me.

"Hey, Mr. Winston," I called over to him. "I'll be right with you once I'm done helping these customers."

He gave a nod that he'd heard me and began browsing the aisles like it was his first time in the store.

"I think we might have something like that in the back," I said to Xander and Cody.

Then I motioned for them to follow me to the storage room. Cody seemed slightly confused, but Xander managed to usher him to the back without saying much.

"Okay, go," I said when we were all alone.

Cody began first. "I wanted to go back to Cappello's house since you said you saw Blabberdeen going down his street, but I didn't know what I'd even be looking for since chances were she wouldn't be back there. But I figured another undercover mission wouldn't hurt just in case."

I thoroughly disagreed, but there was no point in sharing that.

"So," Cody continued, "I asked Xander if he wanted to go with me since he had his own research to do, and he jumped at the chance."

"Jumped is a bit of hyperbole. More like cautiously acquiesced because I wanted to ensure you didn't do anything too impetuous."

"Stop using big words to confuse me," Cody said.

"They're normal words."

"Can you two tell me what you found out already?" I said.

"Yes, sorry," Xander said.

But before he could continue, Cody blurted out, "You were right about there being a connection between Aberdeen and Cappello. Get this . . . They're related."

"Are you sure?" I looked to Xander for confirmation since he was the more reliable of the two.

His face had held his usual stoic expression until now. But with Cody's last revelation, Xander was practically beaming.

"A hundred percent."

"But . . . why didn't you find that when you searched for the two of them online?"

"Because I didn't know what I was looking for. I did a search for each of them individually, and nothing jumped out at me as important. But once I talked to the guy—"

"You talked to him?"

"Well, *you* pretended to blow Cody in front of him."

I didn't know what to say to that, so I stayed quiet and let Xander explain.

"I pretended I wanted to buy a house. Figured if I went onto the property that you guys did, Cappello would eventually come over once he saw me, and it worked. He was extremely friendly to me, though. Probably because I didn't park on his land with my male prostitute."

"I didn't pay for him," Cody said at the same time I said, "Finish, please."

Xander laughed. "I walked around the house and went inside since it was only framed out. I started knocking on some wood or doing whatever people who care about that shit would do."

"They don't knock on wood."

"Okay, then we'll pretend it was for good luck. Whatever it

was, it worked. He came over and asked if he could help me. He seemed annoyed at first, but once I told him I wanted to know if the property was for sale, his whole demeanor changed."

I was skeptical. Maybe Cappello was just playing along because he wanted to do his own sort of investigation.

"He believed a college kid wanted to buy a house that's probably close to a million dollars, if not more?" I asked.

"First of all, I'm not technically a college kid anymore," said Xander. "And also, he knew what kind of money I probably had once I told him who my dad was."

"You gave him your real name?"

"Well, not mine. My dad's. I didn't think Cappello would've known him, so I explained who my father was, what he did for a living, that kind of thing." Xander laughed softly and plopped down on Mark's swivel chair at his desk and began spinning like a child. "Once I said the company name and my father's title, Cappello was more than happy to show me around and discuss floor plans and options."

At first, I wondered if it was a bad idea for Xander to have given his name to the builder, but I decided there really wasn't anything that could come of it that would be worse than what had already happened.

Xander and his dad weren't exactly on great terms anyway, and his dad finding out Xander had used his name to trick someone into giving up information probably would've been pretty satisfying to Xander.

I poked my head out of the back room when I heard the bell on the door jingle again. A woman was pushing a baby in a stroller and trying to corral a boy who looked to be about three. I knew I'd have to help her soon.

"Be right with you," I called to her. Then I turned back to the guys.

"So," Xander said, sounding more dramatic than an actor in a high school play. "It turns out our friend Rich Cappello is Janice Aberdeen's *son*." He brought the swivel chair to a stop and allowed a moment for his words to sink in.

"What? How do you . . . Are you sure?"

Xander nodded slowly. "I told him I wasn't crazy about the floor plan of the house on his street and asked if he had plans to build anywhere else."

"His mother's street!" Cody cut in, too excited to control himself. "He said he's buying land on his mother's street."

Suddenly, I didn't care about Mr. Winston or the mother whose son was probably grabbing dangerous objects.

"That doesn't prove he's Aberdeen's son," I said. "His mom could live anywhere."

Granted, the coincidence would be too hard to ignore since we'd seen her driving down Cappello's street when Cody and I left that day, but she could've had a friend or another relative on the street. She could've even just been driving down it to turn around.

"She could," Xander said. "But she doesn't. Turns out your neighbor has quite a history of husbands. Five, to be exact. And her third was David Cappello. Janice Aberdeen used to be Janice Cappello for the better part of her adult life. Looks like after that divorce she changed her last name back to her maiden one—Aberdeen. She stuck with that through the next two marriages. Guess it's a pain to keep changing it."

"Holy shit," I said to no one in particular. Or maybe I said it to the universe because it had thrown a twist at me that would've made M. Night Shyamalan proud.

"I know," Cody said. "I can't believe she ever got one person to agree to marry her, let alone five."

I was still pondering the implications of this discovery, but it definitely explained why Mrs. Aberdeen was so eager to get me out of the house.

"And get this," Xander added. "Cappello said he planned to build at least five homes on her street. When I looked at public records, there are only two other homes with enough land to subdivide based on township regulations, so I'm sure you're not the only person he approached about buying their property. Makes me wonder if it's an all-or-nothing kind of deal. Like he needs to acquire a certain number of properties to make building there worth it or something."

"I'm willing to bet Cappello is giving his mom a cut of the profits if she can help him acquire some of the houses and land on our street."

Xander smiled. "I'm willing to bet you're right."

"Only one way to be sure," Cody said. "I think a neighborhood meeting is in order. Minus Mrs. Aberdeen, of course."

VERONICA

"Why would you hold a neighborhood watch meeting the morning of the haunted house opening?" I asked. "There isn't even a neighborhood watch."

"There is now," Inez said. She continued arranging little Hawaiian breakfast roll sandwiches in a pyramid on a plate.

Nattie and Owen were putting drinks into a cooler of ice to take out back.

"Yeah," Roddie agreed. "People hear neighborhood watch, and they're immediately interested. They wonder if there's something to be scared of or if someone saw a Peeping Tom or something. They don't wanna be out of the loop."

He'd stated it as fact, and there was probably some truth to it. More people would show for that than a simple neighborhood get-together. They'd just be disappointed once they found out they'd been duped in order to get them there.

"Are you going to tell them they're not there for a watch meeting once everyone arrives?"

"No," Roddie answered. "The plan is for Owen to ask if anyone has concerns about the neighborhood's safety and whatnot, and when people start sharing things, we can lead into a discussion about what's happening with the builder. See if anyone else is being pressed to sell."

"Or even see if Aberdeen has been filing any complaints about anyone else," Owen suggested.

"You think *she* actually filed them?" I asked. "Or did she just have her son call one of his buddies at the township to badger us?"

Once I'd heard Rich Cappello was related to Mrs. Aberdeen, I wasn't convinced that her bitching and complaining was anything more than that, let alone something formal.

"Not necessarily," Owen said, dumping more ice on top of the drinks. "Especially if he's the person who usually handles those things. Let's just see what everyone has to say, and we'll go from there. This can't take more than an hour or so, and then we'll finish setting up the haunted house and get into costumes for tonight."

"Okay," I agreed. "I just don't want to make this a bigger deal than it needs to be. I've been thinking about it, and I don't think we should even worry about Aberdeen. We just need to focus on getting the money we need to stay in the house. The rest of it doesn't matter."

I waited for Owen to reply, and when he didn't, I couldn't be sure he'd even processed anything I'd said. He seemed to be focused on other tasks at the moment—tasks that mattered very little to the main problem he faced. But I'd come to realize that was how Owen's brain coped with stress.

Instead of concentrating on the big picture, he'd break it down into small pieces that were insignificant outside of the whole they were part of. It seemed to be a coping mechanism that served him well and lessened his anxiety about what mattered by projecting onto smaller and hopefully more manageable problems. But I wasn't sure it was the right choice when it came to actually coming up with a solution to anything.

"I know you're worried about the repercussions of Roddie's doggie day care and the haunted house and tenants paying rent," I said, "but I'm pretty sure you don't need to worry about any of that. I was on the township website, and it says you have to have two or more employees for something to be considered a business."

I'd put a call into the township pretending to be a realtor so I could ask more specific questions on behalf of my "client" who was looking to buy in the area, but I hadn't heard back yet. I'd wanted to be completely certain that we were in the clear before I told him about my findings with Owen, but now I felt my hand was forced. If I calmed him down even a little, it was probably worth sharing.

"Owen," I said. "Are you even listening to me?"

My tone must've caught his attention because he immediately looked up at me.

"Yes. I heard you. I just don't have anything to say. You said you're pretty sure, right? You're not positive."

I jerked back at his tone, which I didn't appreciate being directed at me. But my reaction didn't stop him from continuing.

"You don't work for the township. What if I get fined or something? Or we're told Inez, Roddie, and Nattie can't live here anymore? Then what?"

I didn't even want to reply because doing so felt like I'd be giving credence to not only his comments but to the attitude with which he spoke to me.

"I'm sure we could still live here," Roddie said. "We just couldn't pay you rent is all. It's not like we'd be homeless." Poor Roddie had been trying to make him feel better, but Owen glared at him like Roddie had told him he'd been banging Owen's sister or something. Guess Roddie wasn't immune to Owen's grumpiness either.

Gimli looked over from where he'd been waiting for someone to drop some food. It seemed he'd even picked up on Owen's mood.

"You *would* be homeless. We all would because I'm about to lose the house." And with that, he grabbed the cooler and headed out onto the patio.

I didn't plan to follow him.

Chapter Twenty-Three

OWEN

I'd been in a funk for weeks, which was understandable with the stress of the house, among other things. But I'd been a dick to Vee, and she didn't deserve that. Nor did anyone else. But there wasn't anything I could do about that right now.

Most of our neighbors had begun arriving and were all taking seats in the variety of lawn chairs I'd set up in a circle. I was suddenly aware it looked more like an AA meeting.

"Hi, everyone. Thanks for coming," I said over their quiet chatter, which began to die down as I spoke. "I'm Owen Parrish. I live here. Obviously." I was so incredibly bad at this, and it hadn't even begun. "I'm glad you all could make it because I have some things I want to discuss with you all."

"Anyone see that Peeping Tom the other night?" Roddie asked from where he sat beside me.

As soon as it left Roddie's mouth, I regretted not specifically stating that we shouldn't bring that up. I mentally flipped through every curse I could think of. Too bad he couldn't hear any of them.

Over the din of sudden anxious conversation, I heard James McKinney say, "Peeping Tom? Where?" The man looked to be about my father's age with a salt-and-pepper beard, a solid physique, and tan skin. "He better not let me find him, or he's gonna find out what a bullet tastes like."

His wife, Julia, put a hand on his thigh. "Oh, relax. Let him look if he wants to."

"What's a Peeping Tom?" The question came from one of the kids currently sprinting around my yard.

"My name's Tom," another said. "You can call me Peeping Tom. Peeping Tom, Peeping Tom," the boy sang.

"Don't say that!" The order came from the neighbor, Dan, who lived on the non-Aberdeen side of me. They'd brought three kids with them that they could have easily let play in their own yard—which had a trampoline and swing set with a slide and rock wall that could all be seen from my yard—but for some reason, Dan and his wife, Kim, felt the need to bring their three boys over to my yard—which was basically an open field with large patches of dirt where the grass had been worn down from the dogs.

What did I get myself into?

"Does someone have a plan for this . . . Peeping Tom? Has anyone called the police?" It was Mrs. Eisenbach who spoke.

Minnie had always said Mrs. Eisenbach was her favorite neighbor on the street because she didn't give *two squirts of piss.* For some reason, the imagery of that saying always grossed me out, which was strange considering the more common phrase *give a shit* should conjure up more squeamish feelings than the former.

But that was one of the traits I'd learned to love about Minnie—she unapologetically took her own path and forced others to adapt to her rather than the other way around. It had made her some enemies over the years, but it had made her some friends too.

"Oh, you know what?" I said, wanting to ease Mrs. Eisenbach's mind. "We're not even positive it was a person. My roommate Inez thought she saw someone outside one night, but it could've been anything. She can't see a thing without her glasses or contacts in, and it was late at night."

I laughed a little to make light of it, but I didn't think it would do much good. The group already seemed to jump down a rabbit hole of possibilities.

"Is Inez that beautiful girl I see you with all the time, because I doubt she'd like you callin' her your roommate," Mrs. Eisenbach said, thankfully dropping the conversation about the Peeping Tom, though I knew the change in subject would be short-lived.

"No, no, that's Vee. Inez is really my roommate. Or *our* roommate."

"You live with two girls?" James asked with a nod of approval. "Nice."

His wife smacked him, though not as hard as he probably deserved.

"He lives with three," Roddie chimed in. "The other is Vee's cousin, Natalia."

"Is she the one who looks like a witch?" another woman asked.

"No, that was Wynter," I explained. "She doesn't live here anymore. And I'm also pretty sure she *was* a witch."

"I got Wynter's spot," Roddie said with a proud smile like he'd auditioned for the role of a lifetime and beaten out an Oscar nominee.

"Her spot?" the woman asked. "Looks like Janice was right about this being some sort of hotel or something. Where is Janice, anyway? I can't imagine she'd miss a meeting like this." Her voice had grown louder as she spoke, and she'd turned toward Mrs. Aberdeen's yard.

I glanced over to Roddie, who was visibly flustered.

"Oh, no. Owen's not running a hotel. She was probably talking about the hotel I'm running. For dogs," he added, only making the situation worse. "I mean, it's not really a hotel because they don't stay the night. We stay the night. The dogs just stay the day. Like a day care. Only it's not a *day care* day care because it's not a business. I just like hanging out with dogs."

There was a long pause that was so awkward, I swore I could hear people breathe. Even the kids who'd been playing loudly must've sensed the shift in mood, because they were all looking at us from their place nearby in the yard.

Roddie cleared his throat, and for some reason, I felt the need to do the same. Maybe it was to break the silence or maybe it was because I wanted to say something but had no words that would be worth saying.

That left Roddie to keep talking.

He roamed his eyes over the group. "If your dog's lonely, let me know."

It sounded like the canine equivalent of *For a good time, call…*

Our plane had lost one of its engines, but instead of trying to take it down for a smooth landing, Roddie was crashing into trees on his way to a water landing that would most likely lead to a mass drowning. Where were Vee and Inez when I needed them? I could probably do without input from Natalia, but the other two would definitely help. Though there was no way Vee would be going near me by choice anytime soon.

Then the silence was broken by everyone at once. I tried to make sense of the chatter, but there were too many mingling voices to hear any of it clearly until one person took the lead.

He was a man who looked to be in his early thirties with a short beard and unruly brown hair that made him look open, warm even. He was the kind of person you'd approach in the grocery store to ask what they thought about the ripeness of a certain mango.

"I know I haven't lived here for very long, but I grew up visiting it because it used to be my grandparents' house. Some of you I've known since I was a kid, and others I'm meeting today for the first time." He raised a hand as a small wave. "I'm Gregory, by the way."

"Hi, Gregory," most of the group said in unison, and I was reminded of my earlier vision of an AA meeting. Only without the unconditional acceptance.

Gregory nodded before continuing. "So, forgive me if I'm trying to play catch-up here, but why does it matter who's living in Ms. Minerva's house?"

I never knew anyone called Minnie *Ms. Minerva,* but it made me smile inside.

"Because like Janice said, this block isn't zoned for that sort of thing. Or a day care even if it's not for kids." The comment came from the same woman who asked where Mrs. Aberdeen was before Roddie had launched into his long-winded explanation of his love of canines.

I'd hoped she'd forgotten about her curiosity regarding Mrs. Aberdeen's whereabouts, but based on her last mention of her, it unfortunately seemed that she hadn't.

"They're just college kids," Gregory said. "I bet most of us lived with a bunch of people in college. We're not here to talk about what all of *us* are doing anyway, right?" The way he looked around at all of us made me think his question wasn't rhetorical, though I didn't plan to answer it. "It's a neighborhood watch meeting, but we shouldn't be watching each other. We should be watching *out* for each other. My only concern is that this street is as safe for my daughters as it was for me when I was a kid."

"You should bring your kids to the haunted house later tonight," Roddie suggested to Gregory. Then he looked over at my next-door neighbors. "You guys too. It's gonna be awesome!"

"A haunted house?" one of the boys called from out in the yard. "Can we go? Please? I'm old enough this year."

"You're having a haunted house here?" Dan asked. It made sense he'd be surprised because we hadn't really advertised locally. It had been mostly through social media and word of mouth. We'd targeted mainly teens and adults, but I figured ticket sales were ticket sales.

"Yeah. I've always been pretty big on Halloween," I explained. "Usually I do some kind of party, but this is my first year as a homeowner, and I have the room for it, so I figured we might as well try somethin' different this year."

One of the other kids asked to come over, and before I knew it, all of them were begging to come over. Some even asked if they could help us set up or follow people throughout the house to scare them.

"I'm sure they have all that ready to go," Kim told them. "But we'll try to come by and check it out after dinner."

I couldn't tell if she actually meant it or was saying it to appease the kids for the moment, hoping they'd forget about it later. My guess was they wouldn't.

The kids all began discussing Halloween costumes and which houses to hit first for the best candy, but their innocent laughter was interrupted by Inez and Natalia's announcement that the snacks had arrived, which caused all the kids to run to the table where the girls had set down the trays of sandwiches, pretzels, chips, and a plate of brownies with chocolate chunks that had been in the oven when the neighbors had started arriving.

I wasn't sure why they'd waited until everything had been ready before bringing anything outside, but now that the refreshments had arrived, the kids—and some of the adults—had swarmed the table like geese swarm to a slice of bread.

"These brownies are amazing," Gregory said.

Inez shrugged. "Ghirardelli."

Gregory took another bite, swallowing before he replied with, "I totally would've said they were homemade."

"Well, anyone who knows me knows I don't make anything unless it's out of a box."

"I've seen you make lasagna," Roddie said. "And it was damn good too."

I wondered if Roddie had said something for the sole purpose of ensuring Gregory didn't get to have a conversation with Inez.

"I'm a huge lasagna fan." Gregory smiled at her.

Even I noticed Gregory's dimples. There was no way Inez would be immune to them.

"Been to Italy and everything."

"Wow, that's some serious commitment to pasta."

As I left the two of them to continue whatever it was

they'd just begun, I heard Gregory say something about being committed to everything special in his life. If he didn't strike me as so genuinely corny, I would've thought it was a line.

Once people were up and moving, chatting with people they hadn't been seated next to before, it became easier for me to engage with some of them further. I'd always been more of a one-on-one guy, preferring the intimacy of a few people than a large gathering, especially if I had to be the person running the show. So when Mrs. Eisenbach came up to me and thanked me for organizing this, I felt more at ease.

"Yeah, of course. My pleasure. I figured it was a good way to introduce myself to the neighbors I haven't met yet."

Lines spread across the skin around her mouth as she smiled, even though it wasn't very broad. "You aren't missing much," she said with a little more humor in her eyes. "Most of them are dull. And the ones who aren't dull aren't very nice."

"Minnie told me something similar," I said, laughing a little. "No real details, but just a general vibe about the neighborhood."

"I'm surprised she *didn't* give you details. Minnie wasn't one to mince words."

"No. No, that she wasn't," I said, figuring the reason she hadn't been so forthcoming with the neighborhood details was that she didn't want to focus on the negative when she knew one day I'd be living here.

"Did she tell you Aberdeen's the worst of 'em, or'd you figure that one out yourself?"

"A little of both," I said with another laugh, reaching down to grab a bottle of water from the cooler. "Can I get you something to drink?"

Mrs. Eisenbach politely declined before continuing.

"She's always had her nose in everyone's business, and poor Minnie took the worst of it, what with all those rumors about her, Milton, and June going around. Then she had to live next to the woman for most of her life. Minnie'd be out weeding her garden, and Janice would be peering through the trees like she was trying to catch her growing something she shouldn't have been."

I wondered if Mrs. Eisenbach knew about Minnie's little side hustle, not that Minnie had grown the stuff herself or anything.

She chuckled like she'd thought of a joke and only she was in on the punchline.

"What?" I asked, smiling.

She leaned in closer to me. "Maybe Aberdeen's the Peeping Tom. That'd be an interesting twist, wouldn't it?"

For some reason, I felt the need to be honest with this woman who'd been a good friend to Minnie during all the time that others hadn't been. She seemed sincere, genuine.

Still, I hesitated before saying, "So we may have made up the Peeping Tom thing," I said, feeling the embarrassment on my face.

"What? Why?" There was a chair nearby, and she sat down in it. I figured it had more to do with her age and physical condition than it did with what I was about to tell her.

I sat down in a chair next to her and sighed. Then I told her all of it: the taxes I owed, Cappello's offer, our efforts to earn money so I didn't have to sell, even how we'd done a little investigating and come to find out Mrs. Aberdeen was Rich Cappello's mother.

Mrs. Eisenbach listened without judgment, or at least she didn't offer any opinions as I shared everything with her.

I wasn't sure why I felt the need to tell this woman I barely knew all the crazy things our Scooby Gang had done to help me keep the house, especially when I hadn't even wanted to tell someone like June or my family. But maybe unloading on a stranger seemed safer.

Either way, I couldn't help but hope she told me what I wanted to hear. I felt so guilty about ending up in this position and wanted her to tell me it wasn't my fault—that it could've happened to anyone. Or maybe I secretly hoped Mrs. Eisenbach would have some sort of magical solution that none of us had thought of. Or maybe I just missed Minnie and my own grandmother, and this sweet, old, down-to-earth woman reminded me of the parts of both of them I loved.

Once I finished talking, Mrs. Eisenbach leaned back against the white plastic chair and said, "I'm sure you'll figure it all out. You seem like a pretty bright kid. Aberdeen tried to convince me to sell to Richie too. She told me I couldn't live in that big house by myself much longer, which is true, but I'll be damned if I'm gonna let her son buy it and build some McMansion next to it."

Mrs. Eisenbach was one of the neighbors who had quite a bit of land, and it seemed Rich had tried to capitalize on that.

"He even called my daughter and told her I'd fallen taking my trash out." She let out a brusque laugh. "Like my daughter's naïve enough to blindly believe that one fall's going to put me in some old person's home."

"So you *did* fall?"

"I fell," she said, sounding almost proud. "But it was because I stepped in a divot in the yard. Twisted my ankle too. But it could've happened to anyone, at any age. It didn't happen to me because I'm too old to take care of myself."

She pointed at me as she spoke, it seemed, to emphasize her point that she was as independent as she'd always been. "The important thing was that I got myself back into the house on my own, rested it, iced it... I forget what the *C* stands for in RICE, but the *E* is for elevate, and I did that too."

"I don't know what the *C* stands for either," I said, more as a way to bond with her than make her feel better. Mrs. Eisenbach's confidence didn't need a boost, especially from someone as unprepared for life as me. "So what did your daughter say about your fall?"

"Nothing. I told her Rich and Janice made it up. Wasn't hard for her to believe since she went to high school with him. He was a storyteller back then too, and time hasn't changed him."

"Why didn't you tell her the truth?"

Mrs. Eisenbach's thinning eyebrows pressed together like my question confused her. "No point in her worrying about me needlessly. Molly's got three kids, a full-time job as an elementary school principal, and a husband who's less help than the feral cat her youngest found under their deck. Last thing she needs to think about is me and my ankle."

Her warm laugh made me laugh too.

"So, listen," she continued. "I honestly wouldn't worry about Rich Cappello. He talks big, but when it comes down to it, he can't make any of us move if we don't want to."

That much was true at least. Her property was safe, and so was everyone else's in the neighborhood. Me, though...

"Maybe not, but the township's a different story. I have three weeks left to come up with... I'm not even sure how much because we've all spent money to make some." I let my forearms rest on my thighs and hung my head. "I'm so bad at this adult stuff."

Mrs. Eisenbach's smile had a way of making me feel better. Like a mother's hug after a scraped knee. It didn't help to heal the wound itself, but it had a way of making the problem fade into the background.

"I got a secret for ya." She leaned in closer to me. "Most of us are. We spend our whole childhood wishing we weren't children and then most of our adulthood wishing we were."

She paused as she let her words sink in, and I did my best to let them. I wasn't the only one who didn't have it all figured out.

"Greener grass and what have you," she said before settling back into her chair again. "Lucky for you, you have a lot more years left to figure it all out."

"I'm assuming you mean life in general, because I only have twenty-three days to figure out how I'm gonna keep this house Minnie trusted me with."

"You either will or you won't," she said, putting a hand over my two clasped ones, causing me to look up at her.

"That's like the least comforting thing I've ever heard," I joked, though it really was.

"My dad always used to say it. I kind of always hated it too," she told me. "But it doesn't make it any less true. Don't make things more than they are. All you can do is your best, and sometimes—too much of the time—your best isn't good enough."

I hated I had to hear that—that we could try our best and still fail. But this wasn't a T-ball league where everyone got a trophy. This was real life, where some people were winners and some were losers.

I worried I was the latter.

Inhaling deeply, I did my best to accept that despite my

best efforts, I wouldn't be able to keep the house. It might not go to Rich Cappello, but most likely it would go to someone who wasn't me. And I needed to be okay with that because, when it came down to it, I was the person I was scared to disappoint—not Minnie. She'd lived her life. She'd made her choices. Her mistakes.

Now it was my turn.

"Fuck growing up," I said aloud. "I have a haunted house to get ready for."

Chapter Twenty-Four

OWEN

After the meeting with the neighbors, I'd spent most of the day milling around the house, finishing up any last-minute preparations for the guests and practicing with the band for our fifteen minutes of fame.

I hoped it would literally *be* no more than fifteen minutes, but I had a feeling Brae and Jagger would want us to perform like we were putting on a show that was the next coming of Woodstock—and not the one in the nineties.

Vee and I had interacted a bit, but it was tense and full of unexpressed feelings I knew we'd eventually have to address, though I knew right now wasn't the time.

In the hallway, after I exited Roddie's room, which was now the Room of Doom thanks to Cody's sign, I issued Vee as genuine an apology as I could. I'd momentarily lost my cool and hadn't meant to seem ungrateful. I knew making things okay between us would take more than a rushed apology, but I didn't want her to think I didn't regret how I'd spoken to her.

She thanked me for apologizing and said we'd talk about

it later. Unfortunately, that small amount of closure was about all I could expect for the remainder of the night.

I hated that I'd made her feel like she was feeling right now, but at least both of us seemed to be able to put aside our conversation until we had more time in private. Discussing our issues in the midst of screaming teenagers didn't seem like the most productive option, especially when we needed to focus on the task at hand.

Brae was messing around with the amplifier as I practiced one of the melodies I'd be repeating on my keyboard throughout the night. It did make the mood creepier, though the playlist we'd used for the soft open did the same. But I was sure it would be our music that gave people nightmares. After playing it over and over, I felt like it had already taken possession of me like a demon taking hold of its host.

And speaking of demons . . .

"Wynter?"

Roddie had opened the door to officially open our house to the public, and standing on the front steps staring straight ahead, wearing a tattered wedding dress, was the one person I never thought I'd see again. Or maybe it was just that I hoped I wouldn't.

And I was so focused on *her*, I didn't even notice that Roddie was cowering behind the open door until he peeked out from behind it.

"You're Wynter?"

Bowing dramatically, which made her black veil fall over her face, she said, "The one and only."

Thank God for that.

"What are you doing here?" I asked. "I thought you didn't wanna ever come back."

"Yeah, I'll never live here because your house is freaky as fuck, but tonight it's supposed to be freaky as fuck, so I'm totally into it. Halloween's my holiday," she added with a toothy grin that resembled a jack-o'-lantern more than it did a woman in her early twenties.

From this distance, I couldn't tell if she'd actually lost a few teeth or if she'd put some sort of black stuff on them to make it appear that way. I sure hoped it was the latter, but with Wynter, it was tough to assume anything. Maybe she'd pulled them out as some sort of satanic offering.

"Looks like you had a rough day," Roddie said. "I can't imagine why a dude would've left you at the altar."

Clearly not picking up on the fact that he was teasing her, she gave him an absolutely disgusted look.

"Who even are you?"

"I'm Roddie," he announced proudly. It was his default tone. "I took your spot in the house."

"Well, Roddie." She said his name like it physically hurt her. "This is a Halloween costume I got at Goodwill. I don't believe in socially contrived institutions such as marriage, and I also find it presumptuous of you to assume I'm straight."

"Sorry?" Roddie said quietly, though it sounded more like a question.

I expected him to disappear from the room so he didn't have to interact with Rosemary's Baby, but instead he extended his hand.

"Well, Wynter, it's a pleasure to finally meet the woman I've heard so much about. Do you want to—"

"Don't believe a word of it," she said, stepping inside before Roddie could finish.

"Come in?" he finished, confusion lacing his tone.

Wynter made her way through the living room, and it seemed she intentionally avoided specific areas. It was like watching a runaway bride navigate a laser maze. Every few seconds, she'd stop to smell the air or lick her finger and hold it above her head like she was checking the direction of the wind. Then suddenly she stood tall, her body erect and her eyes wide with terror.

"There are evil spirits among us," she said ominously.

"I think you just caught a glimpse of yourself in the mirror over there," Inez said.

I hadn't even noticed her.

Natalia came into the room and ran to her. "Wynter! You're back!"

Wynter didn't even give Nattie a chance to get close to her, stepping all the way back until she had her back against the wall.

"Don't be weird," Wynter said, causing me to almost laugh out loud. Then she looked over to the rest of us.

"Well, it's nice of you to stop by," Roddie said. "Shame you can't stay to help?"

The way Wynter's eyes lit up as he said it reminded me of a possessed doll.

"What's the plan for tonight?" she asked. "I've got time. Where do you want me?"

Anywhere else but here.

The rest of the group looked equally shocked that Wynter offered to help.

"I guess you could kind of hang outside your old room. You know, really freak people out before they even go in while they're waiting in line or whatever."

"As long as I don't have to go inside it."

I wanted to tell her that she didn't have to be here at all—that her presence here only added to the stress of everything. The last thing I wanted was for people to leave because some weird chick was freaking them out. Though I guessed that was kind of what they'd paid for.

"Whatever you're comfortable with," I told her. "I appreciate the help."

VERONICA

I wasn't sure what I expected the haunted house to be like, but until it was about an hour and a half in, I realized it wasn't this.

Cody and Nattie had surprisingly done an extraordinary job with advertising, because not only had they sold almost all the tickets for each time slot, but there was a line outside that extended to the street in front of Mrs. Aberdeen's place.

Cars were everywhere, and eventually some people even began tailgating while they waited for the line to die down. And since we'd only let in a few people every time some of the ticket holders exited, most people were out there waiting a while.

"Did you see that dude with the van that looked like the Mystery Machine parked across the street?" Brody asked me. "I told him he can't leave without our Scooby Gang taking a picture in front of it."

He blew past me before I could answer, already yelling Aamee's name, probably so he could tell her the same thing.

Aamee was dressed in a witch costume, though lately the choice of attire wasn't as appropriate for her as it would've once been. Somehow, Brody Mason had calmed her down. Being with Brody had been like giving Adderall to an unfocused teen. Somehow the stimulant had had the effect of making her more even-tempered than I'd ever seen her.

I couldn't wait to go to their wedding in the Masons' backyard. Having already sort of attended my own there, I knew that family could throw one hell of a party, and I expected it to be even more of a celebration this time since Brody and Aamee were actually engaged to each other.

They'd also become so sweet and affectionate, it would've been sickening if it hadn't been so darn cute. It made me wish Owen and I could be like that one day.

We loved each other. I knew that much. But lately, we'd seemed to lose . . . whatever we'd had that made us so attracted to each other. Sure, Owen was stressed. And I was stressed watching him. Stressed *with* him. *For* him. But I wondered if we had what it took to go the distance. Or was ours a flame so hot it would burn through all its tinder and fizzle out long before it should?

We were immediately attracted to each other, and we jumped into living together before we even acknowledged our feelings for each other. Or at least before we began to act on them.

Maybe we did things backward and had gotten so comfortable around each other that things between us were beginning to feel stale. I wondered if Owen felt it too—if that was why he'd gotten irritated when I'd only been trying to help.

But my overanalysis of our relationship was interrupted by Sophia.

"Vee, where's the circuit breaker? Xander said something got tripped, and we need to go flip it back."

"It's in the basement."

The basement, which, other than Wynter's old room, seemed to be one of our most popular attractions. Since the unfinished part of the basement was creepy as all hell anyway, we didn't need to make much of an effort to step it up a few notches.

"I'll go take a look."

As I made my way down the steps and past the group of young teenage girls huddled together like a school of fish and communicating through high-pitched squeals, I heard the distinct sound of feedback from an amp and then a muffled voice come over the microphone. After an adjustment to the volume, I could tell it was Owen speaking.

"Hey, everyone. Sorry for the late start with the music here. I want to thank you all for coming out tonight. We hope you have a good time and are so terrified that you consider not coming back next year."

Next year?

"I mean, not really. We'd love for you to come back, but you know what I mean." Then he paused for a moment. "This one's for you, Professor Ted. They're all for you, actually."

Then began the deep melody I'd heard Owen practice on his keyboard more than a few times. This was the first time I'd heard them all together, though, and somehow all the sounds seemed to blend together in a way that made sense.

At least for this event.

Anywhere else, they probably would've been booed off stage, which here was four coffee tables pushed against the living room wall.

I got to the circuit breakers and found the one that had tripped, flipping it back quickly. Then I headed back upstairs and into the living room where Owen and his band members were playing loudly.

In front of them was a middle-aged man with a ponytail and a rolled-up bandana around his head. His bracelets reached halfway up his arm and were made of all different materials: leather, string, rubber, metal. He even had one I was positive was a pipe cleaner.

"You must be Professor Ted," I yelled over the music.

He stopped headbanging long enough to turn toward me. "I am. What gave me away?"

"Pretty much everything. But mainly that you're the only one who seems remotely interested in my boyfriend's band."

He laughed in a way that seemed genuine despite the exaggerated way he threw his head back when he did it.

"Which one's your boyfriend?"

"Keyboard player."

I nodded toward Owen, and his lips turned up into a smile that was so small I almost missed it.

"He's decent for someone who's never really played. Definitely pianist potential."

I tried not to laugh at that, but the way he said it sounded like *penis* potential, especially since it wasn't easy to hear where we were standing.

"Does that mean he gets an *A*?"

Ted shrugged. "Definitely gets the extra credit for finding his own venue. His house or not, he's got a pretty big audience here, so I gotta give him props for that." Ted pulled a pack of Winstons from his shirt pocket. "Cool if I smoke?" He held the pack toward me. "Help yourself."

"Oh, I don't smoke. Thanks, though."

And before I could tell him I didn't think it was a good idea to smoke here since there were some children around, including some of the neighbors' kids, he pulled one out and lit it.

When he brought the lighter away from his face, I realized I'd made a mistake in assuming that Professor Ted had decided to smoke a cigarette in Owen's house. Because he'd obviously decided to smoke a joint.

"Sure you don't want one?" he asked after he must've noticed me staring at him for an awkward length of time.

When I looked at the pack, I saw it didn't have one cigarette in there. Just six joints ready to go and a plastic baggie shoved down, which I assumed held more marijuana. It made me wish we'd known Professor Ted months ago when we'd had to make all those pot brownies Minnie had promised to people before she died.

"I'm good," I told him. "Really."

And then a woman's voice I recognized said from behind me, "I'm good too, but I'll be better once I get one of those."

We both turned around to see who was speaking, and it made me second-guess my choice to decline the opportunity to get high because standing in front of us was the last group of people I thought I'd see at this event.

Did Owen have any clue his family was coming?

Chapter Twenty-Five

OWEN

The haunted house seemed to be going well. There were lines and tailgaters, and our band had managed to come together in a way that didn't sound like a bunch of middle school outcasts playing untuned instruments in their parents' garage.

Professor Ted seemed pleased with our efforts, which meant we'd get some extra credit. Even Roddie's bat house had managed to become a draw for the outdoor crowd as they waited for entry into the house itself.

I had no idea where the bats had come from or when they'd arrived, but they were out there tonight, some of them swooping overhead in the backyard between the trees. Everything had seemed to line up perfectly.

But perfect ended quickly when you noticed your grandmother sharing a joint with your college professor.

Focusing solely on my keyboard, I hadn't even looked up more than a few times since we began playing. I noticed Vee stop to watch, and that gesture, however small, meant something I couldn't ignore. Even when she probably didn't want to be there for me, she was.

And apparently so was my crazy-ass family.

They'd appeared out of the blue, like some sort of spontaneous teleportation that had caused my parents and grandparents to manifest in front of me. It caused my fingers to come to an abrupt stop to the same melodic pattern I'd memorized before they came crashing down onto the keys with a loud crash that startled Brae and Jagger, who stopped playing immediately.

I felt their eyes follow me as I made my way down from the coffee table and onto the living room floor.

"Who taught him to play piano?" my grandfather asked. "This kid doesn't have a musical bone in his body." He turned to Vee, who looked just as surprised as I was to see them.

"I didn't know you were coming," she said to them. "Did you, Owen?"

"No, um . . . no, not a clue. You guys should've called to tell me. We've kind of got a full house right now."

"That's why we came," my dad said. "Natalia told us about the haunted house. You know how we are with Halloween. Couldn't miss an event like this one."

There was so much to take in. So much to comment on that I couldn't decide where to start. Natalia spoke to them? Was it by text or email? Or had she called them? And why hadn't anyone decided to tell me they were coming?

"I didn't mean to keep you all out of the loop, but it's not like you're right up the road, and I didn't want you to feel obligated—"

"Obligated to what? Support my son in all his endeavors?" my dad said. "Too late, because I decided a long time ago I'd be there for everything that was important to you." He glanced at my mom and grandparents. "So, we're here to do just that."

"I don't know if we have room for you to stay, though. We have Roddie in the only spare room that isn't haunted, Inez is in the basement, and we only have one pullout couch, so even if two of you took my bed, there still—"

"Your grandpa and I got a hotel," my grandmother said, a white cloud rising above her head as she spoke. "I heard about your living situation before we came up. I swore to myself I'd never live in a commune again ever since I woke up naked in a tree house surrounded by women wearing corn husks over their tits and asking me if I wanted to shuck them."

Momentarily speechless, I watched as she seemed to replay the memory in her mind.

"Nineteen sixty-six was a year to remember."

My father appeared equally as disturbed as I did, and it made me wonder if it was somehow the first he'd heard of this story. I couldn't imagine it was.

"This isn't a commune," I finally said. Not that it mattered.

"What would you call it?" she asked sternly.

"It's a house. With people living in it. It doesn't need a label."

"You Millennials and your lack of labels," she scoffed.

I managed to not correct her use of the term *Millennial*—though I wasn't one and it was killing me to be mistaken for one, but there was no use engaging with her about this any longer.

"So, how long are you all staying?" I asked, trying not to sound like any length of time would be too long.

"Mom only wanted to stay a couple of days," my dad said, putting a hand on my shoulder. But I didn't have time to feel much relief because he followed it with, "But if we made the drive up, figured we might as well make it a real visit so we can spend some time together."

"Oh." I hesitated. "Well, I'm pretty busy with school and stuff, so I don't know how much time I'll have this week."

"Which is why we're staying through Sunday." My mom reached up to my face and cupped my cheeks in her hands. Then she stood on her toes so she could reach to give me a kiss on my forehead. She obviously meant *next* Sunday, and there was nothing I could do about it but try to embrace the fact that I'd be spending the next week with my family.

There were certainly worse things in the world, though right now I struggled to think of many.

VERONICA

After catching up with Owen's family for a little while, I left Jimi and Professor Ted to listen—or *jam*, as they called it—to Owen's band. Surprisingly, they weren't the only ones who seemed to be enjoying the music.

Turned out the Kenso Gummers had learned a few real songs in addition to the eerie melodies they'd been playing. Every so often they'd bust out with something remotely recognizable, though not exactly identifiable.

I was heading upstairs to check on things in the "haunted" room and see if anyone had earned a free T-shirt yet, when I heard Wynter yell, "You get one try! This isn't a fucking piñata at a kid's birthday party."

When I got to the landing, I saw Owen's mom and dad leaving the room, looking more frightened of Wynter than they did of whatever they'd experienced in the room.

"That one means business," Claudette said as she approached me at the top of the stairs.

"Yeah." I hesitated. "She's kind of... an acquired taste." One I hadn't acquired yet and didn't plan to. "Sorry about that. She used to live here, and she just showed up earlier. I think Owen figured it would be more of a pain to get her to leave than give her something to do."

RJ pointed back toward her. "She's wrapping people's faces up with her veil like she's trying to suffocate them when they leave the room."

"I should probably address that at some point," I said. "Though, it *is* made of lace, so it's not really urgent." Any excuse to avoid interacting with Wynter was one I'd take, I thought, as I watched her pull the veil over some woman's head and wrap it rather tightly around her neck.

Then Wynter pulled her close and kissed her through the black lace, her tongue seeming to trace the floral pattern that was pressed to the woman's cheek.

I weaved through the crowd upstairs to get to her, using only the flashing lights to see in front of me. Once I made it to her, I pulled her back so she and the woman separated.

"Jesus, Wynter! What the fuck are you doing?"

"Ouch! What the fuck am *I* doing? What are *you* doing?"

"You can't make out with the guests. Or try to strangle them," I added, almost as an afterthought.

"I can if they're my girlfriend."

"Your girlfriend?"

"Yes, my girlfriend." Wynter's posture told me she was annoyed, as did her tone. "Summer, meet... I'm sorry, what was your name again? Wasn't it a letter? Like *Y* or *X* or something near the end of the alphabet?"

"Vee. It's Vee," I said, feeling my lips pressing together because I was worried what might come out of them next.

"Oh, right. That's it. Vee is the lady of the household," Wynter explained.

"Pleasure to meet you, my lady." Then Summer—who I just now realized was dating someone named Wynter because why would I expect anything else—curtsied before me like I was seventeenth-century royalty.

Chapter Twenty-Six

OWEN

By the time ten o'clock rolled around, my backyard had turned into something that resembled a cross between a frat party and a...

"Are those tents?"

I struggled to make out what I saw because what light we had didn't make it past the first third of the yard or so.

When I'd asked the question, I wasn't sure who exactly I was speaking to. I was surrounded by so many people, and most I hadn't ever met. It almost felt like I'd asked the question to the universe rather than one person in particular, but the person who responded surprised me more than I'd been ready for.

"Add it to the list of infractions."

It took me longer than it should have to process the comment and its intended meaning, but once I did, I knew exactly who'd said it without having to look. But I did anyway.

"I'm not sure if you're aware, but this is an exclusive event," I said to Mrs. Aberdeen. "You need a ticket to get in here."

"Oh, I'm fully aware. And I find all of this"—she waved around at the scene before her—"disgusting."

And for once I couldn't blame her as I noticed a guy toward the back of the yard probably peeing into a bush. At least Gimli was safe at Brody and Aamee's apartment, so I didn't have to worry about him escaping. Or worse . . .

"This is a haunted house," I told her, hoping to make it sound like an innocent way to entertain the community.

Eyeing the pop-up bar that Brody and Drew had staged in my yard, she said, "Looks more like you're running a homeless shelter. What happened? You run out of room inside?"

"The tents are one of the attractions." It wasn't a complete lie—not that I cared—since now people who'd finished in the house and migrated outside for a drink were walking around the tents trying to peer in through the mesh to see what was inside. "Also, if you don't have a ticket, you need to leave."

She reached into a brown leather bag she had around her shoulder and pulled out a paper.

"Good thing I bought one early, then."

I figured it had probably been her son who bought one and printed it for her since she didn't strike me as the most tech-savvy person.

She gave me what I could only describe as a sneer when I thanked her for supporting the cause—the one she knew helped fund the money to pay my taxes.

"If the preliminary ticket sales are any indication, we should be able to make enough money in time." I had no idea if that was true, but I sure hoped so. Either way, I wanted to give Mrs. Aberdeen her fair share of my anxiety.

"Not if I get this place shut down for selling liquor without a license first."

She seemed pleased with herself, so I was happy to make her aware that the drinks were mocktails and contained nothing other than juices and sodas.

"Want one? Shirley Temple is always a good classic. Though you do strike me as more of a *Dirty* Shirley woman."

And then something happened that was so surprising I wondered if she'd done it intentionally just to throw me off my game.

She laughed.

And that was when I knew for absolute certain that Mrs. Aberdeen was straight-up nuts.

VERONICA

By the time the last group of people had made it through the house and had their drinks in the yard, it was almost two in the morning. Which I guessed was a good thing since it meant we probably made more money because we'd sold tickets at the door in addition to the ones Cody and Nattie had sold in advance. We'd done our best to fit the door sales in between the timed tickets, but it inevitably meant that some of the people had to wait a bit.

There was also a wait to get into the haunted room because most of the people lasted almost the full twenty-three minutes, and a few even made it the full time. We took their pictures to post on the Instagram page Cody and Nattie were running, which we hoped would help develop even more intrigue about the house. Including Halloween itself, we had four more nights of the attraction to generate money.

Some of us had suggested we add Fridays to the schedule,

but Owen thought it would be too much to get ready on a day most of us had school or work, and he didn't want to inconvenience anyone more than he already had.

Somehow, he didn't realize our little Scooby Gang lived for this type of thing. If they managed to help Owen raise the money he needed, it would be their version of winning a Super Bowl. I wouldn't be surprised if someone designed rings for all of us to commemorate the occasion eternally.

Once the last paying customer left, we told our friends they could head home, despite them offering to help clean up. I felt grateful for these people more than I could've ever expressed with words. Luckily, it wasn't something I'd ever need to. They all already knew.

After saying good night to everyone, roommates and non-roommates included, Owen and I ascended the stairs to our room in silence.

I couldn't be sure if the quiet was due to the tension we'd been feeling or if we were both too exhausted to speak. But both of us climbed the steps slowly before collapsing onto our respective sides of the bed. I heard Owen's shoes hit the floor and figured he must've kicked them off. I did the same and then slid up farther so my head could rest on the pillow.

"I wonder how much we made," I said, my gaze fixed on the ceiling above me.

Owen flipped over so he was facing me, which caused me to let my head fall to the side so I could see him. His normally floppy hair was damp with sweat, and his cheeks were flushed a shade of red. His chest expanded with a few deep breaths before he spoke.

"It's not important," he said, moving a strand of wet hair out of where it had fallen in front of his eyes.

Was this man crazier than I thought? "What do you mean? It's definitely important." I realized then that maybe he'd begun to give up, and the possibility caused a fear inside myself that I hadn't noticed was there until something had brought it to the surface.

Propping his head onto his hand as he rested on his elbow, he reached out to take my hand, hesitating a moment before he seemed to realize I wasn't going to resist his touch.

I wasn't sure I ever would.

"It's just... I can only do what I can do. I can't be upset if we don't raise enough money to keep this place because it's not for me to decide. It's up to the universe. Or God. Or whoever dictates the path our lives should take."

"Why are you philosophizing right now?"

He laughed softly, but it sounded as hollow as I would've expected a laugh to sound right about now.

"It's what I do."

"No, it's not." I knew we had different ways of looking at the world sometimes, but I hadn't realized we'd differed on this. "So, what does that mean exactly? That you're just gonna fold before you even look at all your cards?"

"I'm not folding." I could tell from his tone that I'd pushed a button I hadn't meant to. Probably like he'd done to me earlier. "But I'm done betting on myself having the chance of ending up with four of a kind when I don't even have a pair in my hand."

"You don't know that yet. Maybe we're close to what we need for the taxes from tonight alone."

The way Owen's lips struggled to turn up into even a partial smile told me he didn't believe a word of that. But instead of telling me that, he said, "I'm so sorry about earlier,

Vee. That's one of the reasons I can't worry about this anymore. If it's meant to happen, it will. But all of this stresses me out in a way that makes me act like a douchenozzle to the people I love—the people who are trying to help me."

Somehow that made me laugh. "You're not a douchenozzle. You're human. We all take things out on the people we love most because we know they'll still love us despite it."

I'd been upset with Owen, but it had been more of a momentary reaction than anything else. Owen was a sweet, caring guy who, like he said, was under an immense amount of pressure.

But that was the only Owen I knew. Ever since we'd met, we'd been sailing on a sea filled with storm after storm. And though our ship had capsized a time or two, we were still swimming together.

"That's nice of you to say, but you shouldn't have to put up with me when I act like that."

"I didn't put up with you." I almost laughed at how that sounded. "You walked out, and we barely spoke until a few minutes ago. I think we both needed some time to cool off, that's all."

"That's all?" His raised eyebrow told me he didn't believe that.

So I gave him a kiss and nodded against him. "Yup. I feel like we have to pick our battles." And this just wasn't one I thought was worth wasting any energy on. We all got emotional or angry, and I wouldn't want Owen getting overly angry when my emotions got the best of me. "I mean, it's not like you went out and married someone else."

"Aww, that was a low blow," he said. Then he rolled onto me, pinning my hips beneath him as he sat on me.

As he leaned in to tickle my sides and breathe in my ear, I squirmed beneath him as I tried to escape . . . but not actually wanting to.

"Okay, okay, mercy," I huffed, trying to catch my breath.

At that, Owen stopped his sweet torture and looked down at me with eyes so warm and kind, I wondered if I might melt from his gaze alone.

"Thank you," he said with a slight cock of his head, like he was trying to understand something about me that he'd been struggling to.

"For what?"

"For fighting with me and not against me. I needed that. I need *you*."

I let the words settle into me after he said them, like my mind needed a moment to *feel* what he'd said in addition to hearing it.

"You have me," I said.

With that, he planted kisses on my lips and forehead and neck. And when he moved lower—over my collarbone and down to the sensitive flesh of my breast just above my nipple, I knew I'd made the right decision to let Owen slide on this one.

We both needed this. Needed each other. And I was glad we had that.

Chapter Twenty-Seven

VERONICA

I was heading out of the Preston building when my phone rang. I hadn't meant to leave the sound on, so I was relieved it hadn't gone off in class.

Dr. Mantilli never hid the fact that she hated phones. She'd said that if we couldn't be bothered to leave them off during class, then we'd never be able to leave them off in the courtroom. I thought the correlation was fairly weak, but my opinion didn't matter much.

But what surprised me more than getting a phone call was whose name I saw on the screen when I finally managed to fish the phone out of my bag.

"June?" I'm sure she recognized the surprise in my voice because I'd definitely heard it. "Is everything okay?"

I heard her laugh, though it wasn't very loud. "Yes, yes, everything's fine with me. That's sweet of you to ask. I was calling to ask you the same, though. Have you and Owen managed to figure out the whole tax issue?"

I hadn't spoken to her since that time we'd sat down to

chat, and it hadn't occurred to me to update her on the status of everything, especially since it wasn't her problem, and I didn't want her to worry about us any more than she already had. But since she'd called and asked...

"Not exactly. I think we're still about four thousand short, according to the tally we did after the official opening of the haunted house."

"I feel like there's a lot to discuss there. You opened a haunted house?"

"Oh, um, yeah." I wondered if she'd view marketing her former home as a haunted house as offensive now that I'd said it aloud. "Owen's a big fan of Halloween, and we were originally only going to do a party, but we figured we could use the money, so it kind of spiraled into something more."

I waited for her to reply and took a seat on a nearby bench.

"Minnie would've loved that," she finally said. I imagined she was smiling on the other end of the line, and the image of it made me smile too.

"Really?"

"Absolutely. I'd like to think she was there for it in spirit." Laughing again, she said, "Which I guess is appropriate since it's a haunted attraction. If I didn't think I'd have a heart attack and die on your property, I'd come check it out for myself."

I wasn't sure what to say to that.

June must've noticed my silence, so she said, "I'm kidding. Well, not really. I've never really been a fan of people jumping out at me or anything of the sort, but I'm not about to die just yet. At least not that I know of."

That made me let out a breath I hadn't realized I'd been holding. "That's good."

"What I can do is put some flyers or something at the café

if you're still selling tickets. I'm assuming you're running this through Halloween?"

"Yeah! Yes, that would be amazing if you could put some out."

June's café got a ton of traffic, so having the flyers there with the QR code that linked right to the ticket purchase would definitely help get the word out even more.

"Of course. I'm happy to help however I can."

It was a nice thing to say, especially since I knew she'd meant it. But I couldn't help feeling like we'd already asked more of June than we'd be able to repay. Though I was pretty sure she didn't feel that way.

"Any chance you're free tonight for dinner?"

OWEN

Wednesday was my only day completely off from classes, and I usually worked at the hardware store most of the day. But when Mark had heard my family was visiting, he'd offered—or more like forced—me to take off early.

It wasn't that I didn't want to spend time with my parents and grandparents, but I needed the extra cash work would've provided. Still, I couldn't turn the offer down without feeling ungrateful, so I thanked him, grabbed some supplies I needed for the house, and headed home early.

When I arrived around two, I found my parents, grandparents, Inez, Nattie, and Roddie in the kitchen surrounded by today's canine unit: Buffy, Kramer, Phoebe, and Fury.

Of course, Gimli wasn't far away, but since he was the

only one allowed to sit on the furniture, I found him curled up in his favorite chair near the window in the next room. It didn't take me long to realize why all the dogs had congregated in this spot—my grandpa was standing over a huge pot of chili, stirring and tasting, tasting and stirring.

"Would you get away from that?" my grandma scolded. "It's not ready yet. Doesn't need spit all over it."

I expected my grandfather to snap back with a witty comeback of his own, but a knock at the door stopped him before he got the chance to. And then the doorbell rang a few seconds after that.

"Coming," I called, wondering what the urgency was.

When I opened it, I was staring right into the angry face of Mrs. Aberdeen. I felt like a teenager who'd walked into his room to find his parents standing there ready to launch into a diatribe about how they'd found a homemade bong and a bottle of Jack Daniels under my bed.

I knew that look because that exact scenario had happened to me right after my sixteenth birthday.

"Hi, Mrs. Aberdeen. What can I do for you?"

She stepped inside without waiting for the invitation she wasn't going to get.

"What you can do for me," she said, her eyes somehow narrowing even more without closing completely, "is take down your social media page."

I hadn't realized that everyone had followed me into the living room. They must've heard it was Mrs. Aberdeen at the door and came in to find out what was happening.

"I'm sorry?"

Roddie's eyes caught mine when I looked his way. Evidently, we were both thinking the same thing. Roddie's doggie day care page had somehow been discovered. But I needed to hear it from her to be sure.

"What social media page? You're going to have to be more specific. I have a Facebook page, Twitter account, Instagram," I said, counting them off on my fingers. "Oh, and Snapchat, TikTok, and what was that one everyone used when we were in like fifth grade? Oh! Chat Roulette. That's the one! I don't know if I still have it on my phone, but the account still exists, ya know? Those things are impossible—"

"Don't be smart," she said. "The one that portrays me as a petty old bitch."

Roddie leaned in to me, his arms folded casually over his chest. "You think she's confusing your account with her own?"

"I heard that," Mrs. Aberdeen squawked.

"You were supposed to," Roddie said back in a singsongy voice.

Mrs. Aberdeen scoffed at him and pulled the silk shawl tighter around herself. "Well, one of you knows what I'm talking about, and if I had the stupid thing myself, I'd be able to show you." She pointed her finger toward each one of us as she spoke, reminding me of a second hand as it made its way around a clock. "But I'm sure one of you, if not all of you, are behind this, and I'll have you know I've already notified my lawyer so he can look into a case against you."

I gulped, probably too loudly. "A case? For what?"

The laugh that came from her was sharp, cutting in a way that was difficult to describe. "Libel, of course. You're defaming my good name in this town with all your pictures."

Shaking my head, I tried to imagine what she could even be thinking of, but nothing came to mind. I'd thought initially she'd been talking about Roddie's business account, but it seemed now like that would've been preferable to whatever she was describing now.

"I'm sorry, but I honestly don't know what pictures you're talking about."

"No?" she replied in a way that made it clear she thought I was full of shit. "So you didn't take a picture of me swatting a broom at that bat thing you have on my tree? Or photo-edit my face onto the witch from *The Wizard of Oz*?"

"No, I didn't."

"I think you mean Photoshop," Inez chimed in.

"Was it even the bad witch?" Roddie asked. "Because the other one is sort of a compliment, right?" He looked around at the rest of us for confirmation.

"What's going on here, Owen?" my grandmother asked, suddenly appearing by my side.

I almost expected her to have her shotgun when I looked over to her. Instead, she was armed with only her piercing glare and witty tongue. Mrs. Aberdeen didn't know it yet, but she'd met her match.

"I'm sorry, who are you?" Mrs. Aberdeen asked.

"Jimi. This one's grandmother."

"Jimmy's a man's name."

My mom muttered "uh-oh" beside me and then asked my dad if we should do anything. I didn't hear him answer, but I doubted there was much we could do anyway. My grandmother wasn't going to listen to anyone other than herself. She never had.

"No one asked you," she said, still sounding fairly calm. "But I do have something to ask you. What is it you're bothering my sweet grandson about?"

Her comment would've been embarrassing if she'd been

speaking to anyone I'd cared about. But since it was directed at Janice Aberdeen, I internally fist pumped the air.

Go, Grandma!

"Your grandson and his friends have been starting illegal businesses in a residential neighborhood and portraying me as a bitter old woman."

"Aren't you?" my grandma asked.

Mrs. Aberdeen's head jerked back like the question was a ridiculous one. "Of course not."

"Sure you are. We all are. Those of us of a certain age are all bitter about something."

Mrs. Aberdeen appeared as though she was going to say something to counter that but decided against it for some reason.

Leave it to my grandma to make this woman speechless.

After a minute or so, my grandmother said, "I think you're mistaken, so you should probably take your accusations elsewhere."

Mrs. Aberdeen pressed her lips together so hard that they wrinkled even more. When she finally relaxed them, she said only, "I'm not mistaken. I saw it with my own eyes. But I'll leave anyway."

And with that, she turned toward the door.

Natalia stepped forward, placing a hand on Mrs. Aberdeen's shoulder as she escorted her out. "Janice, I really do think you're mistaken. Are you sure you took your medication this morning?"

"What do you know about my medication?" she snapped. "You got a picture of that too? Maybe you can ask your audience or whatever to guess what my diagnosis is."

"Okay, yeah," Natalia said quickly. "I think you should

probably take a nap when you get home."

"It's five thirty."

"There's nothing wrong with listening to your body. It's one o'clock somewhere."

That definitely was not the saying, and while I appreciated Natalia escorting her out, she was acting weird as hell. Even for Natalia.

So as soon as our lovely neighbor had left and the door was shut behind her, I turned my attention to Natalia.

"What the hell did you do?"

Chapter Twenty-Eight

VERONICA

I'd texted Owen a few times throughout the day and even called him to let him know that I'd invited June over for dinner, but I hadn't heard from him yet. Not that I thought it would be a big deal, necessarily, but I didn't want Owen and his family to be surprised when she showed up.

It turned out I was the one who was surprised, because when I got home, I found Owen arguing with Natalia and Cody. What was stranger was that Owen's family and Inez and Roddie were sitting in the living room watching them like they'd bought tickets to some sort of sporting event.

I dropped my bag on the floor and took everything in for a moment as I tried to make sense of the scene taking place before me.

Natalia and Cody were standing together on one side of the room, and Owen was on the other, scrolling through his phone and muttering random things like, "You really said she measured the length of our grass with a plastic ruler she stole from a child walking home from school?"

"She did that!" Cody argued adamantly, and then with much less enthusiasm, he added, "The measuring part at least."

Looking up from his phone, Owen said, "So you're *not* sure she pilfered it from an elementary schooler?"

"Not a hundred percent, no," Cody admitted. "Though it would help if I knew what pilfered meant."

Owen shoved his phone into his pocket and tugged at his hair. By the looks of it, it probably wasn't the first time he'd done it tonight.

Walking over to Owen, I took what I felt like was my place beside him. Right now it was two against one, and I'd always take the underdog's side. Especially when the underdog was Owen.

"What's wrong?"

"Our friends are completely insane is what's wrong."

When no one said anything to expound upon that, I asked, "Can someone elaborate, please?"

"Owen's being completely unreasonable," Nattie said to me. "We were only trying to help."

Famous last words.

"What did you do?" I said the words slowly, like I was removing a Band-Aid and was worried it would hurt if I pulled it off too quickly.

Nattie threw her arms up dramatically before letting them fall abruptly to her sides. "This is what we get for trying to help," she said, as if the throwaway comment served as some sort of explanation.

I had no choice but to look at Owen. Grabbing his bicep, I said, "Can you please tell me what happened?"

With that, he turned to face me, letting out a frustrated

breath before speaking. "Gladly. These two," he said, gesturing toward Cody and Nattie, "decided to start an Instagram account—"

"We didn't *decide* to start it," Cody interrupted. "You asked us to."

Owen's head turned toward them like something out of *The Exorcist*. "I didn't ask you to bully Mrs. Aberdeen on social media."

"Well, she'd have to be on social media herself for us to do that," Nattie said. "All we did was document her actions that were already public in an even more public way. We can't help it if our followers took a liking to her."

"Yeah," Cody said. "We gave the people what they wanted. You can't be mad at us for that."

"I can definitely be mad," Owen said. "We have enough to deal with without adding to the list of shit she has to complain about."

"Let her complain," Nattie said. "She can't do anything. She has no right to privacy when everything we publicized was already public to begin with."

Owen's family hadn't said anything, but they might as well have had buckets of popcorn on their laps as they watched the three of them with rapt attention.

I looked to Owen, who appeared absolutely defeated, not only because of this conversation, but most likely because of everything that had transpired over the past couple of months.

"She might be right about that," I told him. "Can I see what they posted?"

Reluctantly, he reached into his pocket and pulled out his phone, unlocking it before handing it to me.

I took a minute or so to look through the account Cody

and Nattie had been running. Originally it had begun as a promotional account for the haunted house, but then they'd made a joke about the biggest attraction being the witch next door. There was a picture of Mrs. Aberdeen pointing at them—and seemingly yelling—on her front lawn.

She'd no doubt seen the phone and one of them taking her picture. Then I saw some others: the grass measuring one, which was on *our* lawn, and a couple of photos that were drawings that appeared to be done by some of their followers.

There were a few other pictures of Mrs. Aberdeen peeking through the bushes and even one of her meeting with Rich Cappello in her driveway. I wondered if that was before or after Owen and Cody had found out that Rich was her son. Not that any of that mattered.

I scrolled a bit more and looked at some of the comments—most of which were funnier than the pictures themselves—before handing the phone back to Owen. Everyone was quiet, probably waiting for me to give my semiprofessional opinion.

"As much as it causes me physical pain to say, I think Nattie's right. There aren't any pictures of her inside her home or even in her car. She was outside for all of them. She can't expect any right of privacy when she's in plain view of the public."

Cody and Nattie threw their hands up in triumphant celebration, high-fiving, fist-bumping, and hugging out their apparent win. Once they were done with their victory dance, Cody turned to Owen and me again.

"We haven't even told you the best part yet! We were waiting until the whole gang was here again for Halloween night, but we may as well do it now so you don't freak out any more than you already have."

Owen's posture relaxed slightly, but I could tell he was still stressed by the whole thing. Even though Mrs. Aberdeen probably wouldn't win any libel case against us should she actually decide to file one, what Cody and Nattie had done would only make whatever time we had to interact with her that much worse.

"The *best part*?" Owen said dryly. "What could possibly be better than gaslighting our already cranky neighbor?"

The two partners in crime smiled at each other before they seemed to silently decide that Nattie could share whatever their big news was.

"So," she said, not bothering to hide the excitement in her voice. "I know you thought a GoFundMe would be a bad idea, but it turns out it was an amazing one!"

"Thanks to Mrs. Aberdeen," Cody added. "We didn't want to look like bullies picking on some innocent, elderly neighbor, and since everyone knew the haunted house was to help raise money for the taxes, we added a GoFundMe link to our bio. People had already asked where to donate because they wanted us to stay just so we could continue to piss off Blabberdeen."

"How much did you raise?" Owen asked cautiously.

Cody and Nattie glanced at each other again before Nattie continued.

"A lot," she said with a raise of her eyebrow that made her seem humble about the whole thing.

"Yeah," Cody said. "People either really love you or they really hate Blabberdeen. We started a couple of weeks ago with a few hundred followers, which we thought was pretty good, but then the followers were tagging people in our posts, and then they were sharing stories about their own experiences with crazy neighbors. And it just kinda . . . grew."

I could tell by Owen's expression that he hadn't noticed how many followers they had when he'd looked at the pictures they'd posted. I hadn't either. We'd probably been too focused on the content to pay attention to anything else.

"Grew to what?" Owen asked slowly.

"Last time I checked, earlier this morning, we were at a little over twenty-eight thousand," Cody told him.

"Actually," I said, looking up from Owen's phone, "it's almost thirty now." I widened my eyes when I looked closely at their bio. "You started a YouTube channel!"

"Yeah, didn't we tell you that?" Cody asked in a way that told me he knew the answer. "We told them, didn't we?" he said to Nattie. "I could swear . . ."

"I thought so," Nattie said with a shrug. "It started as edited videos of the haunted house and the Room of Doom, but once Aberdeen made an appearance . . . Oh, well, that's not important."

"Nope," Cody agreed. "The important thing is that it turns out when you ask tens of thousands of people to donate as little as one dollar and even half of them do it, you end up with thousands of dollars." He said it casually, but I could tell he was struggling to maintain his nonchalant attitude. Inside, he was probably bursting with excitement.

"How many thousands of dollars?" Owen and I asked practically in unison. I heard the awe in both of our voices—the complete disbelief.

We waited, seemingly unable to speak as Nattie searched on her phone. "We're currently up to eleven thousand five hundred and sixty-three dollars."

"Eleven thousand dollars," Owen said, his face

expressionless even though I imagined he was filled with emotion. "We were only four thousand away from paying off the taxes."

Nattie smiled. "I know. And we're planning to leave it open until Halloween night's haunted house is done. Now that you know about it, we can promote it even more. We'll put some QR codes around the house."

"I can't take anyone else's money. I already have more than enough to pay the taxes."

"It's not taking the money when they're giving it to you," I said.

Owen's mom, Claudette, spoke up, and for the first time since I'd arrived home, it occurred to me that his family must know now about the tax money.

"Honey, I think you should take it. It's not like you can return what they already gave you."

"Yeah," Cody agreed. "And we had the goal amount on there, and they passed that a long time ago, so they know you don't *need* the money anymore."

"Maybe they saw from the pictures what a piece of—" RJ's comment was interrupted when Claudette elbowed him. "What a fixer-upper this house is and thought you could use the money to work on it."

"Maybe," Owen admitted.

"Really, Owen," his grandfather said. "I've lived long enough to know that it's not often that people offer their help to you unconditionally. Usually they expect something in return, even if it's not until years later. So if people are willing to make your life easier now without making their own harder, you should take 'em up on it."

"I doubt they're missin' any meals over donating a couple

of bucks," Jimi said. "It's a lot of money to *you* when it's all put together, but it's not a lot to them or they wouldn't have given it to a stranger."

Owen took my hand and looked over at me. "What do you think, Vee?"

It seemed like his decision depended heavily on my own opinion of the situation, and I didn't know how I felt about that. On one hand, it felt like a compliment that Owen valued my opinion, but on the other . . . well, *with great power comes great responsibility.*

"I think you should take it if they're willing to offer it," I told him because it was what I truly believed.

Owen was so giving of himself so much of the time. There was no harm, I thought, in allowing others to give to him for a change—to let them make things easier instead of harder.

He looked weary, like he'd just woken up from a nightmare and was scared that if he closed his eyes, he might have another bad dream. Glancing around the room at all of us, he breathed in deeply before finally taking a seat on a nearby chair and allowing his muscles to relax.

"Okay," he said, finally sounding sure of himself. "Guess I should go pay off those taxes."

OWEN

After accounting for the money we'd earned from the haunted house so far and paying my friends back for what they'd put out for supplies and decorations, I could easily pay off the tax debt and still have money to start paying back what my friends had loaned me. Once I'd fully accepted that my biggest concern was no longer one, I relaxed enough to call the rest of the gang so I could tell them my news.

I got a hold of as many of them as possible and suggested we meet at Drew and Brody's new bar to celebrate. It hadn't officially opened yet, and wouldn't for some time, but what better way to christen it than with our group of friends—and June, who'd come over for dinner and had been so happy to hear I could pay off the debt she said there was no way she'd miss the celebration.

Unfortunately, Drew decided against it, not wanting to have everyone over to a building that was currently being renovated and had no working plumbing at the moment. I had a feeling he just didn't trust us not to dance on the bar or fuck up any progress that had already been made.

So I invited them over to my place—since it would remain *my* place—so we could celebrate with beer and s'mores.

Inez went out to get the ingredients for the s'mores along with some other snacks and drinks, and within an hour, everyone had arrived. Toby and Carter cuddled next to each other on one of the logs, and the other couples found a space for themselves too. Sophia and Drew laid out a blanket on the lawn so my parents and grandparents could have some of the chairs, and Aamee and Brody shared a fold-up beach chair, which barely fit one of them, let alone both. And I sat on a tree stump with Vee on my lap and a gooey marshmallow on a stick in my hand.

And suddenly, as I looked around at everyone, I found myself filled with so much love and happiness, it felt as if my soul was expanding with it.

I'd been so wrapped up in my own bullshit, it was then—surrounded by my closest friends, my girlfriend, and my family, and June, who'd become like family—that I realized how lucky I truly was. Without the fog of getting out from under an enormous debt, I could finally appreciate everything I had instead of focusing on everything I didn't.

And then, between everyone's laughter and the crackle of fire, I heard it: the sound of a chainsaw or something like it coming from Aberdeen's side of the yard. I couldn't see what was going on because of the dark and all the bushes she had lining the fence, so it wasn't until I saw the large branch that hung over the fence begin to shake that I realized what was happening.

"What the . . ."

I hadn't gotten to finish my thought before the branch, which was probably about ten inches in diameter, came crashing down onto the fence. It smashed against the metal with its weight and then tipped back onto Mrs. Aberdeen's side of the property, squishing one of her precious shrubs and ripping off some of the branches on its way to the ground.

"My bats," I heard Roddie yell before I saw him sprint past me over to the scene of the crime.

Once I got close enough to the fence and was able to see what was going on, I saw Rich Cappello up on a ladder with a chainsaw in his hand and a look of absolute satisfaction plastered across his face. When he spotted me, he held the chainsaw high like a trophy as he balanced on the ladder.

"It's gettin' cold lately. Thought I might chop up some firewood for the upcoming winter. Sure you don't wanna sell the place?" he said, sounding like he already knew the answer.

He and his mother had tried their best to make it miserable for us, but the joke was on them.

"Not necessary," I told him. "I'm going over to the

township building tomorrow to pay the tax debt."

"Maybe while we're at it," Roddie said, "we'll put in a complaint that you cut down the branch that wasn't technically yours."

Mrs. Aberdeen scoffed. "Well, it's certainly not yours! The tree is on *my* property. Just because part of it's hanging onto your air space doesn't make it your property. And I'm tired of all those bats flying around."

"Can I at least have the bat house back?" Roddie asked, sounding like a kid who just got his lunch taken from a schoolyard bully. "I'd like to put it up somewhere else."

She and Cappello exchanged glances like they were giving Roddie's request some thought, even though I'm sure all of us knew they weren't. Cappello looked down at the branch below him on their side of the fence.

"I'm thinking we'll just hang onto it. It's on our side of the fence now, so I guess it makes it ours," he said with a smug grin.

"That's theft," Vee pointed out.

"Only if you have proof it was yours to begin with," Cappello snapped back.

I saw Cody step closer to the fence. "We do have proof. It's on the YouTube channel we made of your mom!" he yelled up to Cappello loudly.

After he'd finished speaking, Cody slinked back a bit, probably in response to how his comment sounded even though it was entirely accurate.

As Cappello descended the ladder, images of a rung breaking and him accidentally cutting his arm off with the saw flashed in my mind. Or maybe the ladder would tip back from the tree, and he'd fall slowly, like in one of those old cartoons, onto Mrs. Aberdeen, who'd be crushed under the weight of her son and the saw he was holding.

Unfortunately, he made it down unscathed.

"You know," my grandmother said, "you should be ashamed of yourselves for instigating fights with children."

"They aren't children," Aberdeen said. "If they're old enough to own a house, they should be mature enough to deal with everything that comes with home ownership."

"Like dealing with bitchy neighbors?"

Mrs. Aberdeen looked like she'd been slapped, but that was nothing compared to what my grandma was capable of. She could give someone verbal whiplash before they even realized they'd been in an accident.

"You calling me a bitch, *Jim*?"

When Aberdeen stepped closer to the fence, my grandmother did as well. They glared at each other through the holes in the metal like animals caged beside each other.

I heard Aamee say her money was on Jimi.

"I call it like I see it," my grandmother told Aberdeen.

My grandpa moved to stand beside her and said, "She's not worth it, Jimi."

That got Cappello involved too. "Don't you dare try to determine my mother's worth."

"Oh, stop overreacting. No one's impressed with your macho bullshit."

"And no one's impressed with your wife's macho bullshit," Cappello told him.

Suddenly *Hold my beer* was no longer just an expression, because my dad said it to my mom before literally handing her his beer and then scaling the seven-foot fence like he'd been practicing for a prison escape.

But my dad was smart enough not to attack Cappello first. Instead, he'd verbally slay him until the other man hit first.

But I didn't stick around to watch it escalate from my yard.

I muttered a frustrated "Jesus Christ" before climbing up and over the fence myself.

"Dad, leave it alone."

"Owen," Roddie called. "Can you grab the bat house while you're over there?" When I didn't respond, I heard him say, "You know what, it's okay. I'll grab it myself."

Then Roddie ran toward the front of the house, presumably so he could enter from Aberdeen's driveway so he didn't need to hop the fence.

I grabbed my dad's chest and tried to move him toward the front yard to get him away from there. Surprisingly, he let me move him somewhat, but he continued talking shit like a high school lineman until Cappello snapped and charged at him like . . . well, also like a high school lineman.

"RJ!" my grandma called along with my mom, who was also screaming his name. Not because they were worried about him getting hurt but because they were probably worried he'd hurt Rich Cappello. And since we were also on Aberdeen's property and not our own, that didn't bode well for any future litigation we might face.

By the time I got my dad to the front lawn, everyone else was already there, including some of the neighborhood who must've heard the screaming and come out to see what the commotion was. I recognized most of them from the faux neighborhood watch meeting, but I was too focused on what was happening on my front lawn—and Mrs. Aberdeen's, since my dad and Cappello were rolling all over the fucking place.

I did remember Mrs. Eisenbach, though, who'd spotted June in the crowd and gone over to give her a hug. I tried to break up the scuffle, but there was no way I could pull these guys apart on my own, so I didn't even try. Instead, I extracted myself from that part of the yard and jogged over to where June, Vee, and Mrs. Eisenbach were talking.

A few seconds later, another woman emerged from Aberdeen's home, and it didn't take me long to figure out that it must've been Cappello's wife.

She was screaming, "Dicky! Dicky, what are you doing?"

"I love that his wife calls him Dicky," I said with a laugh.

"She's no peach either," June said. "Last time I saw the woman, she told me I should be ashamed of my lifestyle and that I should've never had a home in a community where children could witness my 'taboo tastes.'"

"That's awful," Vee said.

"Uh-huh. And what's worse is the coward said it in my café because she knew I wouldn't say or do anything to her there."

I looked over at June, who was still staring at Dicky's wife.

"Well, we're not in the café now, are we?"

"No," she said. "We're not."

Then June walked slowly across the lawn and punched Cappello's wife square in the face.

Chapter Twenty-Nine

VERONICA

What turned out to be a pretty interesting brawl ended when someone finally called the police. Though most of the physical altercations had ended before they got there, people were still arguing when the cops arrived. They didn't get very far interviewing people since we all basically had different stories, but then Nattie had loudly proclaimed that she'd filmed most of it, and it was already up on YouTube if anyone wanted to watch.

Which they did.

The police ultimately decided that there wasn't any one person to blame, and everyone who'd participated in the fights had done so willingly. And since no one was severely hurt, they agreed to let the neighborhood off with a warning that, should this happen again in the future, there would be charges pressed.

I guessed they didn't want the extra paperwork on a Wednesday night, but they did agree to issue Mrs. Aberdeen a citation for cutting down the branch that hung into Owen's yard. Not because it was his property, but because she'd destroyed the habitat of an endangered species.

Roddie was giddy with excitement when he'd heard that because not only did she need to pay the fine, but she was also ordered to put up another bat house on her own property to replace it and reimburse Roddie for the money he'd spent on his, which meant he could get another one. And this one, he'd promised Mrs. Aberdeen, would be as close to her property as he could get it without touching any of it.

Owen and I woke up early the next morning to make sure we could get to the township building before we had to be in class. We wanted to make sure that the taxes were taken care of as soon as possible—not only to be done with all of it for our own sake, but also so we could inform Mrs. Aberdeen and Rich Cappello that any future efforts to make our lives here miserable or try to push us out would be futile.

"We did it," Owen said to me after we dropped the letter we'd written into Mrs. Aberdeen's mailbox.

We had no doubt she'd share the news with her son as soon as she read it.

"We did. Or maybe Nattie and Cody did."

Since they posted the video of the neighborhood fight, people had donated even more money, pleading with Owen to put an addition on the house so he could get some more roommates or use some of the money to put a kennel in the backyard so Roddie's business venture could be a little more official.

When it was all said and done, and Owen had paid his friends back for every last cent they'd contributed, it was almost difficult to believe all of this was actually over. What had felt like an impossible undertaking when we'd first seen the tax bill had somehow proven we could accomplish almost anything when our group worked together.

By the time both of us returned home that night, we were completely exhausted. The past few months had fed on us emotionally and physically, and the weary looks on our faces showed it. Truth is, we'd probably looked like that for quite a while, run-down and worn out in a way that was usually reserved for new parents.

And so once we'd gotten some rest and successfully managed to go about our semester like typical college kids, we both found a sense of normalcy we hadn't gotten to experience during most, if not all, of the time we'd been together.

We were sharing a quart of vegetable lo mein and fried wontons when Owen looked up at me, a long noodle hanging from his mouth. I could tell he wanted to say something but couldn't with his mouth full.

"You better not ask me to *Lady and the Tramp* you right now," I warned before returning to my own plate of noodles.

He laughed so hard, I was surprised a noodle didn't find its way out of his nose. Once he finally got all his food down, he said, "I like that you used that as a verb, but no, I wasn't going to ask you to . . . *Tramp* me."

"If someone's doing the tramping, it's definitely you. I'm Lady."

"Oh," he replied, looking genuinely puzzled. "That does make more sense." I watched as he picked up another wonton with his chopsticks and dipped it into the broth, still clearly pondering my previous comment. "But why would the boy be the tramp, though? It doesn't—"

"Owen, focus!" I said, snapping my fingers in the hopes that it would literally snap him out of his *Lady and the Tramp* conundrum. "What were you about to say?"

Seemingly already forgetting what he'd been thinking about earlier, he remained silent for a long moment. "I was just gonna say I'm bored. I think."

"You *think*?"

"Yeah. I mean, I know that was what I was gonna say. I just meant I'm bored I think. Or I think I'm bored. Whatever makes the most sense. It's not the syntax that's important though here." He sounded more excited as he spoke. "What's important is that things have been so crazy, I haven't felt bored—or anything close to it—in a really long time."

I didn't know if that was a good thing or a bad thing, even though he seemed pleased by it, so I asked hesitantly, "Do you *like* that feeling?"

"Boredom?" He jerked his head back. "Not really. I feel like you can't like being bored just by definition alone. But then..." He seemed like he was processing a stream of consciousness he was sharing as the ideas came to him. "I don't know. There's a certain level of comfort in it. Like being here with you and not having any worries. It's like eating the same chicken soup my mom used to make for me every time I was sick. I never loved the taste of it because it didn't really have much taste, and also I usually felt like complete shit. But it was comforting, ya know? Like you knew what to expect. No surprises. Does that make any sense?"

I smiled because I knew exactly what he meant. "Yeah," I said. "Yeah, it does." Being with Owen was my chicken soup too.

OWEN

As nice as it had been to spend the rest of the semester focusing only on school and other typical college-y things like my girlfriend and Professor Ted's latest gig—which we got extra credit for attending—I couldn't help but feel like I was missing something, though I wasn't sure what it was until Brody and Drew texted all of our gang to let us know that their bar was finally ready for its first customers.

They'd been so secretive, especially lately, about what stage in the renovation they'd been in and how long it would be until the place opened that most of us had stopped asking about it entirely. Which only made it that much more exciting when they finally invited us to come check it out.

From the outside, Bar None wasn't so big that I could picture it hosting parties or imagining people dancing to live bands or anything. With its red brick exterior that could use some repointing, and a green awning that dwarfed the front door entirely, it struck me as more of a place you'd go to bitch about your boss or complain that your wife was spending your hard-earned money on ebooks and designer leggings.

But inside… Inside, Bar None was exactly what I would've pictured a space of Brody and Drew's to look like. A sleek wooden bar spanned almost the full length of the place. I could picture the two of them making drinks and chatting with regulars while Sophia and Aamee sat in two of the black wooden barstools sipping some sort of fruity drink one of the guys invented just for them.

The high, wide-angled cathedral ceiling had black shiplap and beams, and the light wood floors made the space feel bigger than it was. Most of the wall space was covered with local photos or knickknacks that gave Bar None a homey feel I hadn't been expecting when I'd first pulled up.

"This place looks amazing," I told them, my eyes still taking everything in.

We were the only ones in the bar since it wasn't technically open to the public yet while they waited for their liquor license.

Aamee quickly took credit for the decor selections, silencing Sophia when she tried to say she chose the tables and chairs. The two began bickering while their boyfriends found their place behind the bar and began fixing drinks. It wasn't long before Xander joined them.

The rest of us pushed some smaller tables together until there was room for all of us. Since the kitchen wasn't open, Cody ran out to grab some pizzas—and by habit he brought back some beer, clearly forgetting that we were in a bar.

We fell into our usual routine easily: laughing, eating, teasing each other, arguing about trivial things completely on principle. But as I looked around at our group, I realized not only how little had changed, but also how much.

Aamee and Brody would be married soon, Carter and Toby were discussing which apartment they wanted to rent together, Sophia had a new marketing job in the city, Drew finally accomplished his dream of owning his own bar, Vee and Taylor were on their way to becoming lawyers, and I... Well, I'd finally decided what I wanted to do with the rest of my life.

Or maybe just the foreseeable future. Because, as I'd learned over the past year or so, the only thing predictable about life was its *un*predictability. There was no use trying to hold on to your plans for the future too carefully, because you never knew when you were going to end up divorced from your girlfriend's cousin and raising money with a houseful of lunatics so you can pay off a dead woman's tax debt.

"You okay?"

It took me a moment to realize the question had been directed at me and even longer to realize who'd said it. Mainly because Aamee wasn't known for her empathy.

"Yeah," I said. "I'm good. Better than good, actually." I smiled at everyone seated around the table, but I didn't feel it reach my eyes.

This moment, like many that had come this year, was a bittersweet one. We'd grown so close only to have to grow apart again as we moved on to whatever adventures life had in store for each of us.

"I think I finally figured out what I'm gonna do with some of the money I have left," I said.

Not surprisingly, some of the group looked slightly frightened at what I might say next.

"I think I'm gonna build a treehouse in our yard." I glanced over at Vee as I said *our*, and she smiled warmly at me. "I always wanted to build one as a kid. Like one of those really tall ones that allows you to see over most of the neighborhood, ya know?" I said, not really wanting a response from anyone and thankfully not getting one. "I figured why not do it now. I have the construction knowledge and can make it one of the sickest ones out there."

They listened while I told them how I thought I might be able to run the electric from the basement out there and even put in a small HVAC unit. As I talked about having a loft-style room where a bed could be above the main space, I realized the treehouse was taking shape in my mind as I spoke.

"I figured every classic gang has its clubhouse. The Little Rascals had one, and the kids from *The Sandlot* and *Stand by Me*, George and Harold, the Scooby Gang..." I said. "They all had treehouses."

"Who are George and Harold?" Natalia asked.

I heard Cody answer, but I was too wrapped up in my own thoughts to slow down. "I'm gonna build a treehouse so all of you will have a place to stay when you come back to visit." I made eye contact with everyone as I looked around the group. "If I build it, you will come."

"Okay," Vee said, patting my thigh. "I think we're all movie-referenced out."

"It doesn't even have a bathroom," Taylor pointed out.

"Yeah. No way I'm staying in a tree," Aamee said. And then to Brody, "And you can't make me."

"Your loss," he replied. "That place sounds like it's gonna be sweet!"

I was quiet while I listened to most of the guys talk about how fun it would be to have our own little hideout, and I tried to ignore a few of the girls who seemed like they weren't up for *peeing off the side*. Maybe with time, I could figure out how to get real plumbing up there.

"Seriously, though," I said, quieting the chatter as I spoke. "I know it's crazy, but it'll be a fun project, and maybe if I like it and I'm good at it, I can build custom treehouses for people or something. People pay a fortune for that kind of thing."

I looked around at the group, hoping like hell they wouldn't squash my latest idea because, for some reason, it seemed like one that might have a chance to go the distance. Even if it did feel a little nuts, even to me.

"So what do you guys think?"

And that was one of the things that was so great about this group of people who'd grown to love each other despite all our differences: we could trust each other to be honest. Brutally honest. But as I searched the faces around me for any indication of doubt, all I saw were smiles and, eventually, raised glasses.

"It feels perfect," Vee said.

And I couldn't agree more.

Epilogue

VERONICA

I couldn't remember exactly how long it had been since I'd been at a wedding in the Masons' backyard, which seemed odd because the wedding I'd been to had been my own. Even though it hadn't been real, I still felt like I should've remembered the date of our pretend anniversary.

I wasn't sure how to feel when some of Brody's family remembered me, but most of them had been so kind to me that day, and that hadn't changed. Luckily, I had Owen with me, so he would introduce himself to people, which allowed me to get their names again without having to ask for them.

Owen and I sat silently as Brody and Aamee stood at the altar, holding each other's hands as they said their vows. Brody's mom had been in tears since the ceremony began, and it only got worse when they exchanged rings. I even thought I recognized some sort of emotion on Aamee's mother's face, which surprised me because that much Botox usually ensured a person would be incapable of any sort of expression.

By the time the reception began, it seemed most of the

guests were more than ready to party, including, of course, our friends, who were all seated at one large table. Even though Sophia and Taylor were both bridesmaids, Aamee and Brody hadn't wanted a table for the wedding party. Instead, they'd allowed people to choose their own seats, and it had worked perfectly since the wedding was on the smaller side.

In addition to large, heated tents, the Masons had put a dance floor under one and surrounded it with so many outdoor heaters, we almost forgot how cold it was until it started snowing.

It was light at first but became steadier until it was so heavy it made the air itself appear white. And as all of us danced and laughed and drank and then danced some more, I thought about how perfect this was. We were all together, celebrating the love of two of our close friends, watching the sun disappear into the sky until it got so dark that the snowflakes seemed to glow under the lights.

Owen pulled me in close as we swayed to Elton John's "Rocket Man."

"I still can't believe the Kenso Gummers are a real band now," I said.

"Well, the term *real* is subjective. But yeah, they know a couple of decent covers now that Brae and Jagger found some other people who can actually play instruments."

I laughed against his chest. "Right. Knowing how to play an instrument is definitely an important aspect of having a band. Jagger's voice is pretty, though, and whoever this is on the electric piano really knows what he's doing."

Owen pulled back, and I felt his head tilt down to look at me. "Hey, that better not be a shot at me and my keyboard skills."

"Eh," I said. "You'd have to have some skills for me to take a shot at them."

"Oooh," he teased with a squeeze of my hips. "That was cold."

"I'm blaming the weather."

Owen laughed at that. "Fair enough." And then I watched his eyes grow narrow, like he was straining to look at something in the distance. "Professor Ted?"

OWEN

The wedding had certainly been a unique one so far, but when I saw Professor Ted sprinting down the snowy hill of the Masons' backyard toward us, I thought that was weird, even for this.

"What are you doing here?" I asked him once he was close enough to hear me. He was wearing a baby-blue suit with a metallic hue to it. At least he'd gotten dressed up for the occasion.

"I came to see the Kenzo Gummers," he said, turning toward the small stage at the front of the tent. "I've become a big fan, you know? I try to make it to most of their shows."

I didn't know that I would've considered this a show. "Oh. This is more of a private event. A wedding actually," I explained, as if it mattered one bit to Ted.

He didn't reply to that but instead said, "Almost didn't make it here. That damn van's on its last leg, and the snow is not its friend. Not sure how long it has left, but I've had her since college, and I painted her myself. Always felt like I identified with Shaggy, ya know?"

"Wait," Vee said right as I began to realize the connection.

"Was the Mystery Machine at our haunted house yours?"

"The very same."

I couldn't help thinking that Ted's appearance here, driving a van that represented us, to see a band that wasn't really a band was a type of kismet that only our group of friends experienced.

"Hey, would you mind if we all took a picture in front of your van? Brody was talking about it when you came to the haunted house, but we didn't realize it was yours. We kind of refer to ourselves as the Scooby Gang, and now we're all doing different things and getting married or moving."

"Yeah, man. Say no more. It's right out front. I'll meet you out there." Professor Ted took off from the direction he'd come before I had a chance to ask if he wanted to wait a little bit until Brody and Aamee were ready.

"Should we go get everyone?" Vee asked.

"Might as well, I guess."

It took about ten minutes to get everyone together and convince all of them that we needed to walk out front to take a picture, but once they realized how much it meant to Brody, everyone was happy to comply. And once we were all in front of the van, our arms around each other, dressed in our formal attire and covered in snow, I was sure everyone was glad we'd ended up where we did.

"Thanks, man. This is an amazing wedding gift," Brody told me, as if I'd set up the whole thing in advance and instructed some lunatic to pull onto their front lawn during their wedding.

But instead of explaining any of that, I simply smiled when Professor Ted said, "Say cheese," and told Brody I was glad he loved it so much.

I loved it too. I was pretty sure we all did.

Also by
ELIZABETH HAYLEY

The Love Game:
Never Have You Ever
Truth or Dare You
Two Truths & a Lime
Ready or Not
Let's Not and Say We Did
Tag, We're It
Trivial Pursuits
Duck, Duck, Truce
Forget Me Knot

Love Lessons:
Pieces of Perfect
Picking Up the Pieces
Perfectly Ever After

Sex Snob
(A Love Lessons Novel)

Misadventures:
Misadventures with My Roommate
Misadventures with a Country Boy
Misadventures in a Threesome
Misadventures with a Twin
Misadventures with a Sexpert

Other Titles:
The One-Night Stand

Acknowledgments

First and foremost, we have to thank Meredith Wild for always believing in our writing and inviting us to be part of the Waterhouse team. Working with you the last few years has been so rewarding and so much fun!

To our swolemate, Scott, thanks for making the editing process smooth and for fixing most of our issues so we didn't have to. You're always there to provide insight when we need it, and you've helped make our books the best they could be even when we didn't know how to get them there.

To the rest of the Waterhouse Press team, thank you for the beautiful graphics and for promoting our books. You're an amazing group of people, and we're lucky to have the honor of working with you.

To our Padded Roomers, you all are such a tremendous group of people. It's tough to find people as crazy as we are, and we've truly found our tribe with you. Thank you for everything you've done for us, such as posting teasers, sharing links, reading ARCs, writing reviews, and making us laugh. We don't deserve you, but we're damn glad to have you.

To our readers, there's no way to accurately thank you for taking a chance on us and for your support. Thank you for letting us share our stories with you.

To Google, thank you for providing the means for us to research things including, but not limited to, fraternities, sororities, the difference between a doula and a midwife, township codes, tax laws, alcoholic drinks, legal terminology, and popular clothing trends.

And of course, we need to thank our Scooby Gang, whose personalities created themselves in our minds before they ever came to life on the page. You're such a memorable group of people that we almost forget you aren't real friends of ours. We wish you were.

To each other, for pushing one another forward when we stall. The ride hasn't been easy, but it's sure as hell been a lot of fun. To whatever comes next…

About
ELIZABETH HAYLEY

Elizabeth Hayley is actually "Elizabeth" and "Hayley," two friends who love reading romance novels to obsessive levels. This mutual love prompted them to put their English degrees to good use by penning their own. The product is *Pieces of Perfect,* their debut novel. They learned a ton about one another through the process, like how they clearly share a brain and have a persistent need to text each other constantly (much to their husbands' chagrin).

They live with their husbands and kids in a Philadelphia suburb. Thankfully, their children are still too young to read their books.

Visit them at AuthorElizabethHayley.com